HORROR STORIES

twenty-six scary tales

JA Konrath

INTRODUCTION

I'm a huge horror movie fan, dating back to the creature features and Twilight Zone reruns on UHF Channel 32 in the mid-seventies. If you ever visit a Jaycee's haunted house on Halloween, or ride a roller coaster, you'll hear both screams and laughter. The two emotions are closely tied.

Since writing is about provoking emotion in the reader, I try to use as much fear and as much humor as I can in my stories. Fear is universal. It connects us as human beings. And being scared is a blast.

My bookcase is filled with thousands of horror novels and anthologies, from the traditional standbys of King and Koontz, to the splatterpunk gorefests of Jack Ketchum and Ed Lee, to the British shocks of Graham Masterton and James Herbert.

I tend to jump around sub-genres when writing horror. I don't mind going for the gross out, but I also like to poke fun and make jokes. Even my darkest horror stories could be classified as black comedy if you look hard enough. Though I write some scary and disturbing stuff, it's always done with a wink.

My Lt. Jacqueline "Jack" Daniels thrillers all contain healthy doses of horror. Jack chases some pretty frightening criminals, and if reading those scary sections doesn't make you lock your doors and turn on all your lights you probably have a heart made of stone.

In 2009, I wrote a horror novel called *Afraid* under the pen name Jack Kilborn. Since then I've written two other Kilborn books (they'll be released eventually.) In the meantime, here's a big dose of primal fear, aimed right at your jugular. Make sure your doors are locked…

Joe Konrath – March 2010

CONTENTS

Finicky Eater

This is my very first published story, which was published right after I sold Whiskey Sour. It centers on a theme I've gone back to often in my fiction. This appeared in the magazine Horror Garage, which featured a girl on the cover with her face soaked in blood. My mom didn't pass out copies at her job.

"Eat it."

Billy pushed his plate away.

"I'm not hungry anymore."

A pout appeared on his shiny little face. A miniature version of Josh's. Marge could remember when it used to be cute.

"You haven't even tried it. I made it different today. Just take a bite."

"No."

Marge could feel the tension build in her neck, like cables beneath the skin.

"Billy, honey, you need to eat. Look how skinny you're getting."

"I want an apple."

"We've been over this Billy. There are no apples. There won't be any apples ever again."

He crossed his arms. So thin. His elbows and wrists looked huge.

"I want a Twinkie."

Marge's mouth quivered, got wet.

"Billy, please don't..."

"I want McDonald's french fries, and a Coke."

A deep breath.

"Billy, we don't have any of those things anymore. Since they dropped all those bombs, we have to make do with what's available. Now please, you need to eat."

She pushed the plate back towards her son. His portion of meat was small, scarcely the size of a cracker. Pale and greasy. Marge eyed it and felt her stomach rumble.

It's for Billy, she chastened herself.

But if he didn't want it...

Marge killed the thought and looked away for some distraction.

She failed.

After three months in the shelter, there was nothing left to distract herself with.

She knew every inch of the tiny room like she knew her own body. The shelves, once stocked with canned goods, were empty. The TV and radio didn't work. The three dirty cots smelled like body odor, and the sump hole in the corner had long overflowed with urine and feces. No view, no entertainment, no escape.

Josh had built the shelter because he wanted his family to live. But was this living?

Marge turned to her son, the tears coming. "We're going to make it, Billy. I promise. But you need to eat. Please."

"No." Billy's own eyes began to glaze. "I want Daddy."

"I know you do. But Daddy left, Billy. He knew we didn't have enough food. So he made a sacrifice for you and me."

"I wish Daddy was here."

Tears burned her cheeks.

"He's here, Billy." She patted her chest. "He's here, inside of us, and he always will be."

Billy narrowed his eyes. "You hit Daddy on the head."

Marge recoiled as if slapped.

"No, Billy. Your father made a sacrifice."

"He did not. You hit him on the head while he was asleep."

Billy picked up the small piece of meat and threw it at his mother.

"I don't want to eat Daddy anymore!"

Marge scooped up the meat, sobbing. It tasted salty. She didn't want to take food from her son, but she needed the strength for what came next.

She silently cursed her husband. Why didn't he properly stock this place? Getting nuked would have been better than this.

Her hand closed around the fire axe.

* * *

The scream woke her up.

Marge's face burned with fever. Infection, she knew. In a way, a blessing. Consciousness was far too horrible.

"Billy?"

Whimpering. Marge squinted in the darkness.

"Mommy?"

She shifted, the pain in her legs causing her to cry out. She unconsciously reached down to touch them, but felt nothing.

They'd eaten her legs last week.

"What's the matter, Billy? Are you hungry, honey?"

"I made a sacrifice, Mommy."

He crawled out of the shadows, handing Marge his tiny, dirty foot.

The drool that leaked from her mouth had a mind of its own.

* * *

"You...you have to do it, Billy."

Billy was crying.

"You have to do it for Mommy. Mommy can't cut off her second arm. I can't hold the axe."

"I wish Daddy were here."

"Daddy!" Marge's face raged with anger, madness. "Your father did this to us! He got off lucky!"

She stared a her baby boy, legless, pulling himself along on his hands. Damn the world, and damn God, and damn Josh for letting this...

There was a noise coming from the door.

It was a knock! Someone was knocking!

"Billy! Do you hear it! We're going to be..."

Billy swung the axe.

* * *

"This one's still alive!"

Officer Carlton leaned over the small boy, checking his pulse. He was awful to look at, legless and caked with blood. His mouth was a ruin of ragged flesh.

No—not a ruin. The flesh wasn't his.

"Jesus."

His partner, Jones, made a face.

"Looks like the kid ate his mom. There's another body over here. My guess it's the homeowner. Why'd they come down here?"

Carlton shrugged. "The father had a history of paranoid behavior. Maybe he convinced them it was a nuclear war."

He squinted at the father's corpse. The bones had been broken to get at the marrow inside. Carlton shivered.

"There's a hidden room back here. Look, the shelf swings away."

The hinged shelf moved inward, revealing a large pantry, stocked with canned goods. Enough for years.

"Now, Billy!"

Carlton caught the movement and spun around, in time to see the little creature with the axe bring it down on his partner's head.

Carlton's jaw dropped. The woman—the gory, limbless torso that they thought was dead—was undulating across the floor towards him like a gigantic worm.

He drew his gun. The axe hit him in the belly.

"We're saved!" the mother-thing cried.

Her voice was wet with something. Blood?

When she bit into his leg, he realized it was drool.

* * *

Marge slithered away from the light. It was too bright outside. There was probably radiation coming in, but she didn't pay it any mind.

Her only motivation was hunger. And the food was in the hidden room.

Part of her brain recognized the can goods around her, recognized that they contained edible things. But her attention was focused on the police officer, cowering in the corner, holding the pumping wound in his gut.

Her mouth got wet.

She crawled, inch-worm style, up to him.

"Get away, lady!"

Billy crawled past her, faster because he still had arms. The cop screamed, and Billy hacked at his flailing legs like kindling.

A sound mixed in with the screams, and Marge realized it was laughter. Her son was laughing.

"Billy! Don't play with your food!"

* * *

"You killed Daddy."

Billy had his mouth full of something purple, and his eyes were far away.

"Yes I did, Billy. I killed him so you could have food. But we have enough food now for weeks. And these men have families, who will come looking for them. We'll never be hungry again."

Billy chewed and spit out something hard.

"Daddy is inside me."

"That's right."

"You're a little inside me, too. Your legs and arms."

Marge almost smiled at the child's analogy.

"That's right. Mommy is a little inside you."

Billy narrowed his eyes.

"I want all of you inside me."

Marge watched her son drag himself over to the axe.

* * *

Billy opened his eyes. The sheets were soaked with sweat. He turned in bed and shook his wife, who was snoring softly.

"Jill! Wake up!"

Her eyelids fluttered. "What's wrong, Billy?"

"Get the baby!" Billy rolled over and strapped on his prosthetic legs, snugging the belts tight. "It's happening!"

Jill sat up. The air raid siren cut through their bedroom like a scream.

"The bombs are dropping, Jill! We have to get down to the shelter! Hurry!"

He hobbled out of the room, Jill joining him on the stairs with their six month old son. The siren was louder in the night air. On the horizon was a horribly bright light, and a pluming cloud in the shape of a mushroom.

He opened the door to the underground shelter, ushering his wife and son down the stairs, frightened and anxious and...salivating.

The Screaming

This is from the first anthology I ever appeared in, The Many Faces of Van Helsing, which had nothing to do with the Hugh Jackman film but was released at the same time to capitalize on it. I don't do many period pieces, and don't do many stories set in foreign countries. I also don't do many vampire stories, even though I love to read them. This is set in England in the 1960s, and I paid a lot of attention to vernacular, trying to get it to sound right.

"Three stinking quid?"

Colin wanted to reach over the counter and throttle the old bugger. The radio he brought in was brand new and worth at least twenty pounds.

Of course, it was also hot. Delaney's was the last pawnbroker in Liverpool that didn't ask questions. Colin dealt with them frequently because of this. But each and every time, he left the shop feeling ripped off.

"Look, this is state of the art. The latest model. You could at least go six."

As expected, the old wank didn't budge. Colin took the three coins and left, muttering curses under his breath.

Where the hell was he going to get more money?

Colin rubbed his hand, fingers trailing over dirty scabs. His eyes itched. His throat felt like he'd been swallowing gravel. His stomach was a tight fist that he couldn't unclench.

If he didn't score soon, the shakes would start.

Colin tried to work up enough saliva to spit, and only half-managed. The radio had been an easy snatch; stupid bird left it on the window ledge of her flat, plugged in and wailing a new Beatles tune. Gifts like that don't come around that often.

He used to do okay robbing houses, but the last job he pulled left him with three broken ribs and a mashed nose when the owner came home early. And Colin'd been in pretty good shape back then. Now-frail and wasted and brittle as he was-a good beating would kill him.

Not that Colin was afraid to die. He just wanted to score first. And three pounds wouldn't even buy him a taste.

Colin hunkered down on the walk, pulled up the collar on his wool coat. The coat had been nice once, bought when Colin was a straighty, making good wage. He'd almost sold it many times, but always held out. English winters bit at a man's bones. There was already a winter-warning chill in the air, even though autumn had barely started.

Still, if he could have gotten five pounds for it, he'd have shucked it in an instant. But with the rips, the stains, the piss smell, he'd be lucky to get fifty p.

"Ello, Colin."

Colin didn't bother looking up. He recognized the sound of Butts's raspy drone, and couldn't bear to tolerate him right now.

"I said, ello, Colin."

"I heard you, Butts."

"No need to be rude, then."

Butts plopped next to him without an invite, smelling like a loo set ablaze. His small eyes darted this way and that along the sidewalk, searching for half spent fags. That's how he'd earned his nickname.

"Oh, lucky day!"

Butts grinned and reached into the street, plucking up something with filthy fingers. There was a lipstick stain on the filter, and it had been stamped flat.

"Good for a puff or two, eh?"

"I'm in no mood today, Butts."

"Strung out again, are we?"

Butts lit the butt with some pub matches, drew hard.

"I need a few more quid for a nickel bag."

"You could pull a job."

"Look at me, Butts. I weigh ten stone, and half that is the coat. A small child could beat my arse."

"Just make sure there's no one home, mate."

"Easier said," Colin thought.

"You know"—Butts closed his eyes, smoke curling from his nostrils"—I'm short on scratch myself right now. Maybe we could team up for something. You go in, I could be lookout, we split the take."

Colin almost laughed. He didn't trust Butts as far as he could chuck him.

"How about I be the lookout?"

"Sorry, mate. You'll run at the first sign of trouble."

"And you wouldn't?"

Butts shrugged. His fag went out. He made two more attempts at lighting it, and then flicked it back into the street.

"Sod it, then. Let's do a job where we don't need no lookout."

"Such as?"

Butts scratched his beard, removed a twig.

"There's this house, see? In Heysham, near where I grew up. Been abandoned for a long time. Loaded with bounty, I bet. That antiquey stuff fetches quite a lot in the district."

"It's probably all been jacked a long time ago."

"I don't think so. When I was a pup, the road leading up to it was practically invisible. All growed over by woods, you see. Only the kids knew about it. And we all stayed far away."

"Why?"

"Stories. Supposed to have goblins. Bollocks like that. I went up to it once, on a dare. Got within ten yards. Then I heard the screaming."

Colin rolled his eyes. He needed to quit wasting time with Butts and think of some way to get money. It would be dark soon.

"You think I'm joshing? I swear on the head of my lovely, sainted mother. I got within a stone's throw, and a god-fearful scream comes out of the house. Sounded like the devil his self was torturing some poor soul. Wet my kecks, I did."

"It was probably one of your stupid mates, Butts. Having a giggle at your expense."

"Wasn't a mate, Colin. I'm telling you, no kid in town went near that house. Nobody did. And I've been thinking about it a lot, lately. I bet there's some fine stuff to nick in there."

"Why haven't you gone back then, eh? If this place is full of stealables, why haven't you made a run?"

Butts's roving eyes locked onto another prize. He lit up, inhaled.

"It's about fifteen miles from here. Every so often I save up the rail money, but I always seem to spend the dough on something else. Hey, you said you have a few quid, right? Maybe we can take the train and—"

"No way, Butts."

Colin got up, his thin bones creaking. He could feel the onset of tremors in his hands, and jammed them into his pockets.

"Heysham Port is only a two hour ride. Then only a wee walk to the house."

"I don't want to spend my loot on train tics, and I don't want to spend the night in bloody Heysham. Pissant little town."

Colin looked left, then right, realizing it didn't matter what direction he went. He began walking, Butts nipping at his heels.

"I got old buds in Heysham. They'll put us up. Plus I got a contact there. He could set us up with some smack, right off. Wouldn't even need quid; we can barter with the pretties we nick."

"No."

Butts put his dirty hand on Colin's shoulder, squeezed. His fingernails resembled a coal miner's.

"Come on, mate. We could be hooked up in three hours. Maybe less. You got something better to do? Find a hole somewhere, curl up until the puking stops? You recall how long it takes to stop, Colin?"

Colin paused. He hadn't eaten in a few days, so there was nothing to throw up but his own stomach lining. He'd done that, once. Hurt something terrible, all bloody and foul.

But Heysham? Colin didn't believe there was anything valuable in that armpit of a town. Let alone some treasure-filled house Butts'd seen thirty years back.

Colin rubbed his temple. It throbbed, in a familiar way. As the night dragged on, the throbbing would get worse.

He could take his quid, buy a tin of aspirin and some seltzer, and hope the withdrawal wouldn't be too bad this time.

But he knew the truth.

As far as bad decisions went, Colin was king. One more wouldn't make a dif.

"Fine, Butts. We'll go to Heysham. But if there's nothing there, you owe me. Big."

Butts smiled. The three teeth he had left were as brown as his shoes.

"You got it, mate! And you'll see! Old Butts has got a feeling about this one. We're going to score, and score big. You'll see."

* * *

By the time the rail spit them out at Heysham Port, Colin was well into the vomiting.

He'd spent most of the ride in the loo, retching his guts out. With each purge, he forced himself to drink water, so as not to do any permanent damage to his gullet.

It didn't help. When the water came back up, it was tinged pink.

"Hang in there, Colin. It isn't far."

Bollocks it wasn't far. They walked for over three hours. The night air was a meat locker, and the ground was all slope and hill. Wooded country, overgrown with trees and high grass, dotted with freezing bogs. Colin noticed the full moon, through a sliver in the canopy, then the forest swallowed it up.

They walked by torchlight; Butts had swaddled an old undershirt around a stick. Colin stopped vomiting, but the shivering got so bad he fell several times. It didn't help that Butts kept getting his reference points mixed up and changed directions constantly.

"Don't got much left, Butts."

"Stay strong, mate. Almost there. See? We're on the road."

Colin looked down, saw only weeds and rocks.

"Road?"

"Cobblestone. You can still see bits of curbing."

Colin's hopes fell. If the road was in such disrepair, the house was probably worse off.

Stinking Heysham. Stinking Butts.

"There it is, mate! What did I tell you?"

Colin stared ahead and viewed nothing but trees. Slowly, gradually, he saw the house shape. The place was entirely obscured, the land so overgrown it appeared to be swallowing the frame.

"Seems like the house is part of the trees," Colin said.

"Was like that years ago, too. Worse now, of course. And lookit that. Windows still intact. No one's been inside here in fifty years, I bet."

Colin straightened up. Butts was right. As rundown as it was, the house looked untouched by humans since the turn of the century.

"We don't have to take everything at once. Just find something small and pricey to nick now, and then we can come back and—"

The scream paralyzed Colin. It was a force, high pitched thunder, ripping through him like needles. Unmistakably human, yet unlike any human voice Colin had ever heard.

And it was coming from the house.

Butts gripped him with both hands, the color fleeing his ruddy face.

"Jesus Christ! Did you hear that? Just like when I was a kid! What do we do, Colin?"

A spasm shook Colin's guts, and he dry-heaved onto some scrub brush. He wiped his mouth on his coat sleeve.

"We go in."

"Go in? I just pissed myself."

"What are you afraid of, Butts? Dying? Look at yourself. Death would be a blessing."

"My life isn't a good one, Colin, but it's the only one I've got."

Colin pushed past. The scream was chilling, yes. But there was nothing in that house worse than what Colin had seen on the street. Plus, he needed to get fixed up, bad. He'd crawl inside the devil's arse to get some cash.

"Hold up for me!"

Butts attached himself to Colin's arm. They crept towards the front door.

Another scream rattled the night, even louder than the first. It vibrated through Colin's body, making every nerve jangle.

"I just pissed myself again!"

"Quiet, Butts! Did you catch that?"

"Catch what?"

"It wasn't just a scream. I think it was a word."

Colin held his breath, waiting for the horrible sound to come again. The woods stayed silent around them, the wind and animals still.

The scream cut him to the marrow.

"There! Sounded like hell."

Butts's eyes widened, the yellows showing.

"Let's leave, Colin. My trousers can't hold anymore."

Colin shook off Butts and continued creeping towards the house.

* * *

Though naive about architecture, Colin had grown up viewing enough castles and manors to recognize this building was very old. The masonry was concealed by climbing vines, but the wrought iron adorning the windows was magnificent. Even decades of rust couldn't obscure the intricate, flowing curves and swirls.

As they neared, the house seemed to become larger, jutting dormers threatening to drop down on their heads, heavy walls stretching off and blending into the trees. Colin stopped at the door, nearly nine feet high, hinges big as a man's arm.

"Butts! The torch!"

Butts slunk over, waving the flame at the door.

The knob was antique, solid brass, and glinted in the torchlight. At chest level hung a grimy knocker. Colin licked his thumb and rubbed away the patina.

"Silver."

"Silver? That's great, Colin! Let's yank it and get out of here."

But Colin wouldn't budge. If just the door knocker was worth this much, what treasures lay inside?

He put his hand on the cold knob. Turned.

It opened.

As a youth, Colin often spent time with his grandparents, who owned a dairy farm in Shincliffe. That's how the inside of this house smelled; like the musk and manure of wild beats. A feral smell, his grandmum had often called it.

Taking the torch from Butts, he stepped into the foyer, eyes scanning for booty. Decades of dust had settled on the furnishings, motes swirling into a thick fog wherever the duo stepped. Beneath the grime, Colin could recognize the quality of the furniture, the value of the wall hangings.

They'd hit it big.

It was way beyond a simple, quick score. If they did this right, went through the proper channels, he and Butts could get rich off of this.

Another scream shook the house.

Butts jumped back, his sudden movement sending clouds of dust into the air. Colin coughed, trying to wave the filth out of his face.

"It came from down there!" Butts pointed at the floor, his quivering hand casting erratic shadows in the torchlight. "It's a ghost, I tell you! Come to take us to hell!"

Colin's heart was a hummingbird in his chest, trying to find a way out. He was scared, but even more than that, he was concerned.

"Not hell, Butts. It sounded more like help."

Colin stepped back, out of the dust cloud. He thrust the torch at the floor, looking for a way down.

"Ello! Anyone down there?"

He tapped at the wood slats with the torch, listening for a hollow sound.

"Ello!"

The voice exploded up through the floorboards, cracking like thunder. "PRAISE GOD, HELP ME!"

Butts grabbed Colin's shoulders, his foul breath assaulting his ear.

"Christ, Colin! There's a wraith down there!"

"Don't be stupid, Butts. It's a man. Would a ghost be praising God?"

Colin bent down, peered at the floor.

"What's a man doing under the house, Colin?"

"Bugger if I know. But we have to find him."

Butts nodded, eager.

"Right! If we rescue the poor sap, maybe we'll get a reward, eh?"

Colin grabbed Butts by the collar, pulled him close.

"This place is a gold mine. We can't let anyone else know it exists."

Butts gazed at him stupidly.

"We have to snuff him," Colin said.

"Snuff him? Colin, I don't think—"

Colin clamped his hand over Butts's mouth.

"I'll do it, when the time comes. Just shut up and follow my lead, got it?"

Butts nodded. Colin released him and went back to searching the floor. "Ello! How'd you get down there!"

"There is a trap door, in the kitchen!"

Colin located the kitchen off to the right. An ancient, wood burning stove stood vigil in one corner, and there was an icebox by the window. On the kitchen table, slathered with dust, lay a table setting for one. Colin wondered, fleetingly, what price the antique china and crystal would fetch, and then turned his attention to the floor.

"Where!"

"The corner! Next to the stove!"

Colin looked around for something to sweep away the dust. He reached for the curtains, figured they might be worth something, and then found a closet on the other side of the room. There was a broom inside.

He gave Butts the torch and swept slowly, trying not to stir up the motes. After a minute, he could make out a seam in the floorboards. The seam extended into a man-sized square, complete with a recessed iron latch.

When Colin pulled up on the handle, he was bathed in a foul odor a hundred times worse than anything on his grandparent's farm. The source of the feral smell.

And it was horrible.

Mixed in with the scent of beasts was decay; rotting, stinking, flesh. Colin knelt down, gagging. It took several minutes for the contractions to stop.

"There's a ladder." Butts thrust the torch into the hole. His free hand covered his nose and mouth.

"How far down?" Colin managed.

"Not very. I can make out the bottom."

"Hey! You still down there!"

"Yes. But before you come down, you must prepare yourselves, gentlemen."

"Prepare ourselves? What for?"

"I am afraid my appearance may pose a bit of a shock. However, you must not be afraid. I promise I shall not hurt you."

Butts eyed Colin, intense. "I'm getting seriously freaked out. Let's just nick the silver knocker and—"

"Give me the torch."

Butts handed it over. Colin dropped the burning stick into the passage, illuminating the floor.

A moan, sharp and strong, welled up from the hole.

"You okay down there, mate?"

"The light is painful. I have not born witness to light for a considerable amount of time."

Butts dug a finger into his ear, scratching. "Bloke sure talks fancy."

"He won't for long." Colin sat on the floor, found the rungs with his feet, and began to descend.

The smell doubled with every step down; a viscous odor that had heat and weight and sat on Colin's tongue like a dead cat. In the flickering flame, Colin could make out the shape of the room. It was a root cellar, cold and foul. The dirt walls were rounded, and when Colin touched ground he sent plumes of dust into the air. He picked up the torch to locate the source of the voice. In the corner, standing next to the wall, was...

"Sweet Lord Jesus Christ!"

"I must not be much to look at."

That was the understatement of the century. The man, if he could be called that, was excruciatingly thin. His bare chest resembled a skeleton with a thin sheet of white skin wrapped tight around, and his waist was so reduced it had the breadth of Colin's thigh.

A pair of tattered trousers hung loosely on the unfortunate man's pelvis, and remnants of shoes clung to his feet, several filthy toes protruding through the leather.

And the face, the face! A hideous skull topped with limp, white hair, thin features stretched across cheekbones, eyes sunken deep into bulging sockets.

"Please, do not flee."

The old man held up a bony arm, the elbow knobby and ball-shaped. Around his wrist coiled a heavy, rusted chain, leading to a massive steel ball on the ground.

Colin squinted, then gasped. The chain wasn't going around this unfortunate's wrist; it went through the wrist, a thick link penetrating the flesh between the radius and ulna.

"Colin! You okay?"

Butts's voice made Colin jump.

"Come on down, Butts! I think I need you!"

"There is no need to be afraid. I will not bite. Even if I desired to do so."

The old man stretched his mouth open, exposing sticky, gray gums. Both the upper and lower teeth were gone.

"I knocked them out quite some time ago. I could not bear to be a threat to anyone. May I ask to whom I am addressing?"

"Eh?"

"What is your name, dear sir?"

Colin started to lie, then realized there was no point. He was going to snuff this poor sod, anyway.

"Colin. Colin Willoughby."

"The pleasure is mine, Mr. Willoughby. Allow me. My name is Dr. Abraham Van Helsing, professor emeritus at Oxford University. Will you allow me one more question?"

Colin nodded. It was eerie, watching this man talk. His body was ravaged to the point of disbelief, but his manner was polite and even affable.

"What year of our Lord is this, Mr. Willoughby?"

"The year? It's nineteen sixty-five."

Van Helsing's lips quivered. His sad, sunken eyes went glassy.

"I have been down here longer than I have imagined. Tell me, pray do, the nosferatu; were they wiped out in the war?"

"What war? And what is a nosfer-whatever you said?"

"The war must have been many years ago. There were horrible, deafening explosions that shook the ground. I believe it went on for many months. I assumed it was a battle with the undead."

Was this crackpot talking about the bombing from WWII? He couldn't have been down here for that long. There was no food, no water...

"Mary, Mother of God!"

Butts stepped off the ladder and crouched behind Colin. He held another torch, this one made from the broom they'd used to sweep the kitchen floor.

"Whom am I addressing now, good sir?"

"He's asking your name, Butts."

"Oh. It's Butts."

"Good evening to you, Mr. Butts. Now if I may get an answer to my previous inquiry, Mr. Willoughby?"

"If you mean World War Two, the war was with Germany."

"I take it, because you both are speaking in our mother tongue, that Germany was defeated?"

"We kicked the krauts' arses," Butts said from behind Colin's shoulder.

"Very good, then. You also related that you do not recognize the term nosferatu?"

"Never heard of it."

"How about the term vampire?"

Butts nodded, nudging Colin in the ribs with his elbow. "Yeah, we know about vampires, don't we Colin? They been in some great flickers."

"Flickers?"

"You know. Movie shows."

Van Helsing knitted his brow. His skin was so tight, it made the corners of his mouth draw upwards.

"So the nosferatu attend these movie shows?"

"Attend? Blimey, no. They're in the movies. Vampires are fake, old man. Everyone knows that. Dracula don't really exist."

"Dracula!" Van Helsing took a step forward, the chain tugging cruelly against his arm. "You know the name of the monster!"

"Everyone knows Dracula. Been in a million books and movies."

Van Helsing seemed lost for a moment, confused. Then a light flashed behind his black eyes.

"My memorandum," he whispered. "Someone must have published it."

"Eh?"

"These vampires... you say they do not exist?"

"They're imaginary, old man. Like faeries and dragons."

Van Helsing slumped against the wall. His arm jutted out to the side, chain stretched and jangling in protest. He gummed his lower lip, staring into the dirt floor.

"Then I must be the last one."

* * *

Colin was getting anxious. He needed some smack, and this old relic was wasting precious time. In Colin's pocket rested a boning knife he kept for protection. Colin'd never killed anybody before, but he figured he could manage. A quick poke-poke, and then they'd be on their way.

"I thought vampires had fangs." Butts approached Van Helsing, his head cocked to the side like a curious dog.

"I threw them in the dirt, about where you are presently standing. Knocked them out by ramming my mouth rather forcefully into this iron weight I am chained to."

"So you're really a vampire?"

Colin almost told Butts to shut the hell up, but decided it was smarter to keep the old man talking. He fingered the knife handle and took a casual step forward.

"Unfortunately, I am. After Seward and Morris destroyed the Monster, we thought there were no more. Foolish."

Van Helsing's eyes looked beyond Colin and Butts.

"Morris passed on. Jonathan and Mina named their son after him. Quincey. He was destined to be a great man of science; that was the sort of mind the boy had. Logical and quick to question. But on his sixth birthday, they came."

"Who came?" Butts asked.

"Keep him talking," Colin thought. He took another step forward, the knife clutched tight.

"The vampiri. Unholy children of the fiend, Dracula. They found us. My wife, Dr. Seward, Jonathan, Mina... all slaughtered. But poor, dear Quincey, his fate proved even worse. They turned him."

"You mean, they bit him on the neck and made him a vampire?"

"Indeed they did, Mr. Butts. I should have ended his torment, but he was so small. An innocent lamb. I decided that perhaps, with a combination of religion and science, I might be able to cure him."

Butts squatted on his haunches, less than a yard from the old man. "I'll wager he's the one that got you, isn't he?"

Van Helsing nodded, glumly.

"I kept him down here. Performed my experiments during the day, while he slept. But one afternoon, distracted by a chemistry problem, I stayed too late, and he awoke from his undead slumber and administered the venom into my hand."

"Keep talking, old man," Colin whispered under his breath. He pulled the knife from his pocket and held it at his side, hidden up the sleeve of his coat.

"I developed the sickness. While drifting in and out of consciousness, I realized I was being tended to. Quincey, dear, innocent Quincey, had brought others of his kind back to my house."

"They the ones that chained you to the wall?"

"Indeed they did, Mr. Butts. This is the ultimate punishment for one of their kind. Existing with this terrible, gnawing hunger, with no way to relieve the ache. The pain has been quite excruciating, throughout the years. Starvation combined with a sickening craving. Like narcotic withdrawal."

"We know what that's like," Butts offered.

"I tried drinking my own blood, but it is sour and offers no relief. Occasionally, a small insect or rodent wanders into the cellar, and much as I try to resist it, the hunger forces me to commit horrible acts." Van Helsing shook his head. "Renfield would have been amused."

"So you been living on bugs and vermin all this time? You can't survive on that."

"That is my problem, Mr. Butts. I do survive. As I am already dead, I shall exist forever unless extraordinary means are applied."

Butts laughed, giving his knees a smack. "It's a bloody wicked tale, old man. But we both know there ain't no such things as vampires."

"Do either of you have a mirror? Or a crucifix, perhaps? I believe there is one in the jewelry box, on the night stand in the upstairs bedroom. I suggest you bring it here."

Now they were getting somewhere. Jewelry was easy to carry, and easier to pawn. Colin's veins twitched in anticipation.

"Go get it, Butts. Bring the whole box down."

Butts nodded, quickly disappearing up the ladder.

Colin studied Van Helsing, puzzling about the best way to end him. The old man was so frail, one quick jab in the chest and he should be done with it.

"That small knife you clutch in your hand, that may not be enough, Mr. Willoughby."

Colin was surprised that Van Helsing had noticed, but it didn't matter at this point. He held the boning knife out before him.

"I think it'll do just fine."

"I have tried to end my own life many times. On many nights, I would pound my head against this steel block until bones cracked. When I still had teeth, I tried gnawing off my own arm to escape into the sunlight. Yet every time the sun set again, I awoke fully healed."

Colin hesitated. The knife handle was sweaty, uncomfortable. He wondered where Butts was.

"My death must come from a wooden stake through my heart, or, in lieu of that, you must sever my head and separate it from my shoulders." Van Helsing wiped away a long line of drool that leaked down his chin. "Do not be afraid. I am hungry, yes, but I am still strong enough to fight the urge. I will not resist."

The old man knelt, lifting his chin. Colin brought the blade to his throat. Van Helsing's neck was thin, dry, like rice paper. One good slice would do it.

"I want to die, Mr. Willoughby. Please."

Hand trembling, Colin set his jaw and sucked in air through his teeth.

But he couldn't do it.

"Sorry, mate. I—"

"Then I shall!"

Van Helsing sprung to his feet, tearing the knife away from Colin. With animal ferocity he began to hack at his own neck, slashing through tissue and artery, blood pumping down his translucent chest in pulsing waterfalls.

Colin took a step back, the gorge rising.

Van Helsing screamed, an inhuman cry that made Colin go rigid with fear. The old man's head cocked at a funny angle, tilting to the side. His eyes rolled up in their sockets, exposing the whites. But still he continued, slashing away at the neck vertebrae, buried deep within his bleeding flesh like a white peach pit.

Colin vomited, unable to pull his eyes away.

"He's going to make it," Colin thought, incredulous. "He's going to cut off his own head."

But it wasn't to be. Just as the knife plunged into the bone of his spine, Van Helsing went limp, sprawling face first onto the dirt.

Colin stared, amazed. The horror, the violence of what he just witnessed, pressed down upon him like a great weight. After a few minutes, his breathing slowed to normal, and he found his mind again.

Colin reached tentatively for the knife, still clutched in Van Helsing's hand. The gore gave him pause.

"Go ahead and keep it," Colin decided. "I'll buy another one when—"

Alarm jolted through Colin. He realized, all at once, that Butts hadn't returned. Had the bugger run off with the jewelry box?

Colin sped up the ladder, panicked.

"Butts!"

No answer.

Using the torch, he followed Butts's tracks in the dust, into the bedroom, and then back out the front door. Colin swung it open.

"Butts! Butts, you son of a whore!"

No reply.

Colin sprinted into the night. He ran fast as he could, hoping that his direction was true, screaming and cursing Butts between labored breaths.

His foot caught on a protruding root and Colin went sprawling forward, skidding on his chin, his torch flying off into the woods and sizzling out in a bog.

Blackness.

The dark was complete, penetrating. Not even the moon and stars were visible.

It felt like being in the grave.

Colin, wracked by claustrophobia, once again called out for Butts.

The forest swallowed up his voice.

Fear set in. Without a torch, Colin would never find his way back to Heysham. Wandering around the woods without fire or shelter, he could easily die of exposure.

Colin got back on his feet, but walking was impossible. On the rough terrain, without being able to see, he had no sense of direction. He tried to head back to the house, but couldn't manage a straight line.

After falling twice more, Colin gave up. Exhausted, frightened, and wracked with the pain of withdrawal, he curled up at the base of large tree and let sleep overtake him.

* * *

"This better be it, Butts."

"We're almost there. I swear on it."

Colin opened his crusty eyes, attempted to find his bearings.

He was surrounded by high grass, next to a giant elm. The sun peeked through the canopy at an angle; it was either early morning or late afternoon.

"You've been saying that for three hours, you little wank. You need a little more encouragement to find this place?"

"I'm not holding out on you, Willie. Don't hit me again."

Colin squinted in the direction of the voices. Butts and two others. They weren't street people, either. Both wore clean clothes, good shoes. The smaller one, Willie, had a bowler hat and a matching black vest. The larger sported a beard, along with a chest big as a whiskey barrel.

Butts had taken on some partners.

Colin tried to stand, but felt weak and dizzy. He knelt for a moment, trying to clear his head. When the cobwebs dissipated, he began to trail the trio.

"Tell us again, Butts, how much loot there is in this place."

"It's crammed full, Jake. All that old, antiquey stuff. I'm telling you, that jewelry box was just a taste."

"Better be, Butts, or you'll be wearing your yarbles around your filthy neck."

"I swear, Willie. You'll see. We're almost there."

Colin stayed ten yards back, keeping low, moving quiet. Several times he lost sight of them, but they were a loud bunch and easy to track. His rage grew with each step.

This house was his big break, his shot at a better life. He didn't want to share it with anybody. He may have choked when trying to off Van Helsing, but when they arrived at the house, Colin vowed to kill them all.

"Hey, Willie. Some bloke is following us."

"Eh?"

"In the woods. There."

Colin froze. The man named Jake stared, pointing through the brush.

"Who's there, then? Don't make me run you down."

"That's Colin. He came here with me."

Damned Butts.

"He knows about this place? Jake, go get the little bleeder!"

Colin ran, but Jake was fast. Within moments the bigger man caught Colin's arm and threw him to the ground.

"Trying to run from me, eh?"

A swift kick caught Colin in the ribs, searing pain stealing his breath.

"I hate running. Hate it."

Another kick. Colin groaned. Bright spots swirled in his vision.

"Get up, wanker. Let's go talk to Willie."

Jake grabbed Colin by the ear and tugged him along, dumping him at Willie's feet.

"Why didn't you tell us about your mate, Butts?"

"I thought he'd gone. I swear it."

Jake let loose with another kick. Colin curled up fetal, began to cry.

"Should we kill him, Willie?"

"Not yet. We might need an extra body, help take back some of the loot. You hear me, you drug-addled bastard? We're going to keep you around for awhile, as long as you're helpful."

Butts knelt next to Colin and smiled, brown teeth flashing. "Get up, Colin. They're not going to kill you." He helped Colin gain his footing, keeping a steady arm around his shoulders until they arrived at the house.

In the daylight, the house's aristocratic appearance was overtaken by the many apparent flaws; peeling paint, cracked foundation, sunken roof. Even the stately iron work covering the windows looked drab and shabby.

"This place is a dump." Willie placed a finger on one nostril and blew the contents of his nose onto a patch of clover.

"It's better on the inside," encouraged Butts. "You'll see."

Unfortunately, the inside was even less impressive. The dust-covered furniture Colin had pegged as antique was damaged and rotting.

"You call this treasure?" Willie punched Butts square in the nose.

Butts dropped to the floor, bleeding and hysterical.

"This is good stuff, Willie! It'll clean up nice! Worth a couple thousand quid, I swear!"

Willie and Jake walked away from Butts, and he crawled behind them, babbling.

A moment later, Colin was alone.

The pain in his ribs sharpened with every intake of breath.

If he made a run for it, they'd catch him easily. But if he did nothing, he was a dead man.

He needed a weapon.

Colin crept into the kitchen, mindful of the creaking floorboards. Perhaps the drawers contained a weapon or some kind.

"What you doing in here, eh? Nicking silver?" Jake slapped him across the face.

Colin staggered back, his feet becoming rubber. Then the floor simply ceased to be there. He dropped, straight down, landing on his arse at the bottom of the root cellar.

Everything went fuzzy, and then black.

* * *

Colin awoke in darkness.

He felt around, noticed his leg bent at a funny angle.

The touch made him cry out.

Broken. Badly, from the size of the swelling.

Colin peeled his eyes wide, tried to see. There was no light at all. The trap door, leading to the kitchen, was closed. Not that it mattered; he couldn't have climbed up the ladder anyway.

He sat up, tears erupting onto his cheeks. There was a creaking sound above him, and then a sudden burst of light.

"I see you're still alive, eh?"

Colin squinted through the glare, made out the bowler hat.

"No worries, mate. We won't let you starve to death down there. We're not barbarians. Willie will be down shortly to finish you off. Promise it'll be quick. Right Willie?"

Willie's laugh was an evil thing.

"See you in a bit."

The trap door closed.

Fear rippled through Colin, but it was overwhelmed by something greater.

Anger.

Colin had ever been the victim. From his boyhood days, being beaten by his alcoholic father, up to his nagging ex-wife, suing him into the recesses of poverty.

Well, if his miserable life was going to end here, in a foul smelling dirt cellar, then so be it.

But he wasn't going without a fight.

Colin pulled himself along the cold ground, dragging his wounded leg. He wanted the boning knife, the one he'd left curled in Van Helsing's hand.

When Jake came down to finish him off, the fat bastard was going to get a nice surprise.

Colin's hand touched moisture, blood or some other type of grue, so he knew he was close. He reached into the inky blackness, finding Van Helsing's body, trailing down over his shoulder...

"What in the hell?"

Colin brought his other hand over, groped around.

It made no sense.

Van Helsing's head, which had been practically severed from his shoulders, had reattached itself. The neck was completely intact. No gaping wound, no deep cut.

"Can't be him."

Perhaps another body had been dumped down there, possibly Butts. Colin touched the face.

No beard.

Grazing the mouth with his fingers, Colin winced and stuck a digit past the clammy lips.

It was cold and slimy inside the mouth. Revolting. But Colin probed around for almost an entire minute, searching for teeth that weren't there.

This was Van Helsing. And he had completely healed.

Which was impossible. Unless—

"Jesus Christ." Colin recoiled, scooting away from the body.

He was trapped in the dark with a vampire.

When would Van Helsing awake? Damn good thing the bloke was chained down. Who knows what horrors he could commit if he were free?

Colin repeated that thought, and grinned.

Perhaps if he helped the poor sod escape, Van Helsing would be so grateful he'd take care of the goons upstairs.

The idea vanished when Colin remembered Van Helsing's words. All the poor sod wanted was to die. He didn't want to kill anyone.

"Bloody hell. If I were a vampire, I'd do things—"

Colin halted mid-sentence. His works were in a sardine can, inside his breast pocket. He reached for them, took out the hypo.

It just might work.

Crawling back to Van Helsing, Colin probed until he found the bony neck. He pushed the needle in, then eased back the plunger, drawing out blood.

Vampire blood.

Tying off his own arm and finding his vein in the dark wasn't a problem; he'd done it many times before.

Teeth clenched, eyes shut, he gave himself the shot.

But there was no rush.

Only pain.

The pain seared up his arm, as if someone was yanking out his veins with pliers.

Colin cried out. When the tainted blood reached his heart, the muscle stopped cold, killing him instantly.

* * *

Colin opened his eyes.

He was still in the cellar, but he could see perfectly fine. He wondered where the light could be coming from, but a quick look around found no source.

Colin stood, realizing with a start that the pain in his leg had vanished.

So, in fact, had all of his other pain. He lifted his shirt, expecting to see bruised ribs, but there wasn't a mark on them.

Even the withdrawal symptoms had vanished.

The hypodermic was still in his hand. Colin stared at it, remembering.

"It worked. It bloody well worked."

Van Helsing still lay sprawled out on the floor, face down.

Colin looked at him, and he began to drool. Hunger surged through him, an urge so completely overwhelming it dwarfed his addiction to heroin.

Without resisting the impulse, he fell to the ground and bit into the old man's neck. His new teeth tore through the skin easily, but when his tongue touched blood, Colin jerked away.

Rancid. Like spoiled milk.

A sound, from above. Colin listened, amused at how acute his hearing had become.

"All right, then. Jake, you go downstairs and mercy kill the junkie, and then we'll be off."

Mercy kill, indeed.

Colin forced himself to be patient, standing stock-still, as the trap door opened and a figure descended.

"Well well well, look who's up and about. Be brave, I'll try to make it painless."

Jake moved forward. Colin almost grinned. Big, sweating, dirty Jake smelled delicious.

"You got some fight left in you, eh?"

Colin lunged.

His speed was unnatural; he was on Jake in an instant. Even more astounding was his strength. Using almost no effort at all, he pulled the larger man to the ground and pinned down his arms.

"What the hell?"

"I'll try to make it painless," Colin said.

But from the sound of Jake's screams, it wasn't painless at all.

This blood wasn't rancid. This blood was ecstasy.

Every cell in Colin's body shuddered with pleasure; an overwhelming rush that dwarfed the feeling of heroin, a full body orgasm so intense he couldn't control the moan escaping his throat.

He sucked until Jake stopped moving. Until his stomach distended, the warm liquid sloshing around inside him like a full term embryo.

But he remained hungry.

He raced up the ladder, practically floating on his newfound power. Butts stood at the table, piling dishes into a wooden crate.

"Colin?"

Butts proved delicious, too. In a slightly different way. Not as sweet, sort of a Bordeaux to Jake's Cabernet. Colin's tongue was a wild thing. He lapped up the blood like a mad dog at a water dish, ravenous.

"What the hell are you doing?"

Colin let Butts drop, whirling to face Willie.

"Good God!"

Willie reached into his vest, removed a small Derringer. He fired twice, both shots tearing into Colin's chest.

There was pain.

But more than pain, there was hunger.

Willie turned to run, but Colin caught him easily.

"I wonder what you'll taste like," he whispered in the screaming man's ear.

Honeysuckle mead. The best of the three.

Colin suckled, gulping down the nectar as it pulsed from Willie's carotid. He gorged himself until one more swallow would have caused him to burst.

Then, in an orgiastic stupor, he stumbled from the house and into the glorious night.

No longer dark and silent and scary, the air now hummed with a bright glow, and animal sounds from miles away were clear and lovely.

Bats, chasing insects. A wolf, baying the moon. A tree toad, calling out to its mate.

Such sweet, wonderful music.

The feeling overwhelmed Colin, and he shuddered and wept. This is what he'd been searching for his entire life. This was euphoria. This was power. This was a fresh start.

"I see you have been busy."

Colin spun around.

Van Helsing stood at the entrance to the house. His right hand still gripped Colin's bone knife. His left hand was gone, severed above the wrist where the chain had bound him. The stump dripped gore, jagged white bone poking out.

Colin studied Van Helsing's face. Still sunken, still anguished. But there was something new in the eyes. A spark.

"Happy, old man? You finally have your freedom."

"Freedom is not what I seek. I desire only the redemption that comes with death."

Colin grinned, baring the sharp tips of his new fangs.

"I'll be happy to kill you, if you want."

Van Helsing frowned.

"The lineage of nosferatu ends now, Mr. Willoughby. No more may be allowed to live. I have severed the heads of the ones inside the house. Only you and I remain."

Colin laughed, blood dripping from his lips.

"You mean to kill me? With that tiny knife? Don't you sense my power, old man? Don't you see what I have become?" Colin spread out his arms, reaching up into the night. "I have been reborn!"

Colin opened wide, fangs bared to tear flesh. But something in Van Helsing's face, some awful fusion of hate and determination, made Colin hesitate.

Van Helsing closed the distance between them with supernatural speed, plunging the knife deep into Colin's heart.

Colin fell, gasping. The agony was exquisite. He tried to speak, and blood—his own rancid blood—bubbled up sour in his throat.

"Not...not...wood."

"No, Mr. Willoughby, this is not a wooden stake. It will not kill you. But the damage should be substantial enough to keep you here for an hour or so."

Van Helsing drove the knife further, puncturing the back of Colin's rib cage, pinning him to the ground.

"I have been waiting sixty years to end this nightmare, and I am tired. So very tired. With our destruction, my wait shall finally be over. May God have mercy on our souls."

Colin tried to rise, but the pain brought tears.

Van Helsing rolled off, and sat, cross-legged, on the old cobblestone road. He closed his eyes, his thin, colorless lips forming a serene smile.

"I have not seen a sunrise in sixty years, Mr. Willoughby. I remember them to be very beautiful. This should be the most magnificent of them all."

Colin began to scream.

* * *

When sunrise came, it cleansed like fire.

Mr. Pull-Ups

Prior to being published, I'd often go to open mike night and read stories at a venue called Twilight Tales in Chicago. They sporadically publish short story collections, and for their latest anthology, Tales From The Red Lion, asked me for one. This is what I gave them.

Horace checked the address he'd written down, then walked left on Fullerton. Chicago was dark, but far from quiet. Summer meant people stayed out late. Though it neared 10pm, the sidewalks remained packed with college kids, bar hoppers, tourists, and the occasional homeless man holding out his filthy Styrofoam change cup.

Straight ahead he saw the sign; The Red Lion. Horace contemplated walking away, realized he didn't have any choices left, and entered through the narrow door.

The bar resembled a traditional English pub, or what Horace assumed one would look like. Dark, smoky, with stools older than he was and a large selection of scotch bottles lining the wall. He scanned the room, saw one man sitting alone, and approached him cautiously, the stained hardwood floor creaking beneath his feet.

"Are you Dr. Ricardo?"

The man—old, grizzled, red-eyed—glanced up at Horace over a half-empty rocks glass. He drained the remainder and stared, not saying anything.

"My name is Horace Gelt. You're a plastic surgeon, right?"

Ricardo sniffed the empty glass, looking mournful.

"I don't like talking about the past." The doctor's voice was rough, as if he didn't use often.

Horace looked around, saw that none of the bar's four customers were paying attention to him, and sat at the table across from the doctor. He leaned forward on his elbows, getting a closer look. The results didn't impress him. Sallow pallor. Sunken eyes. A fat tongue that protruded between thin lips. The doctor looked like he'd died a month ago but no one had bothered to tell him.

Again, Horace considered walking away. Then he thought about the record book, about his life's dream, and forced himself to continue.

"I was told you might be able to help me."

Ricardo's red eyes squinted. "Help you how?"

This wasn't illegal. At least, not on Horace's end. But he still felt as if he were making a drug deal, or soliciting a prostitute.

"I need...surgery."

"I need whiskey."

Horace caught the attention of the bartender and pointed at Ricardo. A moment later, the doctor had a fresh glass in front of him.

"How about you?" Ricardo asked. "Don't drink?"

"I'm training."

Ricardo's shoulders flinched in what might have been a shrug, or a snort. He sipped his new drink and leaned forward. The smell of booze coming off this guy made Horace want to recoil, but he didn't move.

"What are you? Tranny? Want me to lop off the goods, shave the Adam's apple, give you boobies?"

Horace made a face. "No."

"I'm good at it. Making little boys into little girls. Had talent. A kind of sixth sense. They shouldn't have revoked my license. I helped a lot of people."

Horace had done his research, and didn't mention the patient that had sued Ricardo out of a license. The guy had gone into surgery expecting a nose job, and had walked out with a vagina. Rhinoplasty on the wrong protrusion.

"I don't want to be a woman." Horace pulled the book page from his pocket, unfolded it carefully. Brett Gantner's smiling face stared up at him, mocking. Horace showed the doctor.

"What is that? I don't have my glasses on."

"Page 43 from the Shawley Book of World Records. Brett Gantner is the record holder for pull-ups. Seven-hundred and forty in an hour."

"I'm sure it makes his mother proud." Ricardo leaned back and sipped more booze. The bartender returned with a basket of food—fish and chips— and set it before the doctor. Without bothering to look at it Ricardo stuck his hand in and began to munch.

"I'm second place. See?" Horace pointed at the printing. "Horace Kellerman. Seven-hundred twenty-five."

"Only missed by a few," Ricardo said, his open mouth displaying half-chewed fish. "Damn shame. Maybe you should work out."

Horace bit back his reply. He worked out all the time, eight, sometimes ten hours a day. He ate all the right foods, supplemented with the right products, treated his body like a shrine. But no matter how hard he worked, how much effort he gave, he couldn't do more than seven-hundred and twenty-five pull ups. It didn't seem humanly possible.

The quest to be number one had become such an obsession with Horace that he actually flew to Phoenix to meet Brett Gantner, to see what he had that Horace didn't.

As it turned out, it was what Brett didn't have that made him the World Record holder. Brett was missing his left leg, above the knee.

"Car accident," Gantner had told him over wheat germ smoothies. "I get around okay with the prosthesis. It hasn't slowed me down any. Don't you agree, Mr. Second Place?"

Horace felt his bile rise at the memory. Gantner had beaten him not because he was the superior athlete, but because he weighed less. About fifteen pounds less. The weight of one leg.

After that meeting, Horace had gone on a crash diet. But his body fat percentage was already dangerously low, and the diet caused him to lose muscle: he couldn't even break six hundred. That led to steroid injections, which led to heart palpitations and perpetual shortness of breath, which made him give out at just over five hundred. He finally went back to his old regimen of diet and supplements, and again regularly hit the seven hundred mark, but he couldn't reach seven-forty. The last time he tried he'd hung on the bar, tears streaming down his face, putting so much effort into his last few pull ups that he shit himself. But seven twenty-five was as high as he could go.

But then inspiration struck. Epiphany. All Horace needed was a doctor who would be willing to perform the surgery. He'd been searching for two months straight, and so far had gotten nowhere. Doctor after doctor turned down his request. One had even told him his problem wouldn't be solved by plastic surgery, but by psychiatry. Asshole.

An internet forum on body modification and voluntary amputation eventually led him to Dr. Ricardo and this dinky little bar.

Horace wasn't sure if the whack-jobs on the website were telling the truth. One guy bragged he had his hands removed. If he did, how could he be using a computer keyboard? Was he typing with his face? But if the forum people were right, Dr. Ricardo might be able to help him.

"I want you to cut off my legs," Horace told the doctor.

Ricardo didn't miss a beat. He drained his whiskey and then used a fork to roughly bisect a golden fried fillet of perch. He only answered after his mouth was full of fish.

"Ten thousand. Cash. Up front."

Horace was overcome by a surge of joy, but mingled in were feelings of wariness, and oddly, remorse.

"Five beforehand, five after the operation."

Ricardo dunked a greasy bit of fish into some mayo and popped it into his mouth.

"That's fine. But why stop at your legs? Human's have lots of unnecessary body parts weighing them down. A kidney is a few ounces. You don't need all of your liver. Appendix, tonsils, gall bladder, half your stomach and a few yards of intestines—that's several pounds of material."

Horace's face fell, and he realized that the man sitting in front of him wasn't simply an incompetent drunk—he was insane. Much as he longed for the surgery, he wasn't about to subject himself to...

Ricardo's body shook, and it took Horace a moment to realize the doctor was laughing.

"Just kidding, Mr. Kellerman. Let's talk dates. The sooner you lose those legs, the sooner you can break your record. When are you free?"

* * *

Horace stared up at the operating room lights. Actually, this was a bedroom, and the lights were the kind do-it-yourselfers used when repairing drywall. He turned his gaze to Dr. Ricardo, who was fussing with a tank of anesthetic, turning the dials this way and that.

Upon arriving at the building—a crumbling brick duplex with empty beer bottles and used syringes decorating the front porch—Horace almost decided to forget the whole thing. But the inside seemed much cleaner than the exterior, and the ersatz surgery theater was extremely white and bright and smelled like lemons; courtesy of the can of disinfectant on the counter. The doctor had walked Horace through the whole procedure, and he seemed to know what he was doing. Tourniquets would restrict massive blood loss, veins and arteries would be tied off one at a time, and an extra flap of skin would be left on each leg to cover the bone and form an attractive stump, just below the buttocks.

Dr. Ricardo poured a fresh bottle of rubbing alcohol over a hacksaw blade, and Horace looked down the table at his legs, one last time.

They were good legs, as legs went. Perhaps a bit thin, but they'd treated him well for twenty-six years. Horace felt no remorse in losing them. His goal to become the world record pull-up holder was more important than petty things, like walking. And his job had amazing disability insurance. Horace would make do in a wheelchair just fine.

"Are you ready?"

Dr. Ricardo had on his surgical mask, and to Horace's eye seemed sober as a judge. Horace nodded, and Ricardo fit the gas mask over his face.

"Take a deep breath, and count backwards from one hundred..."

Horace began to count, but not from one hundred. He began at seven hundred and forty.

By the time he reached seven hundred and twenty, he was asleep.

* * *

Recovery was harder than Horace might have guessed. The pain was minimal when he was lying down, but moving, sitting, taking a shit—these all brought agony.

Ricardo had given him drugs, both oral meds and morphine to inject into his stumps. He only used them once, and as a result slept all day. That was unacceptable. Horace couldn't afford to miss a work out.

While in bed, he stuck with barbells, but after a week he was ready to hit the pull-up bar again.

The results were impressive. On his first attempt, he hit six-hundred and fifty. Not bad after major surgery and seven days on his back. His balance was a little off, but he was thrilled by the results. Ricardo had warned him against resuming activity so soon, and Horace did manage to rip a few of his stitches, but he knew—knew—that the world record would soon be his.

A month after his double amputation, Horace felt great. His stamina was back, and constantly moving around on his hands had made his arms stronger than ever. He set up his video camera, used a step ladder to reach the pull-up bar, and prepared to break the record.

The first two hundred pull-ups were candy. They came smooth, easy. Horace didn't even break a sweat.

The next two hundred were harder, but he still felt good. No leg pain, good breathing, good stamina, and a full half an hour left on the clock.

Horace paced himself for the next two hundred. Fatigue kicked in, and the familiar muscle pain. He also felt a bit of dizziness. But he still considered himself better off than he did while still having legs, and knew he'd make it no matter what.

When he reached seven hundred, he wasn't so sure anymore. He became extremely dizzy, and nauseous. While his grip was strong, the up and down movement had begun to make his stomach lurch. Perhaps it was still too soon. Perhaps he needed more recovery time, more workouts.

At seven hundred and ten Horace threw up, lost his grip, and fell hard onto his stumps, sending lightning bolts of pain up his spine that made him throw up again.

He waited a week before giving it another shot. Made it to seven hundred and thirty, then hung there for ten minutes until the time ran out, unable to do any more.

The week after that he could only manage seven hundred and twenty-five. A few days later he ran out of time at seven hundred and thirty-two. In the following month he posted numbers of 722, 734, 718, 736, 728, 731, 734, 729, and a tantalizingly frustrating 737. But he couldn't reach seven hundred and forty. No matter how hard he tried.

Depression set in. Then anger. Then a plan. Dr. Ricardo had mentioned all of the extra organs in a human being, extras that amounted to several pounds.

If Horace were five pounds less, he could easily get over 740.

* * *

When Horace rolled up to Dr. Ricardo at his usual table in the Red Lion, the good doctor was tilted back in his chair and snoring. Horace shook him, hard.

"I need help. I still weigh too much."

Ricardo took a few seconds to focus. When he spoke, the booze on his breath burned Horace's eyes.

"I remember you. Howard something, right? You needed your legs amputated for some reason. What was it again? Some sort of fetish?"

Horace roughly grabbed Ricardo by the shirt.

"You mentioned that people have extra organs. Kidney, liver, appendix, stuff like that. I want them taken out."

Ricardo blinked, and his eyes began to glaze. Horace gave him a shake.

"Remove it, Doctor. All of it."

"Remove what?"

"Everything. Take away everything I don't need. All of the extra stuff."

"You're crazy."

Horace struck the doctor, a slap than sounded like a thunder crack. The Red Lion's three patrons all turned their way. Horace ignored them, focusing on Ricardo.

"I got a disability settlement. Half a million dollars. I'll give you ten thousand dollars for each pound of me you can remove."

Ricardo nodded. "I remember now. You want to weigh less. Some sort of world record. Sure, I can help. A few yards of intestines. Half the stomach. The arms."

"No! The arms and the muscles stay. Everything else that isn't essential to life can be removed."

"When?" Dr. Ricardo asked.

Horace smiled. "Doing anything tonight?"

* * *

Horace awoke in a drug-induced haze. Thoughts flitted across his drowsy mind, including his last instructions to the doctor.

"Leave the arms, leave the eyes. Everything else goes."

Like a fire sale on body parts.

He squinted at the table next to him, saw the mason jars lined up with bits and pieces that used to be his. Pounds and pounds of flesh and organs.

Several large loops of intestines, floating in formaldehyde.

A kidney.

A chunk of liver.

So far, so good.

An appendix and a gall bladder, though Horace didn't know which was which.

A jar of fat, suctioned from his buttocks.

Part of his stomach.

His penis and testicles.

When Horace saw that, he gasped. No sound came out—in the next jar were his tongue, his tonsils, his vocal chords, and a bloody half moon that he realized was his lower jaw.

Doctor Ricardo had gone too far. The drunken bastard had turned Horace into a monster, a hideous freak.

But...Horace still had his arms. And even as maimed and mutilated as he'd become, he could still do pull-ups, still break the...

Horace's eyes focused on the last mason jar. Horace filled his remaining lung with air and screamed, and he was absolutely sure he made some noise, even though he had no ears to hear it.

The last jar contained ten fingers.

The Shed

Just about every horror mag in the world rejected this story. I'm not sure why. Sure, it's a standard EC Comics supernatural comeuppance, but I think it's fun. It eventually sold to Surreal Magazine.

"That's gotta be where the money is."

Rory took one last hit off the Kool and flicked the butt into a copse of barren trees. The orange firefly trail arced, then died.

Phil shook his head. "Why the hell would he keep his money locked up in a backyard shed?"

"Because he's a crazy old shit. Hasn't left the house in thirty years."

The night was cold and smelled like rotting leaves. They stood at the southern side of Old Man Loki's property, just beyond a tall hedge with thorns like spikes. The estate butted up against the forest preserve on the east and Lake Fenris on the west. Due north was Fenris Road, a winding, private driveway that eventually connected with Interstate 10 about six miles up.

Phil peered through the bramble at the mansion. It rested, dark and quiet, a mountain of jutting dormers and odd angles. To Phil it looked like something that had been asleep for a long time.

"Even crazy people know about banks."

Rory clamped a hand behind Phil's head and tugged the smaller teen closer. "If it's not money, then why the hell does he got that big lock and chain on it? To protect his lawnmower?"

Phil pulled away and glanced at the shed. It stood only a few dozen yards away, the size of a small garage. The roof was tar shingles, rain-worn to gray, and dead vines partially obscured the oversized padlock and chain hanging on the door.

"Doesn't look like it's been opened in a while."

Rory grinned, his teeth blue in the moonlight. "All the more reason to open it now."

It felt all wrong, but Phil followed Rory onto the estate grounds. A breeze cooled the sweat that had broken out on his neck. Rory pulled the crowbar from his belt and swung it at a particularly tall prickle-weed.

"Yard looks like shit. Can't he pay someone to cut his goddamned grass?"

"Maybe he's dead." Phil chanced another look at the mansion. "No lights on."

"We woulda heard about it."

"Could be recent. Could be he just died, and no one found the body yet."

Phil's words bounced small and tinny in the open air. He felt a rush of exposure, as if Old Man Loki was sitting at one of the dark windows of his house and watching their every move.

"You turning chicken shit on me? Baby need his wittle bottle?"

"Shut up, Rory. What if he is dead?"

"Then he won't mind us stealing his shit. Damn—will you check out the size of that lock!"

The padlock was almost as big as Phil's head. An old-fashioned type with a key-shaped opening on its face, securing three lengths of thick, rusty chain which wrapped around the entire shed like packing tape.

"You gonna try to bust that with just a crowbar?"

"Won't know until we try." Rory raised the iron over his head, and Phil set his jaw and cringed at the oncoming sound.

The clang reverberated over the grounds like a ghost looking for someone to haunt.

"Sonuvabitch! First try!"

The lock hung open on a rusty hinge. Rory pulled it off and the chains fell to the ground in a tangle. Phil eyed the door. It was some kind of heavy wood, black as death. Next to the doorknob was a grimy brass plaque.

"Welcome," Phil read.

"How about that shit? We're invited."

Rory laughed, but Phil felt a chill stronger than the night air. He'd heard stories about Old Man Loki. Stories of how he used to live in Europe, and how he hung around with that creepy Mr. Crowley guy Ozzy sang about.

Reflexively, Phil looked over his shoulder to see if anyone was watching.

There was a light on in the house.

"Shit! Rory, there's..."

The light winked twice, then went off.

"There's what, Phil?"

"A light. On the second floor."

Rory pulled a face and made a show of squinting at the mansion. His mouth stretched open in horror, lips snicking back over years of dental neglect.

"Run, Phil! Jesus Christ! Run!"

Phil took off in a dead sprint, fighting to keep his bladder closed. He was forty yards away when he noticed Rory wasn't next to him.

That's when he heard his friend's laughter.

Phil looked back over his shoulder and saw Rory holding his stomach, guffawing so loud that it sounded like a barking dog.

Phil felt his ears burn. He took his time walking back to the shed.

"You should have seen your face!" Rory had tears in his eyes.

"Shut up, Rory. That wasn't funny."

"I swear, you ran like that during football tryouts you woulda made the team."

Phil turned away, shoving his hands in his pockets. "I wasn't scared. You told me to run, so I did."

"Okay, tough guy—prove you aren't scared." Rory pointed at the black door. "You go in first."

Phil chewed his lower lip. If he didn't go in, Rory would never let him forget it. The teasing would last for eternity.

Why the hell did he hang out with Rory anyway?

"I knew you were chicken."

"Kiss my ass, Rory."

Phil grasped the knob and pulled.

The massive door opened with a whisper, moving smoothly despite its weight. Warm, stale air enveloped Phil, and the sound of his own breathing echoed back at him.

So quiet.

Rory switched on the flashlight. The small beam played over four bare walls.

"It's empty."

"Shine the light on the floor."

The cone of light jerked to the center of the room, bending over the edge of a large, round pit and disappearing into the darkness.

"What the hell is that?"

Rory crept up to the edge, holding his flashlight out in front of him like a sword. He peered down into the pit.

"Do you smell that?"

"Yeah. Rotten eggs. I think it's coming from the hole."

Phil glanced over his shoulder again, taking a quick peek at the house.

The light was back on.

"Rory—"

"There's a rusty ladder going down."

"The light is—"

"Shh! Do you hear that?"

Both boys held their breath. There was a quick, rhythmic thumping, coming from deep within the pit.

Bump...bump...bump...bump...bump...

"What is that? Footsteps?"

...bump...bump...bump...bump...

"It's getting louder."

The sound quickened, like a Harley accelerating.

"I think something's coming up the ladder."

Phil decided he'd had enough. This was the part in the movie where the stupid kids got their guts ripped out, and he didn't want to stick around for it. He spun on his heels and hauled ass for the entrance, just in time to see a very old man with a pulpy, misshapen face slam the door closed.

Phil grabbed for the knob and pushed, but the door held firm.

"He locked us in! Old Man Loki locked us in!"

Rory kept his focus on the pit. "I think I can see some..."

A black hairy thing sprang out of the hole and yanked Rory downward. The flashlight spun in the empty air for the briefest of seconds, and then fell into the pit after Rory, the light dimming until the room was drenched in pitch black.

Phil stood stock-still in the darkness.

A minute passed.

Five.

He heard whimpering, and realized it was his own.

This can't be happening, he thought. Why was this happening?

Bump.

A sound. Coming from the pit.

The thing was climbing the ladder.

Phil forced himself to back up until he was pressed against the door.

"Hailmaryfulofgracethelordiswithyou—"

...bump...bump...bump...bump...bump...

"—blessedartthouamong—"

The noise crescendoed, then stopped.

The silence was horrible.

Phil couldn't see anything, but he could feel the presence of something large and warm coming towards him. Something that smelled like rotten eggs and wet dog.

He screamed, and kept screaming when it wrapped its prickly tentacles around his face, a thousand hooks digging in and pulling. Phil's hands shot up to push the pain away, and similar barbs shot into his palms.

His screaming stopped when the barbs filled his open mouth.

Then, with a quick tug, Phil was dragged down into the pit.

There was a sensation of falling, skin burning and tearing away, consciousness blurring into a darkness as complete as the one that surrounded him.

And suddenly, Phil was watching a movie in his head. A shaky, black and white film of him and Rory breaking into Old Man Loki's mansion. Rory had the crowbar, and they used it on Loki, breaking his bones, bashing his face, demanding his money. Old Man Loki moaning the whole time, "The shed! The shed!" Repeating it over and over, even when Rory jammed the crowbar down the old man's throat.

The movie abruptly cut to Phil as a much older man, clad in an orange prison uniform. He was strapped to a chair, a guard swabbing electrolyte on his temples and his left leg. The switch was thrown and Phil's blood began to boil within his veins, every nerve locked in agony.

Phil watched the prison doctor pronounce him dead, watched as his own soul left his body, transporting him to Loki's estate.

A terrifying deja vu ensued as he viewed himself acting out the same scenario he'd experienced only moments ago. Breaking into the shed—the thing grabbing Rory—getting dragged into the pit—

When Phil finally caught up with himself, he discovered he was in a small, stone dungeon.

Next to him, a forty-year-old version of Rory was chained to a medieval torture rack, naked and stretched out until his shoulders had separated. His body was a haven of slithering, spiny worms, which burrowed underneath his skin.

"Hi, buddy." Rory offered a bloody smile, his teeth filed down to exposed nerves. "Be nice to have some company."

Phil remembered that Rory had been executed eight years prior.

"What's going on? What happened to the shed?"

Rory whimpered, a worm tunneling into his ear. "Old Man Loki didn't have no shed. That's why we beat him to death. Kept saying it over and over, when we asked him where his money was."

"But we just broke into the shed."

The worm stitched out of Rory's nose, trailing crimson mucus. "The shed is the doorway to this place. I remember breaking in, too. Right after I died."

Phil squeezed his eyes shut. His temples still burned where the electrodes had been attached. But the memory of his own death dwarfed the fear he felt right now.

He opened his eyes and tried to bolt, panic surging through him. But, like Rory, he found himself tied to a rack. His eyes fell upon a fire pit, where a dozen branding irons glowed white.

A squat, hairy man entered the room. He had sharp horns sticking out of his head where ears would normally be, and his skin was a dull shade of crimson.

He picked up a hot iron and gave Phil a fanged grin.

"Welcome to eternity, Phil. Let's get started."

Them's Good Eats

I had this terrible little story idea stuck in my head for almost twenty years, and finally put it down on paper for the collection Gratia Placente published by Apex Digest. One of my rare jumps into science-fiction, though this is more horrific black humor than sci-fi.

"Damn, Jimmy Bob, these are damn good cracklins."

Earl's face—wrinkled and sporting three days' worth of gray whiskers—glistened with a fine sheen of lard. A hot Georgia breeze blew smells of tilled earth and manure, but the overpowering scent was pig skins, fresh from the deep fryer. Earl eagerly reached for the plate Jimmy Bob held out, a pile of pork rinds stacked onto a grease-soaked paper towel.

"Thanks, Earl," Jimmy Bob said. "Got me a new way of preparation."

"Tell me." Earl scooped two more into his mouth and chewed so fast he risked a tongue severing. "I been eating cracklins since I was weened off the tit, ain't never had any this good before."

"It's a secret."

"Chicken shit. Tell me or I'll beat it out of you."

Jimmy Bob snorted, a sound not unlike a fat bullfrog croaking. He slapped Earl on the back, hard enough to make the old man's dentures slup off his gums and out of his mouth. The teeth bounced onto the dirty wooden porch.

Jimmy Bob stared down at Earl, a man half his weight and forty years his senior, and smiled big.

"Well, I wouldn't want to take a beating, Earl. The secret, my good buddy, is skinning the piggies while they still alive and kicking."

"Doe thip?" Earl said. He'd been going for "no shit" but hadn't stuck his teeth back in yet.

Jimmy Bob held up his hand, preacherman-style. "That's the God's truth, Earl. Something about them porkers struggling and squealing before they die, tenderizes their skins and imparts that extra tangy sensation. Longer they struggle, tastier they get."

Earl wiped his falsies on his bib overalls and slurped them into his eating hole.

"You're putting me on," Earl said.

"You got a dead spider in your bridgework, Earl."

Earl picked out a dry Daddy Longlegs and flicked it over his shoulder, then repeated his prior statement.

"I'm honest as the day is scorchin', Earl. Ain't just the cracklings, neither. Bacon comes out so juicy it melts in your mouth, and you can cut the pork chop with a spoon they're so tender."

"Now I know you're funning me, Jim Bob. Ain't no way you can carve up a hog while it's still kicking. It would run like the dickens, and the blood would make it all slippery."

"I built me a hog rack, out of wood. Keeps it locked in place while I do the carving. Put on the salt and vinegar while they're still wiggling, so it soaks in. Louder then hell, but you're tasting the results. Want another one?"

"Hell yeah."

Earl was reaching for more when the big silver saucer flew out from behind a fluffy white cloud, situated itself over Jimmy Bob's porch, and hit the two men with a beam of light.

There was a moment of searing hot pain, then darkness.

* * *

Jimmy Bob awoke on his back. His head hurt. His last memory was of Earl, who had come over with a mason jar full of his rotgut corn shine, and he figured he had himself a granddaddy hangover. But Jimmy Bob couldn't remember drinking any of the shine. All he could recall was eating cracklins.

He stared up at the ceiling, and realized it wasn't his ceiling. It was silver, and curvy.

Then he noticed he was naked. Even worse, Earl was on the floor next to him, similarly declothed.

"Oh sweet Jesus, how drunk did we get?"

Jimmy Bob reached for his nether regions, but nothing down there seemed to ache from use. Thank the lord for that.

He sat up, the metal floor smooth and cool under his buttocks, and looked around. The room they were in was all silver. No furniture. No carpet. No doors or windows. No lights, even though he could see just fine. It was like being inside a giant metal can.

Then Jimmy Bob jerked, remembering the spaceship in the sky, the blinding bright light.

An unidentified flying saucer. A UFO.

Lordy, him and Earl had been ubducticated.

He nudged his old buddy.

"Earl! Get your ass up. We're in some shit."

Earl didn't move.

"Goddammit, Earl!"

He shoved Earl again. Earl remained still. Jimmy Bob noticed his friend wasn't breathing, and had taken on an unhealthy bluish tint.

Jimmy Bob knew about CPR from watching TV, and much as he didn't want to touch lips with the older man, especially since they both were nekkid, he forced Earl's mouth open and blew hard down the old geezer's throat.

His breath didn't go nowhere, no matter how hard he gusted, and Jimmy Bob squinted down and saw the big bulge in Earl's neck.

Earl has swallowed his falsies.

Jimmy Bob stuck his finger into Earl's mouth, tried to fish the teeth out, but they were down too far and Earl's throat was cold and slimy and disgusting and after ten or so seconds Jimmy Bob realized he didn't like Earl that much to begin with so he took his hand back and wiped the spit off on Earl's thick tangle of gray chest hairs.

Jimmy Bob wondered if he should say some words, but he didn't know no prayers and then he got really scared because he was alone—all alone—in an alien spaceship, so he tried to give Earl CPR again.

It didn't work no better the second time, and then Jimmy Bob got up and started pacing back and forth, terrible thoughts bouncing around in his bean.

He'd seen all the movies. Starship Troopers. Independence Day. War of the Worlds. Alien. Predator. Alien vs. Predator. No good ever came out of being abducticated. The aliens were always bad guys who wanted to take over the world or eat people's guts or hunt humans for sport or get folks pregnant in their bellies or give painful probes up the brown place.

Jimmy Bob didn't want none of that to happen to him. He wondered why those guys that made movies never made one about an alien who came to earth and gave a lucky farmer a brand new plow. He'd watch that on the cable, for sure. But instead it was always death rays and cut-off heads.

Jimmy Bob yelled for help, loud as he could, so loud his ears hurt. No one answered.

He ran to the nearest wall, pushed against it. The surface was slippery, almost like it was covered with a fine layer of grease. He grunted with effort, but the metal was solid, immobile. Jimmy Bob walked around the room, trying to find some sort of seam, some sort of crease. Everything he touched was rock solid and perfectly smooth.

Jimmy Bob sat in the center of the room and hugged his knees to his chest. He wondered if they was still flying over earth, or if they was already in another universe, about to land on some weird planet with rivers made of acid and trees that looked like rib bones. He wondered what the aliens looked like. Tall and gray with big glowin eyes? Green and scaly with sharp fangs? Or did they have fish heads, like that commander guy in Star Wars? And what did they want from him?

Was it the butt probes?

He looked at Earl. Earl got off easy, the lucky bastard. Maybe Jimmy Bob could fish out those false teeth and choke on them himself. Not a bad idea, considering. He began to crawl towards his dead friend when he heard a buzzing sound.

It sounded like a pissed off hornet, and seemed to come from everywhere at once. Jimmy Bob looked around, tried to find the source, and noticed a pinpoint of white light on the wall. First it was a real tiny, and then it grew into a larger and larger circle until it was the size of a manhole cover.

Death ray.

Jimmy Bob crabbed backwards, trying to get away from the death ray, but there was no place to go. He retreated until he was up against the opposite wall, fists and teeth clenched, waiting for the final ZAP that would make his skeleton light up then turn him into cigarette ashes.

The ZAP didn't come. In fact, the more he looked at the light, the more Jimmy Bob began to think it looked more like a door than a death ray.

Was this some kind of alien trick? If he went through the door, would he be hunted down like a deer, aliens in big orange coats chasing him through the woods? Would he have to fight in some alien gladiator battle? Would he be forced to squat on a probe the size of a fire plug?

Maybe none of those things. Maybe this was a chance to escape.

Jimmy Bob took a quick look at lumpy-throat Earl, then sprang to his feet and ran for the circle of light. He was almost upon it when something flew out the doorway at him.

It was large, and red, and hit him in the chest with the force of a football tackle. Jimmy Bob tumbled backwards, the weight of the thing pinning him down, blanketing him in a warm, wet goo.

Jimmy Bob screamed.

The thing on top of him also screamed, and Jimmy Bob bucked and pushed and got it off and scurried away, his eyes focusing on a creepy crimson alien, completely hairless, dripping head to toe with some kind of blood-like fluid.

No, it wasn't blood-like. It was actual blood.

And the creature wasn't an alien.

"No more," it whimpered. Its voice was thick and wet.

Like Jimmy Bob, it was naked. A man. A human man. Or what was left of one. Every square inch of his body was bleeding, thick and viscous like he'd been dunked in raspberry preserves. The man lay on his back, trembling, red smudges coating the floor where he had rolled.

"Hey buddy, you okay?" Jimmy Bob asked, knowing how ridiculous it must have sounded.

"No more...please...no more..."

Jimmy Bob chewed his lower lip and looked the man over. There didn't seem to be any main wound. Instead, his whole body was a wound. He hadn't been skinned—Jimmy Bob didn't see any exposed muscle or fat on the man. No, this man looked more like he'd been worked over with a cheese grater. Every square inch was raw and bloody. Even his eyelids looked scraped.

"What happened to you?" Jimmy Bob asked.

The man's chest rose and fell. "Kill me," he said.

"Who are you?"

"Please...kill me. I tried to...kill myself...by breaking open my head...but I always knock myself out first."

The bleeding man lifted his head then rammed it viciously into the floor, making a hollow pinging sound.

"Are we on an alien ship?" Jimmy Bob asked.

The man's eyes opened, startlingly white compared to the redness of his body. His eyes locked on Jimmy Bob.

"I'm begging you...kill me..."

Jimmy Bob crawled over to the man.

"Answer my questions."

"I want to die."

Jimmy Bob slapped him. The man howled like a dog with a toothache.

"Keep it together. I need to know what's going on."

Rather than reply, the man began to sob. Jimmy Bob slapped him once more. And a few times after that. It was like hitting a wet fish.

"Damn it, tell me what's going on! Answer me!"

"I'll...I'll tell you...if you promise to kill me after."

Jimmy Bob considered it. He'd never killed a man before, but if anyone needed killing, this poor bastard did. He figured he could snap his neck, if'n he got a good hold of it. Couldn't be any harder than breaking hog necks, which he did with tasty regularity.

"Deal. Now tell me what's happening."

"Appealing. It's appealing."

The man began to sob again, and Jimmy Bob smacked him on the chest to get his attention.

"What's appealing?"

"They...pulled them all off."

"You're not making sense. Start at the beginning."

"They...caught me when I was in the woods...hunting coon. Ship. A big white light. At first I didn't know where I was...didn't know what had happened. They left me in this room. I don't know...for how long. But then...they came."

"Who?"

"Aliens. Short...like midgets. Big heads and tiny mouths. Scales instead of skin. They took me...took me to the room and..."

The man began to cry again. Jimmy Bob dug his fingernails into the man's shoulder to help him focus.

"And what?"

"And they put me...in the machine. It...it scraped my skin off."

"But why? Why torture you? Did they ask you questions?"

"No."

"Were you," Jimmy Bob winced, "probed?"

"They...they kept me in there...just long enough."

"Long enough for what?"

"For me to bleed. Then they took me here. I thought it was over. But they came back. They always come back."

"For what? What do they want?"

The buzzing sound began again, and the pinpoint light on the wall began to grow.

"Kill me! You promised!"

Jimmy Bob backed up to the other side of the room, fear oozing out of every pore. Two figures stepped through the light. They were short, green, with heads like watermelons and tiny little black eyes. True to form, they wore little silver suits, and held little silver ray guns.

"Get away from me, you stinking space iguanas!" yelled Jimmy Bob.

They shot their little guns, and Jimmy Bob was paralyzed where he stood, his muscles locked by an unpleasant tingle of electricity. Space tasers.

He strained to move but couldn't.

The aliens approached, walking in a strange, waddling gait, as if their oversized heads were threatening to tip them over. Jimmy Bob noticed childlike, almost delicate, noses and mouths on their broad faces, and their black rat eyes had a glint of red to them. He watched as they went to Earl, poked him with their clawed fingers, and then spoke rapidly to each other in some foreign space language that sounded a lot like that singing chipmunk cartoon. They didn't look happy.

Jimmy Bob tried to speak, but his jaw felt like it had been wired shut and he could only manage a few grunts. If only he could talk, maybe he could get out of this. Reason with them. Or bribe them. Maybe they'd like Jimmy Bob's complete collection of state quarters, each coin in mint condition and sealed in a protective plastic case. Or maybe they'd want his grandma's antique sterling silver serving set, complete except for a single salad fork that he broke adjusting the carb on his Chevy.

Jimmy Bob tried to say, "Silverware," but only a grunt came out. They didn't seem impressed. Their little iguana claws latched onto his wrists and pulled him forward with amazing ease. Jimmy Bob noticed for the first time that he was floating a few inches about the floor, and they tugged him along as if he were a balloon. The aliens maneuvered him through the opening, and he caught a last glimpse of his bleeding cellmate, who had resumed bashing his own head into the floor.

Jimmy Bob was pulled through a large metal tube, first right, then left, then down a gradual incline sort of like those tube slides at Chuck E. Cheese. The aliens kept chittering to each other, and one of them patted Jimmy Bob on the thigh and smiled.

Maybe this will be okay, Jimmy Bob thought. Maybe they won't hurt me.

A few seconds later, Jimmy Bob was placed into a large upright box, which closed around him like a coffin and dipped him into complete darkness.

Then, agony.

At first, it felt like being burned alive. But there wasn't any heat. The pain was the same, though, every nerve in his body firing at once. It was as if someone was using a power sander on his body, scraping every inch from head to toe. There was even a probe, but it felt more like a giant drill bit, coring out his unhappy place. Jimmy Bob screamed in his throat, screamed until he was sure it bled like the rest of him.

After an unknown amount of time, Jimmy Bob passed out.

He came to while being pulled back through the hallway, and then shot, like a rocket, back through the doorway and back into the original room. He hit the floor with a wet splat, and rolled onto his belly, the pain driving him mad, eating him alive. He was no longer frozen by the ray gun taser, but he dared not twitch because even the slightest movement was torture.

"Kill me," someone said.

He glanced right, his eyes already crusting with dried blood, and saw his cellmate.

Jimmy Bob asked, "Why are they doing this?" but it came out garbled— even his tongue had been scraped raw.

"Been here...weeks...maybe months. They use...an IV...so we don't die..."

"Why?" Jimmy Bob asked again.

"Snacks."

Jimmy Bob wasn't sure he heard right.

"What?"

"We're snacks."

"How? They suck our blood?"

His cellmate sobbed.

"Scabs. They wait until we heal, then peel off the scabs and eat them. Like beef jerky."

Jimmy Bob moaned. Those little iguana bastards were going to wait until his scoured body began to scab over, and then tear off the scabs? He couldn't bear it.

"A dozen of them come in with pliers," the man said, even though Jimmy Bob didn't want to hear no more, "They peel off every last piece. They're slow eaters, too."

"Jesus, no."

"And..." the man became full blown hysterical, "they dip us in salt and vinegar so we taste better!"

Jimmy Bob squeezed his eyes shut. He could already feel the sores on his body begin to heal, begin to clot. The light on the wall appeared, and began to get bigger.

"You promised to kill me!" the man shrieked at Jimmy Bob.

A bunch of space iguanas filed in, chirping at each other like Alvin and the band, snapping gleaming metal pincers. One of them held up a bottle of hot sauce.

"NOOOOOO!" Jimmy Bob began to scream before the space taser froze his vocal parts.

Then the snacking began.

Jimmy Bob hadn't thought his pain could get any worse.

But it did.

First Time

I wrote this when I turned thirty. I never was able to sell it, perhaps because it's a bit too obvious. This is also one of the few shorts I've ever written with an omniscient narrator, popping into the heads of more than one person in the same scene.

"Were you nervous your first time?"

Robby didn't break stride. He could clearly remember that smelly hotel room, Father paying the money, the girl naked and waiting.

"A little," he answered his brother. "Everyone's nervous the first time."

"I guess I am too. A little."

Pete looked it. Thirteen and small for his age, lost in one of Robby's old T-shirts. But that's how Robby was at thirteen, walking into that room. And ten minutes later, he walked out a man, ready to take on the whole damn world. Robby wished their father was there, then cursed himself for the thought. He was the man of the family now, since Father had gone away. It was his job to initiate Pete.

"How long do I have?" Pete asked.

"Long as it takes. Once you pay, you're there 'till it's done."

"Is it a lot different from animals?" They lived on a farm, so both boys had a lot of experience with animals.

"A lot different. Think about it. A real woman, like in one of those magazines. Naked and all yours. Maybe I'll even do one too."

"Really?" Robby knew he wouldn't. They didn't have enough money for two. Besides, Robby did it enough at home. He was eighteen, and picked up women whenever he liked. His boyish good looks, just this side of full-blown manhood, attracted girls like flies to compost. Robby was a real lady killer.

"Are we almost there Robby?"

"Almost."

The neighborhood was seedy, all cracked sidewalks and graffiti and urine soaked winos. It hadn't changed at all since Father brought him here, those years ago. He could still picture the face of his first girl—oval, with high cheek bones and bright red lipstick that made her mouth look like a wound. Her eyes were vacant, wasted on some drug, but not so wasted that she didn't moan when he stuck it in.

You never forget your first.

The boys cut through an alley, rats scurrying out of their path. Pete moved a little closer to his brother. He was nervous, but didn't want to show it. Robby was his hero. He wanted to make him proud. He relished every story Robby told him about his times with women, forever caught between awe and envy. Now it was his turn.

"Did Father watch you?" Robby asked.

"Yeah. He watched. Afterward he said he was real proud of how I gave it to her."

Pete's face bunched up.

"I don't remember Father so good. Before they took him away."

"Father's a great man. We'll see him again some day. Don't worry."

Pete looked up at his older brother. "Will you watch me, Robby?"

"If you want me too."

"I want you too."

"I will then. Here we are."

The alley door was brown and rotten. Robby kicked it twice.

"I got money!" That was what Father had said five years ago, and Robby's chest swelled saying the same words. After a moment the door inched open. A red eye peered through the crack.

"You the ones called earlier?"

The boys nodded.

"You cops?" Pete giggled.

"Hell no, we ain't cops!"

The door opened, revealing a short, thick man with hairy arms.

"Thirty bucks."

Robby took six fives from his pocket and laid them out one at a time. They quickly disappeared into the man's dirty jeans.

"You or the kid?"

"It will be Pete tonight," Robby said.

They followed the man through a hall lit with single bare bulb, down some stairs, and into a basement thick with mold. Against the wall, naked and waiting, was the girl. She was fatter than Robby's first one, with dirty knees and smeared lipstick and so much blue eye shadow she looked like a peacock. But there was some life in her eyes, a tiny spark that hadn't been totally dulled by the drugs.

"Hey, hey guys," she said, her voice slurring. "Untie me and we can party, okay?"

"You bring your own?" the man asked Pete.

Pete nodded, patting his pocket. The man spit on the floor, and then left the basement.

"What's you name, beautiful?" Robby asked. He put a hand on her cheek and she nuzzled against his touch.

"Candy. Can you untie my hands? I'm better when I can use my hands."

"Hi Candy, this is Pete. You're gonna be his first."

"Hey, Petey," she flashed him a whore's smile, a curved mouth without any trace of warmth. "Come get some Candy, baby."

Pete licked his lips and gave his brother a glance. Robby nodded his approval, and backed away.

"She's all yours, Pete. Do her good."

Pete looked at her, hanging there by her wrists, and couldn't believe this was really happening. It was almost as if he wasn't there, but rather above himself someplace, watching everything going on.

She protested when she saw the knife. The protest was soon replaced by crying. Pete made some tentative cuts at first. Her screams were so loud that it freaked him out.

"No one can hear," Robby assured him. "Just mind the blood."

Getting brave, Pete jabbed deeper and harder. It was just like Robby had told him. She cried. She begged. And every sound made Pete hate her even more. The excitement built and built, and he cut faster and harder, and finally he lost control and stuck the knife in her neck and there was a gurgling choking sound and then she wasn't moving.

Pete took a step back, his heart hammering, the thick smell of blood filling his nostrils. He was excited, but disappointed that it ended so fast. Robby patted his shoulder.

"Nice job. I'm proud of you. Father would be proud too."

"It wasn't...too quick?" Robby laughed.

"The first one is always quick. You'll be able to last longer the more you do it."

The door opened behind them. It was the short man, with a mop and bucket. Pete looked at the dead girl, wishing he could take her home as a trophy. He settled on the left breast, putting it in a plastic bag we brought with for the purpose.

"A breast man," Robby laughed. "Just like Father."

"When can I do it again, Robby?"

"Whenever you want. I'll teach you how to get women, just like Father taught me. It gets more and more fun each time. Remember to wipe off your knife. We'll ditch it down a sewer grate on the way home."

Robby made a show of eyeing the body.

"Good work. You really wrangled some screams out of her. Didn't I tell you it was more fun than slaughtering a pig?"

"A lot more fun. I'm gonna write Father in prison, tell him I finally did it."

"Good idea. He'd like that. Now I think you deserve—some ice cream!"

Pete grabbed his older brother and hugged him.

"Thanks, Robby."

Robby took a deep breath, filling his lungs with pride. He thought about Tommy and Ed and Jasper, all younger than Pete, all anxious for their first times.

"After the ice cream, let's tell our brothers. Tommy's turn is coming up in October."

"He's gonna love it," Pete said, and the two of them walked out of the basement, through the building, and down the alley, searching the seedy neighborhood for a place that sold soft serve.

Forgiveness

The toughest horror magazine to get into is Cemetery Dance, and I sent them a few things before they finally published this one. Odd thing though, they never gave me a formal acceptance, or a contract, or a check. I only knew it saw print because some guy at a writing convention brought a copy up to me to sign.

The woman putting the tube into my penis has cold hands.

She's younger than I am—everyone is younger than I am—but she betters me in the wrinkle department; scowl lines, frown lines, deep-set creases between the eyebrows. The first woman to touch my peter in fifty years, and she has to be a gargoyle.

I close my eyes, wince as the catheter inches inward, my nostrils dilating with ammonia and pine-lemon disinfectant and something else that I knew so well.

Death.

Death has many smells. Sometimes it smells like licking copper pennies out of used public washrooms. Other times it smells like cold cuts pickled in vinegar, left in the sun to rot.

On me it smells sour. Gassy and bloated and ripe.

"There you go, Mr. Parson." She pulls down my gown and covers me with the thin blanket. Her voice is perfunctory, emotionless.

She knows who I am, what I've done.

"I'd like to talk to someone."

"Who?"

"A priest."

She purses her lips, lines deepening around her mouth in cat whisker patterns.

"I'll see what I can do."

The nurse leaves.

I stare at the white cinder block walls over the hump of my distended stomach. Edema. My body can no longer purge itself of fluid, and I look ten months pregnant. The morphine drip controls the worst of the pain, the sharp stuff. But the dull, cold ache of my insides rotting away can't be dampened by any drug.

The room is cool, dry, quiet. No clock in here. No TV. No window. The door doesn't have bars, but it is reinforced with steel and only opens with a key.

As if escape is still an option.

Time passes, and I go into my mind and tried to figure out what I want to say, how to say it. So many things to straighten out.

The next thing I know the priest is sitting beside the bed, nudging me awake.

"You wanted to see me, Mr. Parson?"

Young, blond, good-looking, his Roman collar starched and bright. Youthful idealism sparkles in his eyes.

Life hasn't knocked the hope out of him yet.

"Do you know who I am, Father?"

He smiles. Even white teeth. Little points on the canines.

"I've been informed."

I watch his face. "Then you know what I've done?"

"Yes."

I see patience, serenity. Old crimes don't shock people-- they have the emotional impact of lackluster history books.

But the crimes are still fresh in my mind. They're always fresh. The images. The sounds.

The tastes.

"I've killed people, Father. Innocent people."

"God forgives those who seek forgiveness."

My tongue feels big in my mouth. I speak through trembling lips. "I've been locked up in here since your parents were babies."

He rests his elbows on his knees, leaning in closer. His hair smells like soap, and he's recently had a breath mint.

"You've spent most of your life in this place, paying your debt to society. Isn't it time to pay your debt to the Lord?"

And what of the Lord's debt to me?

I cough up something wet and bloody. The priest gives me a tissue from the bedside table. I ball it up in my fist, squeeze it tight.

"What's your name, Father?"

"Bob."

"Father Bob—I've got cancer turning my insides into mush. The pain, sometimes, is unbearable. But I deserve that and more for what I've done."

I pause, meet his eyes.

"You know I was once a priest."

He pats my hand, his fingers brushing my IV.

"I know, Mr. Parson."

Smug. Was I that smug, when I was young?

"I'm in here for killing twelve people."

Another pat on the hand.

"But there were more than twelve, Father."

Many more. So many more.

His complacent smile slips a notch.

"How many were there, Mr. Parson?"

The number is intimate to me, something I haven't ever shared before.

"One hundred and sixty-seven."

The smile vanishes, and he blinks several times.

"One hundred and—"

I interrupt. "They were children, mostly. War orphans. No one ever missed them. I'd pick them up at night, offer them money or food. There was a place, out by the docks, where no one could hear the screams. Do you know how I killed them?"

A head shake, barely perceptible.

"My teeth, Father. I tied them up—tied them up naked and filthy and screaming—and I kept biting them until they died."

The priest turns away, his face the color of the walls.

"Mr. Parson, I..."

The memories fill my head; the dirty, bloody flesh, the piercing cries for help, the wharf rats scurrying over my feet and fighting for scraps...

"It isn't easy, Father, to break the skin. Human teeth aren't made for tearing. You have to nip with the front incisors until you make a small hole, then clench down hard and tug back, putting your neck and shoulders into it. It took a long time. Sometimes hours for them to die."

I sigh through my teeth.

"I'd make them eat bits of themselves..."

The priest stands, but I grab his wrist with the little strength I had left. He can't leave, not yet.

"Please, Father. I need Penance."

He takes a breath, stares at me. Watching him regain composure is like watching a drunk wake up in a strange bed. He manages it, finally, but some of that youthful idealism is gone.

"Are you sorry for what you've done?"

"I'm sorry, Father." The tears come, a rusty faucet that has gone unused for years. "I'm sorry and I beg for God's forgiveness. I'm...so...alone. I've been so alone."

He touches my face as if petting a crocodile, but I'm grateful for the touch.

The tears don't last long. I swat them away with tissue.

Together we say the Act of Contrition.

The words are familiar on my tongue, but my conscience isn't eased.

There's more.

"Rest now, Mr. Parson." He makes the sign of the cross on my forehead with his thumb, but his eyes keep flitting to the door, the way out.

"Father..."

"Yes?"

I have to proceed carefully here. "How strong is your faith?"

"Unshakable."

"What if...what if you no longer needed faith?"

"I will always need faith, Mr. Parson."

For the first time since his arrival, I allow myself a small smile. "Not if you have proof."

"What do you mean?"

"If there is proof that God exists, you'd no longer need faith. You would have knowledge— tangible knowledge."

He narrows his eyes. "You have this proof? A lapsed priest?"

"Defrocked, Father. My title was stripped."

"Of course it was. You killed..."

I sigh, wet and heavy. "You misunderstand, Father Bob. They didn't defrock me because of the murders. My vocation was taken away from me because I knew too much."

I lower my voice so he must lean closer to hear me.

"I KNOW God exists, Father."

The priest frowns, folds his arms.

"The great mystery of Faith is that we accept God without knowing. If God wanted us to truly know, he would appear on earth and touch us."

I raise my hand, point at him.

"You're wrong there, Father. He has come down and touched us. Touched me." This is the tricky part. "Would you like to see the proof?"

I almost shout with glee when he nods his head.

"Sit, Father Bob. This story takes a while."

He sits beside me, his face a mixture of interest and wariness.

My mouth is dry. I take a sip from a cup of tepid water, soak my tongue.

"Fresh from the Seminary, I was sent to Western Samoa, a group of islands in the South Pacific. It's tropical paradise, the population predominantly Christian. A garden of Eden, one of the most beautiful places on earth. Except for the hurricanes. I arrived after a particularly devastating storm wiped out most of Apia, the capitol."

It comes back in fragments, a series of faded snapshots. After a twenty hour plane ride, I landed in little more than a field. The island air and deep blue beaches were a stark contrast to the wholesale destruction throughout the land. I saw livestock rotting in trees. Overturned cars with little brown arms jutting out crookedly beneath them. Roofs in the middle of streets, and jagged pipes planted in piles of rubble where schools once stood.

Worst of all was the constant, keening sob that hung over the city like a cloud.

So many ruined lives.

"It looked like God had smashed His mighty fist down on that country. How could He have allowed this? I had to assist in the amputation of a man's legs, without anesthetic because there was none left. I had to help mothers bury their babies using gnarled traffic signs to dig graves. I gave so much blood I almost died myself."

"Natural disasters are a test of one's faith."

I shake my head.

"It didn't test mine. I was sure in my faith, like you are. But it made me question God's intent."

"We cannot question God, Mr. Parson."

"But we do anyway, don't we?"

I sip more water before I continue.

"In Western Samoa, I did God's work. I helped to heal. To rebuild. I restarted the parish. I preached to these poor, proud people about God's grace, and they believed me. Things slowly got back to normal. And then the murders began."

I close my eyes and see the first body, as if it is in the room with me now. The eyes jut out of the bloody, ruined face like two golf balls pushed into the meat of a watermelon. The flesh is peeled away, in some places exposing pink bone. A rat pokes its greasy head out of a lacerated abdomen and squeals in gluttonous delight.

"Every seven days, another mutilated body was discovered. The police didn't seem to care. Neither did my congregation. They accepted it like they accepted the hurricane; sad but unavoidable."

Father Bob folds his arms, eyebrows furrowing.

"Were you killing those people, Mr. Parson?"

"No...it turned out to be one of my parishioners. A fisherman with a wife and three kids. He came to me just after he butchered one—came into my Confessional drenched in blood, bits of tissue sticking to his nails and teeth. Begged me for forgiveness."

The man had been short, painfully thin for a Samoan. His eyes were the eyes of the damned, flickering like windblown candles, both insane and afraid.

"He claimed he was a victim of a curse. A curse that had been plaguing his island for millennia."

"Did you dismiss his superstitions?"

"At first. While Christians, the islanders had a distant connection to paganism, sometimes fell back to it. I tried to convince him the curse wasn't real, to turn himself in. I begged him that God didn't want any more killing."

I was so earnest, so full of the Word. Convinced I was doing God's work.

"He laughed at me. He said that killing is exactly what God wanted."

The priest shakes his head. He speaks with the sing-song voice of a kindergarten teacher. "God is all-loving. Killing is a result of free-will. We had the paradise of Eden, and chose knowledge instead of bliss."

I scowl at him.

"God created mankind knowing that we'd fall from grace. It's like having a child, knowing a child will be hungry, and then punishing the child for that hunger."

Father Bob leans in, apparently flustered. "God's grace..."

"God has no grace," I spit. "He's a vengeful, vindictive God. A sadist, who plays with mankind like a child pulling the wings off of flies. Samoa was Eden, Father. The real Eden, straight out of the Bible. The murderer, he showed me a mark on his scalp."

I lift up my bangs, reveal the Mark at my hairline.

"Witness, Father Bob! Proof that God truly exists!"

The priest opens his mouth. It takes a moment before words came out.

"Is that...?"

I nod. I feel inner strength, the strength that had forsaken me so long ago.

"It's the Mark of Cain, given to the son of Adam when he slew Abel. But the Bible was inaccurate on that point—Cain didn't wander the earth forever, but his curse did, passed on from man to man for thousands of years. Passed on to me from the murderer in Samoa."

The Mark grows warm on my head, begins to burn.

"This is your proof of God, Father."

He stands abruptly, his chair tumbling backwards. I grin at him.

"How does it feel to no longer need faith?"

Father Bob falls to his knees, weeping.

"My God...my sweet God..."

Abruptly, blessedly, the burning sensation disappears. I laugh, laugh for the first time in decades, laugh with a sense of perfect relief.

Father Bob presses his hands to his forehead. He screams, just once, a soul shattering epiphany that I understand so well.

"The Lord be with you, Father Bob."

And then he falls upon me, mouth open.

I try to push him away, but am no match.

His first few bites are awkward, but he quickly learns my technique.

Nip.

Clench.

Pull.

The pain is exquisite. So much worse than cancer.

So much better...

Redux

Another story for a Twilight Tales anthology. This was the first story of mine they ever accepted, for the collection Spooks. I'm mixing genres again, this time PI noir and ghost stories.

"Let me get this straight—you want me to murder you tonight?"

She nodded. "At midnight. As violently as possible."

I leaned back, my office chair creaking in distress. The woman sitting across from me was mid-thirties, thin, well groomed. Her blonde hair, pulled back in a tight bun, held a platinum luster, and the slash of red lipstick she wore made her lips look like a wound. There was something familiar about her, or maybe it was my whiskey goggles.

I blinked at my watch. 11:00am. I'd been soused since breakfast.

"And this decision is because of your dead husband?"

"Yes."

"You want to be—" I paused. "—reunited with him?"

A tricky word to pronounce, reunited, even when sober. But being a semi-professional drunk with some serious pro potential, it came out fine.

"I need to die, Mr. Arkin."

"Call me Bert. And you haven't offered your name yet, Miss..."

"Ahh...Springfield. Doris Springfield."

"Are you trying to atone for some sin, Ms. Springfield?"

Another tough sentence, but it slid out like butter.

"No. The death has to be violent, because a person needs to die violently in order to become a ghost."

I blinked. Then I blinked again. Before my face gave anything away, I broke her stare and went looking through my desk drawer for the Emergency bottle. I took two strong pulls.

A frank look of pity, perhaps disgust, flit past her eyes.

I shrugged it off. Who was she to judge me? She was the one who came in here wanting a violent death.

The bottle went back into the drawer, and I wiped my mouth on the back of my jacket sleeve.

"It's medicinal." I didn't care if she believed it or not. "So...you want to die to become a ghost?"

"Yes. He haunts me, my husband does. Not in any of the clichéd methods you've heard about; I mean, he doesn't break dishes or rattle chains. Instead, every night, he comes to me and holds me when I'm in bed."

Her eyes went glassy, and I frowned. Tears made me uncomfortable.

"We're both so very alone, Mr. Arkin. I want to...I must...be with him."

"Ms. Springfield, I'm sorry for your loss. But murder is—"

"I have thirty-six thousand dollars."

The number gave my weak resistance pause. I could put money like that to good use.

Since I'd gotten kicked off the force, a grievous wrong since half the guys in the CPD are alkies, employment opportunities nowadays were slim. I work as a night watchman four times a week at a warehouse, and do the private investigator thing in my free time, mostly lapping up scraps that my friend Barney throws me. Barney is still on the Job, and whenever something minor comes along that the cops don't have time for, he funnels it my way. Mostly cheating spouses and runaway kids.

But Barney never sent me anyone who wanted to die.

"Just how did you find me, Ms. Springfield?"

"I...I heard about your problem."

"Which problem is that?"

Her eyes, tinged with red, locked onto me like laser sights.

"You're being haunted, too."

This time there was no hiding my reaction, and I recoiled as if slapped. My shaky hands fumbled with the desk drawer, unable to open it fast enough.

The whiskey burned going down, but I fought the pain and sucked until my eyes watered.

Rather than face her, I got up and walked over to the window. My third floor view of the alley didn't change much from winter to summer, but it did offer me a brief moment to collect my thoughts.

"Who told you?" I managed to say.

"I'd...I'd rather not say. I'm asking you to do something illegal, and if something should happen...well, I wouldn't want it getting back to him."

I searched my mental Rolodex for people I'd blabbed to about my problem. Hell, it could have been any bar jockey in any of three dozen gin joints going back two years.

When I drink, I talk.

So I wind up talking a lot.

"Does this person—the one who sent you here—know that you want to die?"

"No. I simply asked around for someone who believes in ghosts, and your name came up. Who haunts you, Mr. Arkin?"

I shut my eyes on the view.

"My mother," I lied.

"She died violently?"

"You could say that."

The booze made my tongue feel big in my mouth, and I began to forget where I was. Usually a good thing, but now...

"I can't do this, Ms. Springfield."

"There's no way to link it to you. You can use my gun."

"That's not the problem. I just don't want this kind of thing on my conscience."

"Is thirty-six thousand enough?"

"Yes. No. I don't know."

"I also have these."

I turned to look at her. She opened her purse and took out a small, white envelope.

"Diamonds, Mr. Arkin. About six carats worth. My husband was a jeweler, and he assured me they're worth over twenty thousand dollars. I was going to leave them to charity, but..."

"Look, Ms. Springfield—"

"I'll leave you the papers on these. That's almost sixty-thousand dollars, Mr. Arkin."

Sixty grand for my conscience?

Who was I kidding? My conscience wasn't worth sixty cents.

"Congratulations, Ms. Springfield. You've hired yourself a killer.

* * *

I stumbled out of Harvey's Liquor on Diversey and took a nip right there in the middle of the street.

Chicago winter wind bit at my cheeks and face, making all the broken capillaries even redder. I stuck the bottle in my jacket and climbed into my car.

Driving was a blurry, dreamlike thing, but I managed to make it home.

Truth be told, I'd driven a lot worse. At least I could still see the traffic signals.

My apartment, a little shoe box in Hyde Park, had the smell to go along with the ambience. Checking the fridge revealed just a dirty pat of butter and some old pizza crusts.

So I had a liquid lunch instead.

Part of me wanted to sober up so I wouldn't make any mistakes tonight.

The other part wanted me to get drunk enough so I wouldn't remember the details later.

I took a spotty glass from the sink and poured myself three fingers and sat down at my cheap dinette set and drank.

I had to admire the lady. She had guts, and her plan looked like it would work.

At 11:45pm I arrive at her house on Christiana off of Addison. Park in the K-Mart lot across the street. Access her place from the alley; she'll leave her gate and her back door unlocked. The house will look like it had been robbed—drawers pulled out and pictures yanked off the walls. She'll be in the bedroom, hand me the gun. A quick blam-blam in the brain pan, and I can leave with the diamonds and the cash. No witnesses, no muss, no fuss.

I got to pouring another drink when the screech of tires raped my ears and made me drop the bottle.

There was a room-shaking, sickening crunch of motor vehicle meeting flesh, followed by the thump-thump of a skull cracking under the front and rear tires.

"Leave me alone, you little bitch!"

She came out of the wall and hovered before me. Her glow was soft and yellow, a flashlight bulb going dead.

I avoided looking at her face, even as she moved closer.

"You're a bad man, Mr. Arkin."

I bit the inside of my cheek, refusing to be baited.

"A very baaaaaaad man."

She touched my arm, and I jerked back, slopping my drink all over the table. Being touched by a ghost was like getting snow rubbed into your bare skin—so cold it was hot.

"Go away!"

I turned to get up, but she already stood in front of me. No more than five feet tall, her head a crushed pumpkin leaking brains instead of stringy seeds. One eye was popped out and dangling around her misshapen ear by the optic nerve. The other one stared, accusing.

"You can still turn yourself in."

I stumbled away, heading for the bedroom, bottle in hand.

"Call the police, Mr. Arkin. Confess...confess..."

I pulled the door open and screamed. My bedroom had become a winding stretch of suburban highway. Speeding at me at fifty MPH, a swerving, drunken maniac unscrewed his bottle cap rather than paid attention to the road.

Me. It was me driving.

The car hit like a slap from God, knocking me backwards, smearing my face and body against the phantom asphalt in a fifteen foot streak.

I lay there, in agony, as I watched myself get out of the car, look in my direction and vomit, and then get right back into the car and drive off.

The image faded, and I found myself lying on my stained carpet.

"Confess, Mr. Arkin."

I sought my dropped bottle, the worst of the nightly terror over for the time being.

"Confess?" I spat. "Why should I? Haven't you tortured me enough for the last two years? I ran you over once. You've done this to me how many times? Two hundred? Three?"

She stood next to me now, the loops of intestines hanging out of her belly giving me cold, wet slaps in the face.

"Go to the police and confess."

"Go to hell, or heaven, or wherever you're supposed to go."

I rolled away and struggled to my feet.

"I can't go away until my business here is done."

I drank straight from the bottle now, trying to tune her out. Confess? My ass. Going to the cops meant going to prison. And that just can't happen. I couldn't survive in prison.

They don't let you drink.

"You can't die without resolution, Mr. Arkin. If you do..."

"I know! You've said it a thousand times!"

"Your soul will be mine if you don't atone."

She cracked a bloody smile, all missing teeth and swollen tongue.

"I don't think you'll like eternity with me in charge."

I spun on her, jabbing a finger into her spongy head.

"I'll have money soon! Lots of money! I'll hire someone to exorcize your preachy little ass!"

She laughed, a full, rich, deep sound that made the hair on my arms vibrate.

"I'll be seeing you, Mr. Arkin. Soon."

And then she faded away, like a puff of cigar smoke.

I drank until I started to puke blood.

Then I drank some more.

* * *

My hands perspired in the latex gloves Ms. Springfield had provided. The alley behind her house was deserted, except for a rat scurrying into an old Pepsi box.

I walked up to her gate—it was the only one that was unlocked—and let myself into her modest backyard.

Dark ,silent, porch light off. Her back door opened with a whisper.

"Ms. Springfield?"

The door led into her kitchen. Drawers had been pulled out and silverware scattered along the floor. I avoided stepping on anything sharp, and made my way through the kitchen and into a hallway.

"Ms. Springfield? It's me."

Silence.

I took a pull from my flask, to calm my nerves. Then another, for luck.

"Ms. Springfield?"

She said to meet her in the bedroom. There were stairs to the right.

I ascended slowly, cautiously. The higher I climbed, the more this seemed like a very bad idea. Even if I could bring myself to murder her—and get away with it—who was to say she wouldn't haunt me too? One ghost was bad enough. Having two...

"Mr. Arkin?"

Her voice came as such a shock that I almost lost my balance on the steps.

"Ms. Springfield?"

"Second door on the right."

Her voice was terribly relaxed.

I took a deep breath, blew it out. Reflexively, my hand went to my hip holster, and I haven't worn a hip holster in years.

"I'll be right there," I said, more for myself than for her.

She was sitting on her bed, dressed in a white night gown. Her blonde hair hung over her shoulders. In her hand was a .38 police special.

I had a momentary flash of panic, but she turned the revolver around and handed it to me, butt first.

"I was worried you wouldn't come."

"Money makes a man do strange things."

I looked on the nightstand, next to the bed. Stacked in a neat pile, so many twenties I'd need a bag to carry them out.

So much money.

"It's almost midnight." Ms. Springfield's voice had a pleasant, almost cheerful lilt. "I want you to shoot me in the heart."

I shuffled from one foot to the other, uncomfortable.

"The head would be better."

"I don't intend joining my husband without a head to kiss him with."

Good point.

"The heart it is."

I moved closer, my gaze flickering between her and the money. Part of me wanted to just take the cash and run. I could make it to Mexico before the cops got on me.

"It's almost midnight, Mr. Arkin."

Her face—calm, so sure.

"This is what you really want, isn't it?"

For the first time since I'd met her, she smiled. "This is all I want."

She tilted her chin upward, thrust out her chest.

I extended the gun.

"This might hurt."

"Just keep firing until it's done. I want messy, remember?"

I chewed my lower lip. The gun shook in my grasp.

A drink. I needed a drink.

My free hand reached back for my flask, and Ms. Springfield's features erupted in pure anger.

"Shoot me, you worthless drunk!"

I fired.

The bullet took her in the center of the left breast, her white nightgown exploding in red fireworks. She pitched to the side, gasping like a landed fish.

I shot her in the back.

Twice.

Three times.

Still twitching. And a high-pitched, whistling wheeze from the sucking wounds in her chest.

"Aw, screw it."

I put the last two slugs in the back of her head.

She stopped moving.

Shoving the gun deep in my jacket, I went for the money. I took a bloody pillow case and began stuffing it full of stacks. The diamonds lay there too, and the papers. I grabbed them and turned to get the hell out of there, but the bedroom suddenly transformed into a highway, and for the second time today I ran myself over.

I tried to brace for the impact, but you can never brace for that kind of thing.

Even knowing it wasn't real, I screamed at the very real feeling of the impact sluicing through every nerve and fiber of my being. Spectral or not, it hurt like hell.

When I was able to move again, the pumpkin head ghost floated above my head, staring down with her one good eye.

But this time she had company.

"I believe you've met my daughter," said the ghost of Ms. Springfield. Her nightgown glowed white, peppered with ugly red starbursts. Bits of brain and bone floated above her hair like a halo.

She held a glowing .38.

The ghostly gun fired, and I felt the bullets rip into my body, gasping in pain and shock.

"It's not real," I told myself.

I lay there, listening to the slurping, keening sound of my lungs leaking air through the holes in my chest. Even though I wanted to move, I couldn't.

Even when I heard the approaching sirens.

* * *

Killing me? It would have been too easy.

Ms. Springfield knew I was the one who ran down her daughter. Her daughter told her.

The only thing stronger than the woman's grief had been her lust for revenge.

She truly did want to die, so she could join her child on the other side.

So they could be together.

So they could haunt me together.

I sat on the cold floor of my cell, hugging my knees.

I've been dry for over a month now, and it's been as bad as I thought. Shaking, vomiting, delirium tremens, pure hell.

But none of it's as bad as the ghosts.

Every day I am treated to an agonizing smearing across the highway, or having large holes blown out of my chest and head.

On some days, I get both.

And without the booze to deaden the pain...

In hindsight, I should have turned myself in after I hit that little girl.

I try to explain that to them. Try to get them to understand that I was just a scared drunk.

They show no mercy.

"And this is just a taste," Ms. Springfield repeatedly tells me. "When you die, your soul belongs to us. We have plans for you, Mr. Arkin."

They have shown me their plans.

Sometimes I cry so hard the prison doctor has to medicate me.

Life now centers on diet and exercise. I watch what I eat. I work out three times a day.

I'm in the best shape of my life.

Which is a good thing.

Because as horrifying as my life is, I want to live as long as I can.

The ghosts can run me over and gun me down a thousand times a day, and that is nothing compared to what they have in store for me after I die.

I don't want to die.

Please, God, don't let me ever die.

Bag

I wrote this for the zombie anthology Cold Flesh. It began as a writing exercise, where someone hands your protagonist a paper bag and says don't open it until midnight. I tried to think of the absolute worst thing a paper bag could contain…

"No thanks."

The bum thrust the bag at me again. Brown paper, bearing the name of a local grocery store, crumpled and filthy and dripping something brown.

"Take it."

I tried to shove him away using my elbows; he was even dirtier than the bag. Strange how these people are invisible until one is in your face, reeking of garbage and body odor and piss. This is what I get for forgoing a cab and deciding to get a little exercise on the way home from work.

"Take the bag, Jimmy."

I'd pushed him an arm's-length away, but his use of my first name was like a slap.

"How did you...?"

"The answer is in the bag. Take it."

I grinned. Someone I knew must have put this poor sap up to this. Maybe Marky, from Accounting, or my cousin Ernie, who was the only forty-year-old in all of Chicago who still thought joy buzzers were funny.

"Fine. You win. Give me the bag."

The street person smiled, giving me a blast of brown teeth and fortified wine. I took the brown bag, which had surprising heft to it, and reached into my pocket for some change.

"Don't open it until the sun goes down."

"Excuse me?"

He walked away, blending into the rush hour sidewalk crowd, before I could give him his dollar.

My first impulse was to open it right then and there. But there were people all over, and if this was from Cousin Ernie, it was probably offensive or even illegal. Good old Ernie once sent a sixty-eight-year-old stripper to my office, one whose pasties hung at belly button level and whose grand finale included popping out her dentures. If this drippy, heavy thing in the bag was from Ernie, it would be best to open it when I got home.

Home was on the Lake Shore, a high rise condo with a killer view and a 24-hour doorman and mirrors in the elevator. Not too shabby for a South Side kid who used to pitch pennies in back alleys for lunch money. Money had always been the primary motivator of my life, and the stock market was a natural evolution from teenage poker games and fantasy football pools.

I did okay. Better than okay. Enough to keep me in Armani and Cristal. I was on the short list for five star restaurants, and got to bed women of fine social standing, and twice a year I'd fly my mom to Tuscany so she could visit relatives who all worshipped me as a god.

Life was fine.

My condo was cold and smelled like vanilla, some kind of stuff the maid sprayed around after her afternoon visit. I plopped the bag up on the breakfast bar and went to the bedroom to strip, shower, and change into evening wear. Tonight was Molly Wainwright, of the Barrington Wainwrights, and she was ten years younger than me and a foxy little tramp who oozed sex like her daddy oozed real estate.

If all went well, Molly would be notch number ninety-seven on the Jimmy belt. That's ninety-seven runs batted in, out of a possible two hundred-twenty. I did the math in my head.

"Score tonight, I'll be batting .440."

Damn impressive for a South Side kid. And as far a fielding went, I only had one error in my entire career. It was an experience I didn't care to repeat.

I shaved, took the dry-cleaner's plastic from my gray suit, and decided to go with the diamond stud cufflinks. By the time I was dressed and ready to roll I'd completely forgotten about the leaky paper bag on my breakfast bar.

But when I went to the fridge for Evian, there it was, perched on the counter like an old alley cat.

I checked my Bvlgari—a quarter to six. The bum warned me not to open it until the sun went down, but that sounded like stupid Ernie theatrics and I didn't have time to play around. Slowly, gently, I unrolled the top of the bag and peeled it open.

The stench hit me like a sucker punch. Rotting meat masked with something antiseptic. I got an accidental snootful, gagged, and staggered back.

The bag wiggled.

I squinted, held my breath. Whatever was in the bag was definitely dead; the smell was proof. It had to be an air current, or the contents settling, or —

It moved again.

My heart did the pitter-patter thing, like the couple times I'd been caught cheating at five card stud and a beating was about to ensue. The bag jerked to the left, then to the right, then toppled over onto its side.

A tiny red fist appeared from the top, opening and wiggling five miniature fingers.

I knew what this was. I knew, in the depths of my soul.

My fielding error.

The thing cried out, soft and wet. A bulbous, bald head emerged, large fetal eyes locking onto me.

"Daddy."

"Oh, Jesus."

It pulled itself from the bag, dragging along two undersized first-trimester legs and a slimy blue umbilical cord. Though covered in mucus, I could make out the large scars running zigzag over most of its body. Scars that had been sewn up in an ugly Frankenstein stitch.

In its tiny hand was a curved needle, trailing thread.

"Oh, sweet Jesus."

"Not until dark, Daddy. I haven't finished yet." The needle dug into its shoulder, repairing a laceration caused by the abortionist's knife. "I wanted to look pretty for you."

"It wasn't my fault," I managed. "The rubber broke."

My head swam with images of Margo Williams. Young. Sweet. Timid in bed, but I liked them that way. When she called me with news of her pregnancy, I'd had three women since her.

I mailed her a check to get rid of it, and hadn't heard anything of the matter until months later, when I found out she died from complications during the procedure.

"Not my fault," I said again.

The thing on the counter sat up and slumped forward, unable to support its oversized head.

"Mommy says hello. She sent me here so you could take care of me."

The emotions piled one top of another in my chest, fighting for dominance. Guilt. Revulsion. Amazement. Fear. Anger.

Anger won.

"Go back where you came from!"

"Don't you want me, Daddy?"

For an absurd moment, I pictured the bloody, scarred thing sitting on my lap at a baseball game, a tiny cap on its misshapen fetal skull.

"I don't want you! I paid them to take care of you!"

Its tiny face crinkled, tears clearing trails in the mucus.

My decision made, I wondered how to get rid of it. Wrap it in newspaper and drop it down the garbage chute? Flush it down the toilet? It was small enough to fit. But if it was discovered in either case, it might lead back to me. I watched TV. I knew about DNA tests.

I glanced around the kitchen, eyes flicking over possibilities. Microwave. Stove. Compactor. Freezer.

Disposal.

The thing sat right next to the sink, a sink I paid almost two grand for. The garbage disposal could grind up a turkey leg, and this thing wasn't that much bigger. One quick push and—

"Don't grind me up in the garbage disposal, Daddy."

I clenched my teeth. How could it read my thoughts?

"I'm a part of you, Daddy."

It smiled, or tried to smile, with that big scar bisecting its head.

I forced myself to act.

In one quick motion, I scooped it up and shoved it down the sink drain, hard. The bulbous head was too big to fit through the opening, so I smacked it with the edge of my fist, over and over, forcing it down.

"Daddy, don't! I'm your own flesh and blood!"

I pulled my hand free and hit the garbage disposal switch.

For a moment, nothing happened. Then everything happened at once.

The whir of the disposal was surpassed by horrible screaming.

My screaming.

It was like being attacked by hundreds of men with hatchets. My ears were the first to be stripped away, then my nose and cheeks. Clothing was flayed off my body in bloody strips, followed by the meat underneath. Fingers, knees, cock and balls, ground up in a bladed tornado. And a booming voice tore through my head, louder than my own cries.

"I'M PART OF YOU, DADDY!"

How I managed to hit the off switch, I have no idea. My eyes had been cored from my skull. Even more unbelievable, I somehow dialed 911 using only the meaty stump of my hand.

The pain was unimaginable.

It still is.

These days, my son visits me in the hospital. I can't see him, but I can feel him. He's very good at sewing. He practices on me, when the nurses sedate me at night.

I've named him Jimmy Jr.

Looks just like me, I bet.

Careful, He Bites

Another flash fiction piece for the Small Bites anthology. The guidelines were to write a were-creature tale in 500 words or less.

"Careful. He bites."

Malcolm snorted, offering Selma a glimpse of gray teeth. His pants hung around his ankles, the condom dangling like an elephant booger.

"Bites? Damn thing don't even got no feet or wings."

Malcolm banged his palm against the canary cage, knocking the bird across the newspaper-lined bottom.

"I wouldn't do that," Selma said.

Malcolm squinted at her, ugly. "What you gonna do about it, whore?"

Selma shrugged. She swung her legs over the side of the bed and reached for the pack of smokes. Malcolm leaned over and gave her a harsh shove.

"I said, what are you gonna do about it?"

"Nothing. The bird can take care of himself."

Malcolm snorted again, the condom jiggling.

"It can, huh? Let's see what Mr. Birdy can do."

Selma stared blankly as Malcolm opened the cage and stuck in a sweaty fist. The bird tried to wiggle away, but Malcolm managed to get a hold of it quickly.

"Looks like Mr. Birdy is...DAMN!"

Malcolm dropped the bird and withdrew his hand, staring dumbly at the small spot of blood on his palm.

"Damn thing bit me!"

Selma lit a smoke.

"Told you."

Malcolm slapped her across the mouth, smearing bright red lipstick. Then he turned his attention back to the bird.

"I'm gonna..."

"You're not gonna do nothing." Selma's lower lip began to swell, but she seemed calm. "It's a full moon."

"Full moon? What the hell are you talking about?"

"Were-canary," Selma said.

Malcolm frowned, raising his hand to strike her again.

The little feathers growing out of his fingers caused him quite a shock.

Malcolm screamed, bones and tendons snapping and shrinking as the ancient curse of the were-canary mutated his adult human form into that of a tiny, yellow songbird. He perched on the nest of his tangled pants, the condom wrapped around his pointy feet.

"Tweet," Malcolm said.

Selma snatched him up and promptly broke one of his wings. Malcolm sang in agony, flopping around on the bedroom floor in tight circles.

Disoriented and wracked by pain, he didn't notice the cat under the bed until the feline had already pounced.

"He bites too," Selma said.

The next morning, Selma awoke to whimpering.

"...please...kill me..."

She stared at the man, naked and cramped in the birdcage. Roscoe, her former pimp. His legs and arms were missing; it was the only way he'd fit into the cage.

"Morning, Roscoe."

"...please..."

She gave him some fresh water and birdseed, then padded off to the bathroom.

The cat's litter box contained several bowling ball-sized deposits. They didn't come out that big, but once the moon went down, things went back to normal.

That was the price she paid for having pets.

"Hey, Roscoe! How about a little song while I shower?"

"...please...Selma..."

"Do you want me to get the cheese grater?"

Roscoe began "Blue Moon."

Selma smiled. After all, who else had a bird that sang baritone?

Symbios

The closest I've ever come to hard science fiction. I wrote this back in college, and then polished it up a decade later when it was published by Apex Digest. It was originally called Star Vation, but I wisely changed the title.

Voice Module 195567

Record Mode:

Is this thing working?

Play Mode:

Is this thing working?

Record Mode:

This is Lieutenant Jehrico Stiles of the mining ship Darion. I've crash-landed on an unknown planet somewhere in the Eighty-Sixth Sector. Captain Millhouse Braun is dead.

I suppose I'm Captain now.

Captain Braun's last VM concerned the delays we'd been having due to a micro meteor shower while mining Asteroid 336-09 in orbit around Flaxion.

A lot has happened since then. The Brain caught the Madness.

I told Mill a thousand times we shouldn't have used an Organic, but he was willing to take the risks, as long as he had extra cargo space to carry more ore. You know the sales pitch. Why have an interstellar processor that weighs twenty six metric tons and takes up gads of space when an Organic Brain with nutrient pumps can navigate the ship while weighing only three kilograms?

Well, we did fit more ore on the ship. And now Mill and the rest of the crew are dead. When the Brain went bad it thrust the ship into Wormhole GG54 and I got spewed out here.

Mill and Johnson and the rest of the crew were fried when the Brain misfired the photon props. One moment I was watching them on the console viewer, drilling into the asteroid's cortex, and the next moment they were vaporized and the ship was being hurtled toward the wormhole.

The trailer detached before I went through, sending millions of credits worth of iron on some unknown trajectory.

I survived re-entry because the ionic suppressors run automatically and not on Brain power.

The Brain wasn't so lucky. It's dead now, the nutrient containers smashed when we hit the planet's surface. But the Brain had enough juice left in it to seal every hatch and cargo hold before its functioning ceased.

Nothing on the ship works. The com-link is dead. The homing beacon is dead. I can't even open the steel doors to the pantry, and my unrefrigerated food supply is rotting away without me being able to get to it.

The oxygen systems have malfunctioned, but the planet I'm on has an atmosphere I can breathe. The nitrogen level is high, and I'm light-headed a lot, but so far I'm still alive.

The temperature is also hospitable to human life. A bit chilly, but mostly pleasant. Days last about forty hours, and nights about twenty.

I'm surprised this Voice Module still works. It's got a crack in the case, but the batteries haven't leaked. I figure without a recharge, I've got maybe two hours of recording time left.

I'll have to use it sparingly. I've salvaged all I can from this damn ship, and I can't find a lousy pen.

Voice Module 195568

Record Mode:

This is my fourth day on the planet, and I made an impressive discovery. The terrain here tests high for ferrite, making this planet worth a fortune. If no one has staked a claim, I could get funding and mine this place until it's just as gutted as earth is. The planet is large enough that it might even end the Ore Crisis, perhaps for a few years.

The only problem is that I'm starving.

There's a water stream nearby, brackish but drinkable. I waded in deep and searched for hours, but couldn't find animal life in the water, or the surrounding area.

Plant life abounds. At least I think they're plants. Maybe they're fungi. They're reddish in color, lacking chlorophyll, and they have appendages that resemble leaves. The landscape is littered with hundreds of different species, some as high as buildings, some the size of grass.

None have been edible. Everything I've plucked so far contains an acidic enzyme—concentrated highly enough to burn my fingers and my tongue. Swallowing any of it would tear a hole through my stomach.

But at least I have water.

I haven't scouted very far yet, only a few kilometers. Maybe I'll be lucky and there will something to eat on the other side of that big hill that splits my horizon.

Hunger is starting to weaken me. I can't stay awake for more than seven or eight hours. Tried several times to pry open the steel pantry doors, but can't budge them a crack. I think I broke my big toe kicking the panel in frustration.

I hope for rescue, but know the odds against it. If this is truly an undiscovered planet, then no one knows it exists, and no one knows that I'm here.

And I have no way to tell them.

Voice Module 195569

Record Mode:

My hiking boots were a gift from my mother, and came with genuine antique pig-leather laces.

I boiled and ate the laces this morning. My boots won't stay on now, and I've got—I know this sounds funny—a terrible knot in my stomach. But there's nothing else to eat. The only other organic thing on the ship is the Brain, and I'm not touching that. I'd rather starve to death. I'd rather die.

Morals are what make us human.

Voice Module 195570

Record Mode:

I met my new neighbors today.

They are only knee-high, and somewhat resemble the extinct species called dogs. They're covered with a short, rough fur, have pointy ears and yellow eyes, and walk around on underdeveloped hind legs.

I was sleeping in what used to be the control bay, dreaming about food, when I felt something poke me in the ribs.

I opened my eyes, startled, and found six of them in a circle around me. They spoke to one another with high pitched yaps.

None wore clothing or carried weapons. And even when I stood, towering over them by some five feet, none seemed afraid.

One of them yipped at me in what might have been a question. I said hello, and it cocked its head, confused by my voice. I can't recall reading about any life form like these back in school. For all I know they are an undiscovered species.

They half-coaxed, half-pushed me out of my ship and led me further than I'd previously scouted, over the hill.

They took me to their home. There were no structures, just a collection of holes in the dirt. When we arrived, dozens of little brown heads popped up out of the holes to stare at me.

A short time later, I was surrounded.

A kind of collective humming sound rose up within the group, and they all came to me, holding out tiny paws to touch my legs. They took turns, their eyes locked on mine.

For a moment, I felt like a god.

When I reached out to touch them they weren't afraid. And when I did pat a head their dog lips turned into grins and they wiggled their tails.

It was like being around dozens of well-behaved children. For a while I completely forgot how hungry I was.

Voice Module 199571

Record Mode:

They eat the plants. Somehow they're immune to the acid content. They eat many different varieties, raw. Then, out of their droppings, new plants grow.

Nature's perfect symbiotic planet. Ironic that I'd wind up here, considering how my own species has trashed the earth, and the planets of the surrounding star systems.

Perhaps this is a penance of sorts.

I stayed for most of the day in the village, watching the puppies play, patting small heads. I've counted eighty-two dog people in this settlement. Maybe there are other settlements, elsewhere. Staring across the huge landscape with nothing to see but kilometers of horizon, I have to wonder.

Later I left them and tried once again to pry open the metal door that locks away all of the food in the ship's pantry. Once again I was unsuccessful.

Voice Module 199572
Record Mode:

I'm dying. My clothes hang on my body like sheets, and I know I've lost at least fifteen kilograms.

The dogs seem to understand that I'm deteriorating in some way. They try to do funny things to make me laugh, like cartwheels or jumping on me, but I can't laugh.

In fact, when I look at the dogs for too long, I start to salivate.

I wonder what they taste like.

Like that synthetic meat, locked away in the ship's pantry?

I've never had real meat. Could never afford it. My father had a cat steak once, and said it was delicious. My grandfather remembers when he was young and there were still a few cows left, and he used to get meat on holidays.

What do these little dog people taste like?

If I wanted to I could wipe out the entire village in just a few minutes. They have no weapons. They don't move very fast. Their teeth are rounded. I could kill their entire population and not even get scratched.

But I don't. I can't. I won't.

Voice Module 199573
Record Mode:

I ate the Brain today.

I thought it would be rotten, but there was no decay at all. I have a hypothesis why. Decay is caused by bacteria, and perhaps this world has none.

I boiled the Brain, picked out the glass shards, and ate with my eyes closed, trying not to think about what it was.

But I did think about it.

It shouldn't matter. After all, the Brain had ceased operation. Tissue is tissue.

Even if the tissue is human.

Besides, the volunteers who sign up for the Organic Processor Program are elderly, near the ends of their lives. Running a starship gave a brain donor dozens of extra years of sentience, of life.

And, important point, this one did go mad and kill my crew and destroy my ship.

It owed me.

There wasn't any taste to it. Not really. But when I was finished eating, I cried like a child.

Not because of what I had done.

But because I wanted more.

Voice Module 199574

Record Mode:

I can't eat an intelligent life form. Not that the dog people are particularly intelligent. No tools, no clothing, no artificial shelter, though they do have a rudimentary form of communication. I even understand some of their words now.

I can't eat things that speak.

But all I've consumed in the past fifteen days were two shoe laces and a soggy, very small Brain.

I have a few solar matches left. I could spit-roast one of these doggies using a piece of pipe.

What did my grandfather call it? A barbeque.

The village has named me. When I come by, they yip out something that sounds like "Griimmm!"

So to the dog people I am Grim.

They sleep next to me and hug my legs and smile like babies.

Please let a rescue ship find me tonight, so I don't have to do what I'm planning to do.

Voice Module 199575

Record Mode:

I ate one.

When I awoke this morning I had such a single-mindedness, such a raw craving to eat, that I didn't even try to fight it.

I went to the dog people's village, picked up the nearest one, and as it yipped "Griiimmm!" with a smile on its face, I broke its neck.

I didn't wait around to see what the others did. I just ran back to ship, drooling like a baby.

Then I skinned the little dog person with a paring knife.

It was delicious.

Roasted over an open fire. Cooked to perfection. I only left the bones.

When I was done, the feeling was euphoric. I was sated. I was satisfied.

I smacked my lips and patted my stomach and knew how grandfather must have felt. Real meat was amazing. It made the synthetic stuff seem like garbage.

Then I noticed all of dog people around me.

They stared, their eyes accusatory and sad. And they began to cry. Howling cries, with tears.

When I realized what I had done, I cried too.

Voice Module 195576

Record Mode:

Two months on this damn planet, and that's according to these sixty hour days, so it's more like half a year. I haven't recorded anything in a while, because I haven't wanted to think about what I've been doing.

I've eaten fifty-four dog people so far.

I've stopped losing weight, but I can count my ribs through my shirt. One a day isn't enough nourishment for a man my size.

I try to make it enough. I have to ration. And not because of any moral reason.

The population is dwindling.

I don't know why they haven't run away. Packed up and left.

But they haven't.

They don't fear me. Maybe they don't understand fear.

The young puppies still hug my legs when I visit the village.

Everyone else stays inside their holes.

I try not to take the young ones. Instead I dig with my hands and pluck the adults from the ground. They don't fight. In fact, they try to hug me.

I think I'm a little insane at this point.

When I grab them, and they look at me with those sad eyes and say my name...

Sometimes I wish they would run away, leaving me to starve. So I couldn't kill any more of them.

It's like eating my children.

Voice Module 199577

Record Mode:

There are just three left.

They don't even go underground anymore. It's almost as if they've accepted their own deaths.

I wonder sometimes if I deserve to live when so many have died.

But the hunger. The terrible hunger.

I know when my food supply here runs out, I'll have to search for more.

More children to eat.

How can something that sickens make my stomach rumble?

Voice Module 199577

Record Mode:

A ship!

I saw a ship orbiting.

It was night. I was staring at the constellations, trying to remember my astronomy so I could pinpoint where I was in the galaxy.

One of the stars moved.

It circled the planet twice in three hours. I hope against hope it's a manned ship, not a damned probe. Please let there be people on board. I can't last too much longer.

There is nothing left to eat. I've consumed the entire dog village, boiled their bones and eaten the hides, hair and all.

I'm so thin I look like a skeleton with my face.

Voice Module 195578

Record Mode:

The ship landed several kilometers away. I ran most of the way to it, my euphoria bordering on hysterics.

It turned to hysteria when I saw the ship.

Nothing human made it.

It was spherical and grey, like a giant pearl. At first I thought it was some type of meteorite. There were no portals or exhausts, just smooth grey curves, reflecting the world around it.

I hadn't gotten within a few steps when it opened. A hole just sort of appeared in its side. Small and blurry at first, but soon several meters wide. I hid behind an outcropping of rocks.

Then something came out of the hole.

It was twice my size. Vaguely humanoid, but lacking a head. Six yellow eyes stared out from behind the clear visor encircling its chest. The eyes moved in different directions, scanning the terrain. No arms, but under the trunk of the body were four legs, thick and each ending in three long toes.

Its skin appeared reptilian; black scales that shone as if wet.

On the lower half of its body, it wore a bizarre version of pants. Above the eyes was a large and impressive mouth. I instantly thought of old hologramsI'd seen depicting sharks. The rows of triangular jagged teeth encircled the top of the creature like a bastardized crown.

As odd as its appearance was, it seemed to exude a kind of peace. I felt as if I were looking at a fellow intelligent being rather than an enemy from space.

I took a step toward it, and it reared up on its two back legs and waved its front legs at me, making a snorting sound. I suppose my appearance unnerved it. My features probably were just as strange and grotesque to it as it was to me.

"I won't harm you," I told it.

"I won't harm you," it repeated, imitating my voice perfectly. It lowered its front legs and took a cautious step forward. I also took a step.

"Zeerhweetick," it said.

I tried to imitate the sound as best I could. It relaxed its legs and squatted when we were within a meter of each other. I also sat down.

"I won't harm you," it said again.

I recalled my astronaut training. Intelligent Lifeforms 101 was an entirely.hypothetical class about the possibility of communication with an intelligent alien life form. It was in the curriculum because the World Assembly demanded that all space travelers have that training. They believed if we ever did encounter a new race, the first meeting between species would set the tone for all future relations. Making first impressions and all that crap.

Everyone considered it a joke class—we'd visited hundreds of planets, and never encountered any life form smarter than a cockroach.

Now I felt like that was the most important class I ever took.

I began by using words and miming motions. Pointing to myself I said, man. Pointing at its ship I said, ship. And so on.

It watched, and repeated, and within an hour it had picked up several verbs and began asking questions.

"Man here long?" it said in my voice. Then it pointed to the ground.

"Fifty cycles," I said. I flashed fifty fingers, then pointed at the sun, slowly moving across the horizon.

"More men?"

"No."

"Ship?"

"Broken." I pulled up a nearby weed and cracked it in half, illustrating my point.

It gestured at its own ship with a three fingered leg and also yanked a plant from the ground.

"Ship broken." It ripped the weed in two.

"Man," I said again, pointing to myself. Then I pointed at it.

"Zabzug," it said, pointing at itself.

"Hello, Zabzug."

"Hello, Man."

And so began mankind's historic first communication with an intelligent alien species.

I was so excited I wasn't even thinking about the other intelligent alien species I had just finished devouring.

Voice Module 195579

Record Mode:

After communicating for several hours, Zabzug and I went back to my ship. He moved slower than I did, sometimes tripping over foliage. One time I helped him up, getting my first close look at those teeth on his scalp. How he could imitate me so perfectly with a mouthful of fangs like that was anyone's guess.

"Thank you, Man," Zabzug said after getting back to his feet.

I smiled at him. His teeth twitched, which I took to be a smile too.

He was very excited at the sight of my ship, and began speaking rapidly in a series of grunts and snorts. I sat and watched him explore it top to bottom. He stopped in front of the pantry and stayed there a long time, snuffling, trying to open the metal door. Liquid poured down from his head and over his eye plate like tears.

"Hungry," Zabzug said. "No eat long time."

"Man hungry too," I told him.

He beckoned me over and we struggled with the pantry for a while, not budging the door a centimeter. Zabzug's drool smelled like a sour musk, and being right next to him made me realize how big he really was. Three times my mass, easy.

And those appendages of his had incredible strength behind them, putting huge dents in the thick steel door.

But it was all for nothing. The pantry stayed closed.

Voice Module 195580

Record Mode:

Zabzug explained to me how he crashed by drawing a very detailed schematic in the dirt. His ship runs on a bastardized form of fission, using a refined chemical to help control the reaction. I guess the chemical could best be described as a form of lubricant, as oil was used in combustion engines back on ancient earth.

So basically he's stranded here because he ran out of oil, stalled, and got sucked into the same wormhole as me.

We made some limited talk about putting my power supply into his ship, but the parts were so fundamentally incompatible that it proved impossible.

Zabzug tried eating some plants, doing me one better and actually swallowing a few. He became violently ill. I must admit to some perverse amusement at watching black foam erupt out of the top of his head like a volcano, but that only served to remind me how hungry I was.

Two intelligent species, meeting for the first time in history, each with the capability of interstellar travel, and both starving to death.

It might be funny if it were happening to someone else.

Voice Module 195581

Record Mode:

After a week together, I consider Zabzug a friend. He's told me much about his planet, which seems to be located in the Hermida Galaxy. Like humans, his species have used up their natural resources, and have begun scouring the universe for food, fuel, and building material.

He's much better at learning English than I am at learning his language. He's gained such a mastery of it that he made his first joke.

We were resting near his ship, talking as usual about how hungry we were, and Zabzug told me, "If you weren't so ugly, I'd consider eating you."

Funny guy, that Zabzug.

Voice Module 195582

Record Mode:

Zabzug is starving too. His skin has lost its luster, and his eyes are glazed.

We still have animated talks, but the silence often lasts as long as the chatting.

I'm hesitant to tell him about the dog people, about what I consider my genocidal crime.

But they're all I can think about.

I finally spill the story. Hopeful he won't judge. Hopeful that he might know where to search for more.

To my surprise, Zabzug seems to know what I'm speaking about, and he's able to draw an exact picture of their species.

"Hrucka," he told me. He awkwardly explained that the hrucka were like pets to his species.

It made sense. Evolution doesn't create just one species of animal in an ecosystem. The hrucka must have been put here.

Or stranded here.

Which might mean that somewhere, on the planet, there's another ship like Zabzug's.

He's very excited by this prospect, and we decide to conduct a search first thing tomorrow.

Voice Module 195583

Record Mode:

We searched for three days.

We didn't find anything.

Voice Module 195584

Record Mode:

Zabzug came into my ship at night as I slept. The viscous drool from his mouth dripped onto my face and woke me up. In one of his appendages he held a sharp piece of pipe, the one I had been using to roast dog people. Upon my awakening, he yelped and dropped the pipe, hurrying from my ship.

I suppose he's having the same problem that I had with the dog people. Respect for an intelligent life form versus the overwhelming need to survive.

But he's in for a surprise.

I'm going to eat him first.

I stayed awake the rest of the night, standing guard with the pointed pipe. He had the strength advantage. I had the speed advantage. We both seemed to be of similar intelligence, and both had the ability to use tools.

His eyes might be a weak point, but they were always covered by that face plate—Zabzug even wore it to sleep. His skin was covered with scales, and though they looked moist, they were hard, almost metallic, to the touch.

The vulnerable point was his mouth. It was crammed full of sharp teeth, but maybe I could jam something down his throat and into all the soft parts inside.

At the first peek of sunlight I'll go to Zabzug's ship with my spear.

What does alien lizard taste like?

Voice Module 195585
Record Mode:

He didn't come out all day, and I couldn't find a way in. There isn't a seam on the entire ship. No cracks or ridges or anything to pry or beat open. After several hours of trying, I decided to just wait. He'd have to come out eventually.

He wanted the same thing I wanted.

Voice Module 195586
Record Mode:

The bastard ate my hand.

Chomped it off at the wrist. I fell asleep, waiting for him to come out.

But I got him...haha...I got him...jammed the pipe down his throat, into the soft stuff.

Dead. He's dead.

Zabzug, my friend, is dead.

I used my belt as a tourniquet for my hand, but it didn't stop the bleeding.

I had to use the solar matches to close the wound.

The pain...so much pain in my wrist.

But the hunger...the need...is even stronger.

I'm going to cut him open now.

Voice Module 195587
Record Mode:

I'm full! What a wonderful feeling! For the first time since I landed on this planet, I've eaten until I'm ready to burst.

I'm so happy I don't even notice the pain.

Voice Module 195588
Record Mode:

Zabzug lasted for a whole month.

Some parts were delicious.

Some parts, not so delicious.

I ate everything. The inedible parts were boiled into soup until every calorie and nutrient was leeched out.

I even gained a few kilos.

And now, with the last of the soup gone, with the hunger pangs returning, I am afraid.

Voice Module 195589
Record Mode:

Four days since I've eaten anything. Zabzug had stretched out my belly, and I drink a lot to keep it full, to try and fool it into feeling sated.

My belly isn't fooled.

I've managed to get into Zabzug's ship, using a key. It's a tiny sphere he'd been keeping in a pocket. When it touches the ship, the portal opens.

I've fully explored the interior, trying to gain an understanding of how it works. The vessel is a marvel of engineering, with a navigation system light-years ahead of ours. The technology is even more valuable than the iron-rich plant I'm stranded on.

If I can get off this rock, I'll be the wealthiest man in the universe.

The first thing I'll do is get a limb graft...no, the first thing I'll do is have a banquet. A feast that will last a month. I'll gorge myself like the ancient Romans, purging between courses so I can cram in more food.

Such a beautiful picture.

Voice Module 195590

Record Mode:

My wrist isn't healing right. It doesn't seem to be infected, but the wound keeps opening.

I think it's a symptom of starvation. My body is conserving its energy, and deems healing unnecessary.

I'm so weak it's an effort to even stand up.

I have to do something. If I stay here, I'll die. Perhaps there's food somewhere else. I've scouted at least fifty kilometers in all directions, but I need to pick one and keep moving.

I decide to follow the sunset. I'll leave tomorrow.

I have no other choice.

Voice Module 195591

Record Mode:

I don't know how far I've traveled. Perhaps a hundred or a hundred and fifty kilometers. I'm in a desert now, and ran out of water a few hours ago.

My tongue is so thick it's hard to speak.

I fear sleep, because I don't think I'll wake up.

Voice Module 195592

Record Mode:

I can't move another step. Thirst is worse than hunger. I'm hallucinating. Hearing things. Seeing things. I even had a fever-dream, imagining a space ship crashing in the distance...

Voice Module 195593
Record Mode:

A week has passed.

Obviously, I didn't die in the desert. I was rescued. Well, sort of.

That ship I'd imagined I saw—it really did exist. A salvage ship, which had made a run at retrieving the trailer full of ore we'd lost.

They also got sucked into the wormhole, and were spit out here.

Their ship is damaged beyond repair. They'd been here for only a few days, and saw my Voice Module unit glinting in the sun.

They listened to it, unfortunately.

Marta, the woman, said she didn't judge me. She understood.

The man, Ellis, didn't say a word to me.

I received fresh water, medicine for my wrist, and synth rations.

"We have enough synth rations for a month," Marta told me. "And we're hoping for a rescue."

But all three of us knew that a wormhole rescue has never been attempted. It's suicide to go near those things.

I eat, and drink, and try to regain my strength.

I'll need it.

Voice Module 195594
Record Mode:

I got them while they slept.

Ellis, with a large rock to the head.

The rock made a mess. I smothered Marta. Not bloody, but it took a while.

One month rations for three people equals three months rations for one person.

I'm sorry I had to kill them. I truly am.

I'm not a monster.

Voice Module 195595

Record Mode:

Is this thing still working?

Play Mode:

Is this thing still working?

Record Mode:

It's been...how long has it been since I used this? Many months. Perhaps years.

I stopped shaving, and my beard reaches my chest.

Where did I leave off? I think it was with Marta and that guy, I forget his name. The one I killed with the rock.

It was for their synth rations. I paced myself, ate small portions, but still finished them too quickly.

I knew what was next. I knew it from the beginning.

When the rations were finally gone, I ate the people I'd murdered.

Humans, it turns out, are the best meat. Better than dog people. Better than alien lizards.

They sustained me for a while, but then they were gone too.

I began to starve again.

Days, maybe weeks, passed, and I began to whither away. Though I knew hunger well, it didn't make the pain any easier.

At night, I watched the skies. Watched them with a yearning. Hoping for another ship to crash on this planet.

And one did.

Astronomical luck?

Hardly.

Only one survivor this time. Angela something. She explained.

The ore-filled trailer from my ship, the Darion, didn't become lost in space. It's in orbit around Wormhole GG54, daring salvage ships to try and take it.

Many ships have tried. None have succeeded. They get pulled into the wormhole and pushed out here.

It's a giant, baited trap.

According to Angela, five ships have already been lost.

There's a good chance they're somewhere on this planet.

I asked Angela how large her crew was.

She told me there were seven. All dead.

When I killed her, that made eight.

Eight.

Mmmmm.

But that's not enough. It's never enough. I always run out.

I need to find those other ships. And I think I can. The Organic Brain on Angela's ship is still functioning, and it created a partial topographical map of the planet.

The map pinpoints the other crash sites. Some, only a few kilometers away.

I need to move fast. There may be survivors.

The longer I wait, the thinner they get.

A Matter of Taste

Another flash fiction piece for Small Bites. I'm a huge fan of zombie movies, especially the Italian gut munchers. It's pretty obvious with this piece.

"Finish your brains, Phillip."

Phillip pushed the jellied hunk away, using his stump.

"I don't want any more."

Mom squinted in his general direction; her eyes had long since dried up and fallen out.

"Don't you like brains? All little zombie boys need to eat brains. You want to become rotten and putrefied like Dad, right?"

"Arrgghhhhh," said Dad. He didn't have a bottom jaw, so pronunciation wasn't one of his strengths.

"You know I do, Mom. It's just..."

"Just what?"

Phillip folded his arms and picked his nose with the ulna protruding from his stump.

"Phillip!" Mom chided. "Manners!"

"Arrghhhh," his father concurred.

Phillip stopped picking.

"I hate brains."

Mom took a deep breath, and blew it out of the bullet holes in her lungs.

"Fine. Finish your small intestines and you can be excused."

Phillip made a face.

"I don't want to."

"But Phillip, you love intestines. Don't you remember when you rose from the grave? You'd stuff yourself with guts until they were slithering out of your little undead bottom."

Phillip stuck out his lower lip.

"I don't want to eat this stuff anymore, Mom."

"Arrghhhh," said Dad.

"See, Phillip? You're upsetting your father. Do you know how hard he works, hunting the living all day and night, to bring back fresh meat so you can eat? It isn't easy work—he can't move much faster than a limp, and most of the humans left are heavily armed and know to aim for the head."

Phillip stood up. "I don't like it! I don't like the taste! I don't like the smell! And most of all, I don't like eating people I used to go to school with! Last week we ate my best friend, Todd!"

"We're the living dead! It's what we do!"

Phillip's father shrugged, reaching for the child's plate. He dumped the contents onto the edge of the table, and then lowered his face to the organs and bumped at them with his teeth—the only way he could chew.

"I don't want to be a zombie anymore, Mom!"

"We don't have a choice, Phillip."

"Well, from now on, I'm eating something else." Phillip reached under the table and held up a plastic bag.

"What is that?" Mom demanded. "I hear roughage."

"It's a Waldorf Salad."

"Phillip!"

"I'm sorry, Mom. But this is what I'm going to eat from now on. It has apples, and walnuts, and a honey-lemon mayonnaise."

"I forbid it!"

"Arrghhhhh," Dad agreed.

"I don't care!" Phillip cried. "I'm a vegan, Mom! A vegan! And there's nothing you can do about it!"

He threw the salad onto the table and shuffled off, crying.

Dad shoved a piece of duodenum down his throat, then patted his wife on the bottom.

"Arrghhhh."

"I know, dear. But what can we do? Blow off his head and eat him for lunch tomorrow?"

"Arrghhhh?"

"Good idea. I'll fetch the shotgun."

Mom limped in the general direction of the gun closet.

"Waldorf Salad? Not in my house."

Embrace

Written back in college when I thought good writing had to sound flowery and imagery was more important than story. I was wrong on both counts. I can't help noticing, looking over this collection, how many stories of mine have some sort of religious foundation or overtones. That's what happens when you're raised Catholic.

She comes at night.

I push the rocking chair to the balcony so I may watch her, antique cherry that squeaks and protests much like my old bones. This affords me a towering view of my back yard; the hedges trimmed to lollipops, the fountain cherub eternally spitting water, the ocean in the distance.

The sun takes a lazy bow and exits, raking orange and purple fingers across my acres of thick lawn. Years ago, it was champagne cocktails and croquet. Now, I can't even recall the last time I walked the grounds. An acquaintance, deceased like most, once described men as fine single malt—fiery and immature when young, mellowing with age.

I am finally palatable.

The portrait of my younger self hangs above the fireplace, stern face and eyebrows tempered with resolve. Eyebrows that have grown gray and bushy and without direction.

Once, I would settle for nothing less than crushing all opposition.

Now, I'll settle for some honey in my tea.

I watch as the mist arrives, a soft, ethereal blanket, glowing in my yard lights.

She always comes with the mist, and I feel my pulse quicken, warming me. I drop the blanket from my lap—I don't need it anymore.

The first sight of her is magic. Awe and wonder, feelings known only to the young and to me. Worth more than I have ever earned. She is clothed in translucent blue, the color of the moon, a robe that moves like silk. Her face is always peaceful, her movements sure, and I am both enthralled and pacified. Her dance is nature and life, ebb and flow. Slow, languid turns and comfortable poses, arms always beckoning, the tune known only to her.

Beneath my balcony she stops and smiles, as she has for many years.

"Dance with me."

Tonight I shall.

I grip the armrests of my rocker with gnarled hands and tremble to my feet. The thousand pains that plague my days, the gagging pills that keep me beating, the nights of disquiet—all nullified by my resolve. I finally have the strength to know I have none left. The hand has been played, and folded.

Legs shaky, a yearling, knock-kneed and wide-eyed, I lean over the railing. Into her arms I fall, and break...

And then I am free. I bow to my Lady, and take her hand. "May I have this dance?"

The music is crisp in my ears, light and airy. I embrace her, and we waltz on the mist, above my lawn, away from my empty prison. Through the cherub and the hedges, across the beach, over the sea to chase the sun.

Her mouth flutters closer to mine, soft lips parting.

Black teeth. Sharp.

I cry out, my voice muffled by her hungry kiss, ripping at my face, peeling, pulling.

I gaze up at her through lidless eyes, milky with red.

Her maw finds my soft belly, bites, probes deep.

I am tugged into the ground by looping coils of innards.

Down.

Down.

Down to heat so strong the very air sears, baking raw flesh without ever killing nerves.

We dance again on rusty nails, on white coals and fish hooks, my bowels roping us together for eternity.

For another dance.

And another dance.

Trailer Sucks

I almost didn't write this story, because the subject matter is downright disturbing. But I couldn't get the idea out of my head, so I made this humorous rather than straight horror. After writing it I put it away, convinced it would never see print. Incredibly, it was picked up by Cemetery Dance for an anthology of extreme horror. Along with The Confession, this is something I sometimes wish I never wrote. You've been warned.

The night began like any other night at the Galaxy Trailer Park, everyone on lawn chairs in front of Freddie's big double-wide, sharing a bottle of Evan Williams whiskey and setting fire to any squirrel stupid enough to wander into Billy's box trap.

They'd caught three so far, at the cost of one peanut per squirrel. Zeke would yank them out of the box with a leather work glove, sprinkle some of Erma Mae's fancy smelling nail polish remover on its fluffy tail, and then touch a Marlboro to the critter. Damn things ran so fast, they looked like bottle rockets shooting across the lawn, squealing all the way. One even made it all the way up a tree and into its nest, setting that ablaze, little flaming baby squirrels leaping to their deaths and bouncing when they hit the sod.

Good clean American fun.

Jim Bob walked over, a spit covered stogie dead in his lips, smiling like the way he did when he got his weekly check from the gubment, or like that one time when he shit in a box and mailed it to the local porker department because they gave him a ticket for having that rusty Ford up on blocks on his front lawn for over six years.

"Guess what I got me, fellas?"

"A small pecker?" Freddie cackled. Billy thought this was so funny he squirted Evan Williams out of his nose.

Idiots, Jim Bob thought.

"No, you jackasses. I got me a vampire."

More giggling. The giggling turned to guffaws when Zeke, in a show of wit usually reserved for men with more teeth, said, "Well, now...that really sucks."

Jim Bob waited for the laughter to die, showing extraordinary patience, especially considering he broke his ex's nose for sassing back with less conviction. He looked at each of them men in turn, giving them his quit fucking around stare. It only took a few seconds for respectful silence to ensue.

"Here's the deal," Jim Bob said. "You all know 'bout them killings, right?"

The group nodded as one. Some nutbag had been cutting off noggins—one a week—of neighborhood church-going folk. The heads hadn't been found. Last week it was dear old Mrs. Parsons who got herself killed. She had been one of the few women in the community Jim Bob respected, and he often played Mr. Fix-it in her townhouse for eight dollars an hour and homemade apple pie.

"Well, I caught me the killer," Jim Bob said. "Out in the woods, south of Rooney Lake, by that overgrown cemetery. I was hunting coon, discovered this old shack. Outside, in a rain barrel, were all eight heads from the eight people been killed."

Jim Bob paused. Every eye was locked on him, respectful.

"So I go into the shack, and it's got one of them, whatchmacallits, caskets inside. I opened it up, and sleeping in the casket was an honest-to-Christ vampire. Fangs and all. She'd been cutting off the heads, see, to hide the bite marks on the neck. Pretty slick, I gotta admit."

"What'd you do?" Zeke asked.

"You gotta put a stake through the heart," Billy said. "I saw this movie..."

"I'm telling this story," Jim Bob snapped.

"Sorry, Jim Bob. I'll shut up."

"You do that. Anyway, I was thinking the same thing. Put a stake in this bitch."

"Bitch? It was a lady vampire?"

"Hell yeah. And a pretty piece of tail too. Big old titties, and legs that looked like they could wrap around you and ride you until your balls fell off."

"So, what'd you do?"

"I'm getting to that. I was thinking about staking her, but she seemed too damn pretty to kill. Plus, since the Missus left, I haven't tagged a piece of ass."

"You cornholed the vampire?" Freddie asked.

"Can you guys shut up and let me finish the damn story? Jumpin' Jesus on a pogo stick! Do I have to staple your flappers shut?"

"Sorry, Jim Bob."

"Sheesh. Anyway, I'd been riding my 4 by 4, so I hitched a chain up to the casket and dragged it back to my trailer. It was getting dark, and I had to hurry in case the little vixen woke up."

"Did you make it?" Zeke asked.

"No, you idiot. She woke up and killed me."

Silence from the group.

"Hell yeah I made it, you jackass. And I brought her inside and tied her, nekkid, to my bed. Then I gave it to her."

"The stake?"

"The dick."

Billy cocked a head at Jim Bob. "You raped a vampire?"

"It wasn't rape. A vampire ain't alive, dummy. Ain't no laws against humping the living dead."

Zeke winked and gave Jim Bob a nudge. "So how was the little whore?"

"Like fucking an ant hill. That bitch was drier than a box of Grape Nuts. Plus, she woke up in the middle of it, started hissing and snapping those fangs. Could hardly get my nut off."

"Did you stake her?"

"Goddamn, Billy, can you shut up about the goddamn stake for five goddamn minutes?"

Billy nodded, pretending to zip his mouth closed.

Jim Bob chomped on his cigar, swallowed a little piece. "Okay, so I got to thinking. She might be all dried up down there, but her mouth looked all warm and wet and inviting. 'Cept for those long teeth, of course. So I got my five pound rubber mallet and my chisel and I got rid of those nasty teeth. Wasn't easy, neither, bitch spitting and snapping at me the whole time."

"Did it work?" Zeke asked.

Jim Bob broke into a big grin. "Worked like an unwed mother with ten kids. That girl could suck the feathers off a jaybird."

Laughter and spontaneous back-slapping ensued.

"Can we see her?" Zeke asked.

"See her? You can take her for a test drive," Jim Bob said, to cheers. Then he added, "For five bucks."

"Five bucks?" Freddie frowned. "I thought we was buddies, Jim Bob."

"We is buddies, Freddie. But the care and feeding of a vampire costs money. I had to make a deal with Jesse Miller, the janitor over at Covington

Hospital. He charges ten bucks for a pack of blood. So unless one of you guys wants to hook up a straw to your wrist, it's five bucks a bang."

Freddie had to go inside to get some cash. Billy gave Jim Bob a check. Zeke didn't have no money, but had two and a half packs of Marlboros, which Jim Bob admitted was just as good.

They all went over to Jim Bob's trailer, which stank of stale beer and rotten food because Jim Bob hadn't done much cleaning since his wife left.

"She's in my room," Jim Bob said. "It's still daytime, so she's sleeping the sleep of the undead. But the sun is gonna set soon, and then she'll be wild and buckin'."

The quartet crept, quiet as church mice, into the bedroom.

As promised, there was a naked woman tied to the bed, with big old melon titties and fat, red dick-sucking lips, which recessed a bit into her mouth seeing as she had no teeth no more.

"Goddamn!" Zeke removed his John Deere cap and smacked himself on the thigh with it. "Ain't this something!"

"I'm first." Freddie had already undid his overalls. "It's been almost three weeks for me."

"I thought Fat Sue Ellen gave you a handjob behind the church last Sunday."

"Handjobs don't count."

"Wait a second," Billy stepped in front of Freddie. "How do we know this is really a vampire or not?"

Freddie got mean eyes. "Frankly, Billy, I don't give a shit if it's a vampire, my sister, or Mother goddamn Theresa. I'm fucking it."

"You want to go to jail, Freddie? We could all go to jail for this. Is a piece of ass worth prison?"

"Hell yeah."

"Hold up, Freddie." Jim Bob smiled, put a hand on his shoulder. "Billy's right. I don't want to see my good buddies go down on no felony charges. Lemme prove to you this bitch is what I say she is. First of all, any of you see her breathing?"

The three squinted, looking for the telltale rise and fall of the nekkid girl's chest. It didn't move an inch.

"See? No breathing. Now Billy, you want to check to see if you can find a pulse?"

Billy reached out a hand, then hesitated.

"I don't want to."

"Well, shit. You want to stick your peter in her, but you're afraid to touch her wrist?"

Billy swallowed and put two fingers on her wrist, right below where the baling wire bound her to the bedpost.

"Nothing," Billy said. "And she's real cold."

"You sure this ain't just a dead body?" Zeke said. "Because I didn't just pay two packs of smokes to bugger no dead bitch."

"Does a dead body do this?"

Jim Bob reached into his jeans and took out a small silver rosary. He touched the cross to the girl's thigh.

The reaction was instant. The skin blistered and smoked, burning a cross shape into her flesh.

"Goddamn!"

Freddie sniffed the air. "Smells like bacon."

Billy grabbed Jim Bob's wrist, pulled it away from the vampire.

"Jesus, Jim Bob! You made your point. Quit marking her all up."

Jim Bob laughed. "Don't matter none. Bitch heals up the next day. You can get real rough with this little lady, and she's like that fucking battery bunny on TV. Keeps on a'going."

To prove his point, Jim Bob made a fist and punched at her ribs until the left side of her chest caved in.

"Lemme have a go," said Zeke. He picked up the rubber mallet resting on the dresser and brought it down hard on the girl's knee. There was a snapping sound, and the knee bent inwards.

"Son of a bitch! Ain't that somethin'..."

All four men jumped back as the vampire lurched in the bed, her toothless mouth stretched open, crying out like a colicky child.

But no sound came out.

"Shut the fuck up, whore," Jim Bob said, slapping the vampire across the face. She narrowed her yellow eyes at him and hissed, her fat lips flapping.

"Damn," Billy said. "That's some scary shit."

"You kidding? This is the perfect woman. Beat her ass and she can't complain."

Freddie's bibs were already around his ankles.

"I'm first. What do I do? Just stick it in her suck hole?"

Jim Bob slapped her again, then swallowed another piece of cigar. "You could, but it ain't no good. She tries to spit it out."

"Then what do I do?"

Jim Bob put the rosary back in his pants, and his hand came out with a pocket knife.

"Give yourself a little nick on the pecker with this."

Freddie hooded his eyes. "Slice open my pecker? Fuck you."

"Trust me, Freddie. This bitch drinks blood. She goes crazy for just a little taste. Just make a tiny little cut, and she'll suck your balls right out your dick hole."

"No way."

"Don't be a pussy," Zeke said. "Ain't nothing but a little prick on a little prick."

"Then you go first."

"No problem." Zeke shoved Freddie aside and dropped trou. "Gimme the damn knife."

Jim Bob handed Zeke the pocket knife and watched his friend made a tiny slit along the top of his dirty, wrinkled foreskin.

"Now what?" Zeke asked.

"Climb on and give her a taste...and get ready for the ride of your life."

Zeke got onto the bed, causing the vampire to scream again when he kneed her broken ribs. But when his bloody dick got near her lips, she stopped screaming and opened her mouth wide, straining to reach it, tongue licking the air.

"Well, lookee here. Bitch really wants it."

"Shove it in, Zeke. Let her have it."

Zeke did, and the room filled with slurping and sucking sounds. Zeke's eyes rolled up into his head and he moaned.

"Is it good, Zeke?"

"Unngh unghh unghh unghh..."

"Is that yeah?"

"Oh...fuck yeah..."

Zeke's hips were like a piston, gaining speed. Within a minute, his hairy butt clenched, his thighs spasmed, and he was crying out for his mama.

Zeke fell back with a look on his face that was positively fucking angelic.

"I've been boning since I was eleven years old, and that was the best fuck I've had in my whole entire goddamn life."

"I'm next," Freddie said.

Jim Bob handed him the knife, and Freddie gave his pecker two pokes, one on either side of the head, before jamming it in.

Freddie was even quicker than Zeke, finishing up faster than it took most guys to piss.

"That made my nose hair curl," Freddie said, laughing. "Damn, Jim Bob, I think I shot about a gallon into that bitch."

"Goddamn sloppy thirds," Billy swore. But that didn't stop him from stripping off his shit stained underwear, giving his pecker a little cut, and ramming it in those drippy fat lips.

Jim Bob had gotten it four times the night prior, but watching his buddies go at it made his cock so hard he could jack up a car with it. When Billy finished, Jim Bob gave himself a poke-poke with the knife, squeezed to get the bleeding started, and shoved it down her throat.

The sensation was no less incredible than it had been the first four times. This bitch used it all; her lips, her tongue, her cheeks, her throat. She bobbed her head so fast it was a fucking blur. Goddamn, it was good. For five dollars, this was the deal of the century. He should charge at least seven-fifty. Hell, when word got around, there'd be guys lined up out the door for a taste of this. At seventy-fifty a head, twenty people per day...

"Ouch!"

Jim Bob pulled out. While he was mouth fucking her, he felt something pinch.

Sure enough, looking down at his dick, there was more blood than there should have been.

"What the fuck?"

He tried to wipe away the blood, and then noticed the small hole near the base of his pecker.

"What happened, Jim Bob?"

Jim Bob clenched his teeth.

"Fucking bitch bit me."

"I thought you knocked out her teeth."

"I did."

Jim Bob reached over to the dresser, picked up his chisel. He shoved it in the vampire's mouth and pried her jaws open.

There it was, on her upper gums; a new goddamn tooth growing in.

"Son of a bitch!"

Jim Bob flew into a rage. He hit her in the face with the chisel, over and over, cheekbones snapping and jaw cracking. The vampire shook like unholy hell, but that just fueled his fury.

Goddamn women. Can't trust any of them. Even the undead ones.

"Jim Bob..."

Jim Bob didn't pay the boys no mind. He switched his grip on the chisel and began to stab the vampire with it, putting out one of the bitch's eyes with a slurpy pop, then the other.

"Jesus, Jim Bob!"

Someone, maybe it was Zeke, tried to pull him off. But Jim Bob wouldn't budge. After he'd turned the vampire's face into Spaghetti-O's, he began to stab at her chest, puncturing the chisel through her rib cage, driving it into her heart all the way up to the wood handle.

"Holy shit," Billy said.

The vampire began to smoke, her skin cracking and splitting open, exposing red, raw muscle and rotting organs. There was sizzling and snapping and a terrible odor like wet, burning dog.

"Stop it, Jim Bob!"

And then something hit Jim Bob in the back of the head and he was out.

* * *

"Look. He's waking up."

Jim Bob sensed people in the room with him. Without opening his eyes, he knew it was Freddie, Zeke, and Billy.

He could smell them.

His memory was hazy, but Jim Bob knew one thing for certain; I've never felt so good.

His shoulder, which had bothered him every single day since he dislocated it ten years ago hauling bags of cement, didn't hurt at all. He wiggled his big toe, which had an ingrown nail so full of puss it was nearly double the size, but there was no pain.

He felt fan-fucking-tastic.

There was only one problem; he couldn't seem to move his arms.

"Jim Bob? You awake?"

Jim Bob opened his eyes and stared his friends standing around his bed. It seemed to be very bright in his room, even though the only light was the forty watt lamp on the dresser.

"Do you understand me, Jim Bob?"

Jim Bob tried to say Of course I understand you, you idiot, but nothing came out of his mouth.

"Goddamn," Zeke said. "He doesn't understand a damn word."

Billy leaned in close. "Do you remember what happened, Jim Bob? You were killing that vampire bitch, and the Freddie hit you on the head with that mallet..."

"Sorry, man." Freddie shrugged his shoulders. "But you were destroying the best piece of ass I ever had."

Billy shook his head sadly. "Problem was, he hit you too hard."

"My bad," said Freddie.

Jim Bob tried to ask a question, but his lips moved in silence.

"You died, Jim Bob. But since that vampire girl bit you on the pecker, we figured we should keep an eye on you, case you came back. And you did."

Zeke smiled. "You should see yourself, Jim Bob. You got teeth longer than my German Shepherd, Harley. I'd hold up a mirror to show you, but it probably wouldn't do nuthin'."

A vampire? Jim Bob thought. This is crazy.

But then he touched his tongue to his teeth and felt the sharp points.

Holy shit! I'm a vampire. That must be the reason I can't talk—I'm dead, and there's no goddamn air in my lungs.

"Sorry we had to tie you up," Billy said. "But we didn't know what else to do. You...uh...want some of this blood?"

Billy held up a plump unit of plasma, one of the packs Jim Bob had bought from Jesse Miller at the hospital.

Jim Bob's mouth instantly filled with drool. He craned his neck toward the blood, licking his lips, trying to reach it. Never before had he been so hungry. He had to have that blood. Hadtohadtohadtohadto...

"Damn!" Zeke said. "Will you lookit that! I think he wants it!"

"Give it to him, Billy." Freddie nudged him.

Zeke held up a hand. "Hold on, wait a second."

"Give it to him. He's our friend."

"He ain't our friend no more. He's a goddamn monster. Look at him, snapping and slobbering."

Gimmeegimmeegimmeegimmee! I need that blood!

"So what should we do?" Billy asked. "Kill him?"

Zeke grinned, rubbing his goatee. "I got me a better idea. Jim Bob may not have big old titties, but I bet he'll be pretty good just the same."

Zeke picked up the mallet and chisel. Billy smiled, unzipping his pants.

"I got first this time!"

Jim Bob opened his mouth to scream, but nothing came out.

Markey

Flash fiction, a little slice-of-life tale that I posted on my website as a freebie.

Something is in my ear.

It crawled in when I was sleeping. Really deep. I can feel it tickle against the side of my brain.

I tried to kill it with a sharp pencil.

There was a lot of blood. But it didn't come out.

I stuck some pliers in my ear, to pull it out.

But it went in deeper.

Then it started to talk to me.

It didn't sound like words, not at first. More like chirping.

Kind of like a cricket.

But if I concentrated real hard, I could understand.

He says his name is Markey.

Markey talks to me all the time. He tells me he understands me. He knows that I'm different.

Markey says we're going to be famous one day.

He wants me to kill a little girl.

I don't want to. Killing is bad. I tried to get Markey out of my ear by banging my head into the wall, over and over.

Markey didn't like that. He made me hold my hand over the stove burner as punishment.

It hurt a lot, and I had to go to the hospital for a while. The doctors were very nice. They asked me what happened.

I told them it was an accident.

I didn't tell them about Markey.

When my hand got better, Markey was nicer to me.

For a while.

Then he started talking about killing again.

He said I should bring a little girl back to my basement and do mean things to her with a hammer.

Markey said it won't be much different than all the cats he's made me kill. Except this will be even more fun.

Markey has made me kill a lot of cats.

I have a table in my basement with straps on it. The straps are strong, so the little girl won't get away when I'm putting the nails in her head.

I drive a school bus.

It would be easy to grab a little girl.

Better than cats, Markey said.

I was so alone before Markey crawled into my ear.

He's my best friend.

I'll grab the little bitch tomorrow.

Punishment

Another EC Comics inspired tale that I wrote in my younger days. I polished it a decade later for an anthology that never came out, so instead I printed up copies as chapbooks and gave them away for free at horror conventions.

Dominick Pataglia tried to block out the screaming coming from the Punishment Room, but the ceiling mounted speakers were at maximum volume.

The screams came at regular intervals—animal cries, sharp and shrill, only identifiable as human because they were punctuated with pleas for mercy.

Mercy was not known here.

Dominick clamped his fists over his ears, but the terrible sound penetrated the flesh and bone of his hands. From the creaking noise that underscored the screaming, Dominick guessed they were using the screws; wooden clamps, tightened on joints until the bones almost cracked.

Sometimes bones did crack, causing political bedlam in the form of inquiries and written protestations from sympathy groups.

This usually resulted in a sharp fine.

The Law plainly stated that the punishment couldn't inflict permanent damage. The Government was a stickler on that. It interfered with the education process.

Another scream, like a pig being butchered. Dominick squeezed his eyes shut. He had felt the screws before, and other things that were even more horrible.

Dominick had been a guest of the Punishment Room three times since he came here. Each time it had gotten worse.

His first visit had been just after he arrived. Two men in hoods and uniforms grabbed him before he'd even gotten off the bus. They dragged him to the Waiting Room and locked him in, confused and afraid.

There were no windows in the Waiting Room, no furniture, and the floor was cold, gray concrete. It had a sharp, acrid odor, beneath the scent of antiseptic. Dominick would later identify it as the smell of fear.

On the walls of the Waiting Room, tacked up in ranks and files and covering every inch of space, were photographs.

Pictures of people being tortured.

Thousands of photos, thousands of faces, each depicting a moment of grotesque agony.

Dominick opened his eyes and they locked onto a picture of himself. He looked so young in the picture, even in the grip of agony. It was taken only a few months ago.

They had used the rack the first time.

He hadn't done anything to warrant it. It was just to get him acquainted with the way things were done here.

He had screamed until his voice gave out.

That was what seemed to be happening to his comrade in the Punishment Room. The screams were becoming hoarser. Not because the pain was lessening, but because he had been in there for over an hour. Poor bastard.

Dominick let his eyes wander around the room until he saw the photo of the second time he'd visited the Punishment Room. For talking to an instructor out of turn. Dominick couldn't even remember what he had said to him.

Dominick's face in the picture was tear-stained and manic.

They had used the screws on him. On his thumbs, his knees, his testicles.

It had taken him ten days in the infirmary to recover.

His third visit to the Punishment Room was the worst, and warranted three Polaroids, all of which hung on the wall. During a two hour period he was strung up by his feet and beaten with a rubber whip over every inch of his naked body.

Then he was beaten again.

And again.

And again.

The pain reached such an intense level he kept blacking out, and a doctor had to be called in to give him amphetamine shots to keep him awake.

That's what the Torture Man thrived on. There was a rumor one poor girl had been in the Punishment Room for fourteen hours, simply because she kept passing out from the pain.

The Torture Man loved that.

What he loved even more was breaking someone tough.

The Torture Man glowed when someone showed anger or hatred; anything other than total submission. Because then the Torture Man got to break the spirit along with the body.

Where they found people like the Torture Man, God only knew.

Another hoarse cry. It would be ending soon, and then it would be Dominick's turn.

This was his fourth visit. That meant the electricity. From what others had told him, electricity made everything else look mild.

He would have current driven into his teeth, and his ears, and up his anus. The Government had not banned this torture, even though it resulted in burns on the contact points. Burns weren't considered permanent damage.

The screaming stopped. The silence that filled the Waiting Room made Dominick dizzy.

It would be only moments now.

He hugged his knees to his chest and touched the bottom of his left heel for the hundredth time. Rules required he strip before he came in, but Dominick had managed to tape a stubby pencil to the bottom of his bare foot.

He tapped the sharpened point, but it offered him no courage. Even if Dominick somehow found the guts to use it as a weapon, he didn't think it would get him very far. The Torture Man would probably be amused.

And after the amusement would come anger.

Thinking about it made Dominick nauseous. But he thought about it anyway.

Maybe it would work, if he was quick. Maybe it would work, if he stabbed the Torture Man somewhere vital, like the face. Maybe...

The door opened.

The Torture Man filled the doorway, steeped in the stench of body odor and fear. He stood almost twenty inches taller than Dominick, a monster of a man, with a barrel chest and strong, thick fingers.

"Nice to see you again, Mr. Pataglia." His voice was like raking leaves. The black cowl left his mouth uncovered, and his crooked brown teeth smiled with power and certainty. There were stains on his gray shirt from his armpits to his flanks, and a large wet spot soaked the front of his black pants.

Though sexual abuse and rape weren't allowed by the law, the government allowed him to masturbate while torturing.

Dominick palmed the pencil and fought to keep his sphincter closed. He could hardly breathe. The Torture Man produced a clip board and glared at it with little rat eyes.

"Attacked a hall monitor, eh Dominick? Haven't you got the balls?

We'll have to hook them up to the generator, see if we can light them up."

The Torture Man giggled like a young girl.

Dominick stood on rubbery legs and backed into the corner of the room. Dread soaked him to the core. The Torture Man closed in, huge and looming. He grabbed Dominick by the wrist.

"Please," Dominick pleaded. The pencil felt like a strand of spaghetti in his hand, slick and useless.

The Torture Man brought his face close, so close Dominick could smell his rancid breath.

"You're my last assignment of the day, so we'll have plenty of time together."

Dominick looked away, catching a glimpse of his photo on the wall.

"No we won't."

Dominick's voice surprised him. It was low and hard, steely with resolve.

The Torture Man was surprised as well. He went smiley and wide-eyed.

"Why, Mr. Pataglia, did you just contradict—"

Dominick's hand shot out and plunged the pencil into the center of the Torture Man's right eye.

It went in hard, like stabbing a tire, and there was a sucking-slurping sound.

The Torture Man screamed. He released his grip and stumbled backwards, his meaty hands fluttering around his face like birds afraid to land. Blood and black fluid seeped down his face in gooey trails.

Dominick took three quick steps after him and swung his fist at the pencil, managing to knock it deeper into the socket.

The Torture Man made a keening sound, and then crumpled into a large, fat pile on the concrete. His mouth hung open like an empty sack, and his good eye rolled up into the socket, baring the bloodshot white.

Dominick stood over him for a moment, shocked. Had he done it? Had he killed him?

Run! demanded the voice in his head.

But Dominick remained rooted to the floor.

He had to make sure. He had to make sure the bastard was dead.

The adrenalin was wearing off, leaving Dominick sick and shaky. He forced himself to kneel, and then tentatively stretched out a hand to check the Torture Man's pulse.

It was like willfully putting his hand in a fire.

After an eternity of inching closer and closer, Dominick touched the Torture Man's wet, clammy neck. He probed beneath the fat and the stubble, seeking out the carotid.

There was a pulse.

Dominick yanked his hand back as if shocked.

Run, you idiot! If he wakes up...

But Dominick couldn't run. He embraced a chilling certainty; even if he didn't escape, he couldn't allow this evil man to live. Not just for himself, but for all the others.

He chewed his lower lip and reached for the pencil.

The Torture Man groaned.

Dominick sprang to his feet. He needed a weapon of some kind. Side-stepping the Torture Man, Dominick raced out the door and into the hallway. To the left, the door to the courtyard. To the right, the Punishment Room.

Dominick's reaction was visceral—he didn't want to go in the Punishment Room ever again. But there were weapons...

He went right.

The Punishment Room was straight out of his nightmares. Dark and filthy, illuminated by two bare bulbs hanging from the ceiling by greasy cords. The walls were black, and an underlying stink of urine and excrement fouled the moist air. Chains and shackles were bolted to the floor and walls, a rack sat in one corner, and a cabinet full of the Torture Man's hideous instruments yawned open, revealing his tools of pain.

Dominick heard a noise like wind whistling through the trees. He looked back and saw the Torture Man standing in the doorway, wheezing. The pencil was still poking from his eye, and gooey red tears streaked down his face. He pointed a huge finger at Dominick, and took another labored step forward.

Dominick reached into the Torture Man's cabinet and removed a can of lighter fluid. He popped the top and squirted it at the Torture Man's face.

The Torture Man screamed when the alcohol hit his punctured eye. He stumbled backwards and tripped over the generator.

"You little bastard! When I get you..."

Dominick grabbed the nearest object—a digital camera sitting on the cart—and fell upon the Torture Man. He brought the weapon down on his tormentor's face, again and again, the plastic case cracking and splintering as he used it to knock out teeth and break bone.

The Torture Man lashed out, connecting with the side of Dominick's head. Dominick fell onto his back, landing hard. His vision blurred, and something was poking him behind his left shoulder.

Next to him, the Torture Man sat up. He grabbed the pencil and pulled. His eye slurped out of the socket, looking like a tiny red jellyfish trailing its tentacles. The Torture Man howled, dropping the pencil. The eye swung freely down at cheek level, hanging by a coil of optic nerves.

Dominick reached behind his back, seeking the source of his discomfort. He pulled it into view.

It was a steel clamp, almost the size of his hand. He squeezed the ends and it opened its jaws, baring tiny teeth. A cord was attached to the bottom, and Dominick followed it along the floor to where it plugged into the electric generator.

He glanced at the Torture Man, who had managed to find his rubber whip. He smacked it against Dominick's face, the pain instant and staggering.

Dominick rolled onto his side, still gripping the clamp. The whip lashed across his naked back, and he cried out.

"You think you know pain?!" the Torture Man bellowed. "I'll show you pain!"

Dominick spun around onto his bottom, taking another whip stroke in the face. He thrust the clamp at the Torture Man, securing it to his ankle.

Then he stretched out his hand and hit the switch on the generator.

The reaction was instant.

The Torture Man doubled in half like a book slamming shut, and pitched head-first to the floor. A strong whiff of ozone plumed around him as his grotesque body shook in racking spasms. Blood sprayed from his mouth and a piece of tongue escaped his clenched teeth and tumbled down his chin.

Dominick crab walked backwards, putting distance between them. He watched, wide-eyed, as the clamp on the Torture Man's leg began to smoke, and then ignited the soaked-in lighter fluid.

The Torture Man burned like kindling.

Dominick pulled his gaze away and found the drawer next to the cabinet that held his clothes. He tried to ignore the popping sound of blistering flesh and the Torture Man's gurgling moans. By the time he'd tied his shoes the moans had died along with the monster.

The can of lighter fluid was on the cart, next to a pair of tin snips. Dominick shoved the snips in his back pocket and squirted fluid onto the rack. Then he did the same to the Torture Man's dreaded cabinet and the instruments it contained.

They burned well.

Finally, he went back into the Waiting Room and doused the walls, staring one last time at the picture of himself on the rack, watching it burn.

They would be coming. Soon. He had to get away.

The door to the courtyard was open, and amazingly, no one was around.

It made sense—the Hall Monitors hadn't expected to escort him out of there for another few hours.

Dominick stepped out into the fresh air. The sun winked through the trees like an old friend. A light breeze cleared the stench of urine from his nostrils.

The fence was just beyond the basketball courts, locked and topped with razor wire. Impossible to climb over.

But he wasn't climbing.

Two minutes with the tin snips, and he was though the fence.

Freedom enveloped him like a mother's love.

He ran off into the woods, giddy, yet knowing that someday he would return.

But not as a victim.

Dominick had read the forbidden history books. He knew that a hundred years ago there was no torture in America's Public Schools. There was once a time when eleven-year-olds like himself went to school to learn. When education wasn't Government indoctrination. When children were free.

The Torture Man, evil as he was, was just a symptom of the disease. Both a part of the system, and a product of it.

But Dominick knew there were others like himself. Fighters, who sought change.

He would meet up with these people. Grow strong. And in time, when he returned to this place, it wouldn't be as a victim.

It would be as a liberator.

Dominic Patalglia ran through the woods, not looking back at the Elementary Camp. His footfalls were sure and strong, and as he ran he could swear that he heard the sound of a thousand boys and girls behind him, cheering.

The Confession

Beware. This is a rough one. I wrote this story as a dual experiment. First, to do a serious story using only dialog. No action. No exposition. No speaker attribution. Just talking. And second, I always wondered if I could make readers squirm without relying on description. It was written for a horror issue of the webzine Hardluck Stories, at the request of Harry Shannon, and it's as nasty a story as I've ever done.

"From the beginning? The very beginning?"

"Wherever you want to start, Jane."

"Wherever I want to start. Well. I guess you could say it all started when I was thirteen years old, when my father started coming into my bedroom."

"Your father molested you?"

"Molested? That sounds like he stuck his hand under my bra. My father fucked me. Made me suck him off. Called me Daddy's Little Whore. Used to write it on my forehead, in marker. I'd have to scrub it off before going to school. Wretched bastard. Went on until I ran away, at sixteen."

"And that's when you met Maurice?"

"That pimp fucker thought he was so smooth, busting out a white girl. Had no idea my old man busted me out years earlier."

"Was Maurice the one in the pit?"

"No. Maurice was the belt sander."

"Who was in the pit?"

"You want me to tell it, or answer questions?"

"Whatever you're more comfortable with."

"Okay. I'll tell it. Maurice found me at the shelter. Slimy pricks like him can probably sniff out teenage pussy. He talked sweet, hooked me on crack, and the next thing you know I'm blowing guys in their cars for twenty bucks a pop. Wasn't that bad, actually. I know I'm nothing to look at. Even before all the scars, I was fat and dumpy. Plain Fucking Jane, my mom called me. You got a cigarette?"

"Menthol."

"Beats sucking air. Thanks. Anyway, Maurice set me up with this freak. Guy took me back to his place, had a whole torture dungeon in his bedroom. That's how my face got all fucked up. Cigarette burns. Looks like acne scars, doesn't it? Kept me there for four days, then dumped me in a trash can."

"Did you know his name?"

"We'll get to that. You wanted this from the beginning, remember?"

"Take your time."

"Shit. I'm sorry, I can't smoke menthols. Do you have anything else?"

"No."

"Do I have to smoke?"

"No."

"I want to do this right for you."

"It's okay."

"Thanks...Mr. Police-man. Where was I? Oh yeah, after my face got burned, Maurice couldn't give me away. I wound up ass fucking winos in alleys for three bucks a pop. You ever have gonorrhea in your ass? Hurts like a bitch. And fucking Maurice wouldn't give me money for the clinic. Whatcha got there? A picture?"

"Is this Maurice?"

"Jesus! That's disgusting! Is that real?"

"Is this Maurice?"

"Yeah. That's him. Doesn't look too good there, does he? Heard he might live."

"We don't know yet."

"Ha! Be damn tough for him to testify. But I'm getting ahead of myself. After a while, the VD got so bad I couldn't walk. Maurice beat the shit out of me, left me for dead. That's when Gordon found me."

"Reverend Gordon Winchell?"

"He's no reverend. No church would have him. He was just another preacher, screaming scripture at drunks in soup kitchens. Saved my life, probably. Got me to the hospital. Actually came to visit me during my recovery. Seemed like an actual decent guy for a while. Until I learned his kink."

"What did he do to you?"

"On the day of my release, the good Reverend took me to his apartment, tied me to the bed, and began biting me."

"Biting you?"

"Look at this—"

"You don't need to—"

"Don't get all prude on me. See? Nothing there. Bit my nipples right off. If I wasn't in handcuffs I'd show you what he did to my twat."

"Jesus."

"You okay, Mr. Police-man? You don't look so good. You want to take a break?"

"How did you get away?"

"He had it all worked out in his head that he'd kill me. But he couldn't. Didn't have the balls. So he dumped me in front of the same hospital he brought me home from."

"Did you call the police?"

"Are you fucking kidding me? I called fucking everybody. When my dad was raping me, I called DCFS, and he paid the assholes off. When that freak burned my face, I filed a complaint, and you guys didn't do shit. Gordon eats my private parts, one of your finest told me to have my pimp take care of it. Is this turning you on?"

"Stick to the story."

"This is some pretty sick shit."

"Stick to the story!"

"Okay. Sorry. Where was I? I lost my place."

"The cops didn't help you."

"Right. Okay, here it is. That was it for me. I had enough of playing the victim."

"Is that when you started...?"

"Is that when I started grabbing these sons of bitches? Yeah. When I got out of the hospital the second time, I tracked down the freak, watched his house until he was asleep, and then broke in. Used his own handcuffs on him. And his own blowtorch. It was hard to restrain myself, lemme tell you. But even holding back, his balls turned black and fell off after only three days."

"This was John McSweeny?"

"Yeah. He sure was a screamer. Screamed so much, his throat actually started to bleed. Know what the weird part is? He smelled great! Like honey baked ham. When I burned off his face I was actually drooling. Is that funny or what?"

"You stabbed Mr. McSweeny."

"The hell I did. I never killed no one. After a week or so, I uncuffed one of his hands, and gave him a steak knife. Fucker cut his own throat, and that's God's truth."

"After McSweeny came Maurice."

"Nope. Next came my father. I invited him over, got all weepy on the phone saying I forgave him. Hit him with a tire iron when he walked in the door. The freak, McSweeny, had all of these ropes and pulleys and shit, so I stripped Dad naked and hung him up. Then I lowered him down on that hat rack. Right up his ass. Funniest damn thing you ever saw. The more he moved, the lower he sunk, the higher the pole went up his poop chute. He lasted almost a month. I'd bring him food and water. That pole got about two feet up him before he finally died."

"That's murder, Jane."

"That's gravity, cop. If he stayed perfectly still, he would have lived. Blame Isaac Newton."

"Then Maurice?"

"Then Maurice. When I was honey baking McSweeny, he was anxious to make the pain stop. Gave me all sorts of things. His bank account. His stocks. His car. I went to the dealer who used to sell me crack, bought a needle of H, snuck up on Maurice."

"You mentioned you used a belt sander."

"It takes all the skin off, but then gets real slippery. I kept buying belt after belt, until I figured out I could improve the traction if I threw salt on him."

"How long did you torture Maurice?"

"A few weeks. He'd scab over, then I'd start on him again."

"So...the guy in the pit?"

"That was the good Reverend Gordon. He got a heroin poke too, and when he woke up, he was chained up in the hole."

"What did you do to him?"

"Poetic justice. Fucker liked to bite, so I gave him a taste of his own medicine. I went to the pet store, bought a big box of rats. Put them in the pit with him. They were tame at first, but when they got hungry they began to nibble nibble. They started on the soft parts—look, do I have to read anymore?"

"Stick to the script."

"But you've still got your clothes on. You don't seem into this at all."

"I pay the money. I make the rules. I want you to finish reading."

"Look, sugar, I'm the best. Why do you want me to sit here and read when I can make you feel good?"

"Please don't..."

"Are you crying? Don't cry, baby. It's okay. Don't be afraid. Let me just get these pants off."

"I don't want to..."

"I like shy boys. Are you a shy boy? Let's see how shy you are—Jesus!"

"You...you were supposed to stick with the script."

"Where's your cock? You don't have a fucking cock!"

"You read the story."

"The story?"

"Reverend...Reverend Gordon."

"But that was all bullshit, right? Some freaky shit you made up?"

"He...liked to bite..."

"You're bullshitting me."

"I'm...a whore..."

"I'm leaving. Open this door."

"Daddy's Little Whore..."

"Open this fucking door or I'll start to scream!"

"McSweeny's house. Soundproof."

"You psychotic fucking freak! Let me out!"

"I won't hurt you. I want you to understand."

"Get the fuck away from me!"

"You're a prostitute. You're a victim too."

"Let me go!"

"Someone hurt you, right?"

"I want to leave. Please let me leave."

"You didn't choose this. You didn't choose to fuck men for money."

"I...want to leave."

"Who hurt you? Your father? Your pimp? You can tell me."

"I...don't..."

"I won't judge you. It's okay."

"No..."

"Who was it?"

"Don't..."

"Who was the monster that made you this way?"

"My...uncle."

"Your uncle?"

"He'd babysit me. Make me do things."

"I'm sorry."

"I...didn't mean to call you a freak."

"I know. It's okay."

"Jesus, I thought my life was shit. But all you went through..."

"It's okay. From now on, we're both okay. Come on, I want to show you something."

"I...I don't wanna go down there."

"Trust me. I would never hurt you."

"What's that smell?"

"I told you. Smells like ham."

"That was all true?"

"Most of it. Except they're all still alive. Meet Mr. John McSweeny."

"Oh my god..."

"Looks tasty, doesn't he? I use that wire brush on his burns. Still can coax a few screams out of him. Watch your step, there's the pit."

"Oh Jesus..."

"I see the rats finished off most of your face, Gordon. And congratulations! Looks like they also had a litter of hungry babies! You're a papa!"

"What...what is that?"

"That's Maurice. Can't even tell he's a black guy anymore, can you? That belt sander is quite a tool. Want me to pour some vinegar on him, wake him up?"

"This is all...I can't believe..."

"I know. It's a lot to take in. But here's who I really wanted you to meet. Say hello to my father. The person who turned me into the man I am today. Go on, say hello."

"Um...hello."

"He can't talk, because of the gag. But if you want him to answer, just give the pole a little shake. Like this. Hear that? I think he likes you."

"He's...crying."

"Of course he is. He's got two feet of hat rack up his ass. Probably punctured all sorts of vital stuff. You want to give the pole a little shake?"

"No..."

"Go ahead. Not too much, though. Just a little tap like this. See? You can hear him screaming in his throat.

"I don't want to."

"Yes you do. You're a victim, just like me. The only way to stop being a victim is to fight back. Go on."

"I really don't..."

"Stop playing the victim."

"But..."

"Fight back. It's the only way you'll be able to live with yourself. Put your hand on the pole."

"This isn't right."

"Raping children isn't right. Pretend it's your uncle hanging there. Remember all the things he did to you."

"My uncle. That fucking son of a bitch."

"Whoa! Hold on! You're going to kill him, shaking it that hard. Ease back."

"I'm sorry. I didn't mean to..."

"Yes you did. Felt good didn't it?"

"I...I thought of killing him so many times."

"Death is too good for men like that. He doesn't need killing. He needs to be shown the error of his ways. Oh...don't cry. It's okay. No one is ever going to hurt you, ever again. I promise. There there."

"Can we...can we..."

"Can we find your uncle and bring him here?"

"Yeah."

"Of course we can, dear. Of course we can."

Basket Case

Written for an anthology that was supposed to have stories based on Warren Zevon songs. The antho never sold, but the British zine The Horror Express bought this. It's about the things we do for love...

Rust from the crowbar flaked off, coating my palm with orange dust. I tapped the iron against my pants leg, then checked my watch again.

11:42.

Three more minutes.

I wanted to put an ear to the door, but that would only piss me off. I'd lose control, hearing another man grunting inside Leena. Then I might use the crowbar for real, rather than as a prop. The goal was to rob the guy, not kill him.

At least Leena had her limits.

I knew Leena was crazy the first time I saw her, playing pool in a yuppie bar on Rush & Division. She wore a halter top, no bra, her great ass wrapped in a tight leather mini that barely covered her white panties. The guy she was with had his hands all over her, and she seemed to be enjoying it. The slap and tickle went on so long I would have put down money that he was going to nail her right there on the pool table, but it didn't go that way. Instead of getting laid, the guy got a beer mug shattered on his dome when he whispered something to Leena that she obviously didn't appreciate. He hit the floor, covered in blood and Heineken, and Leena kicked him in the stones two or three times until his buddies pulled her off.

After spitting on him, Leena walked up to the bar. Everyone gave her space.

Everyone except for me. I moved in.

"You've been watching me for the last hour," were her first words to me.

"You're something to watch."

She must have liked my response, because she leaned in closer.

"You know what that jackass said to me?"

"He insult your mother?"

"Worse. He asked me how much for the night. Take a look at me."

Leena stepped back, twirled. Her thighs were firm and her hair was blonde and she could have had any man in that bar and she knew it.

"Do I look like a whore?"

"Never saw a whore with a body that nice."

"Damn right. I don't sell it." Then she grinned at me and licked her lips, all red lipstick and pink tongue. "I give it away."

I bought her a few beers, and we soon got into the hot and heavy the same way she had with bleeding boy, except I didn't say anything stupid and managed to seal the deal back at my place a few hours later.

Leena wasn't just hot. She was fire.

I do okay in the chick department. I'm average looking, but have a lot of muscles. Working construction nine months out of the year gives me a deep tan. I go out four nights a week, and I go home with someone about half the time.

But I'd never met a woman like Leena before. It wasn't simply sex. It was SEX. When she was finished with me, I felt melted, like a plastic bottle that had been nuked in the microwave. She did things to me–amazing things, things that blew my mind. And when morning came, and she gathered up her shit to do the walk of shame back home, I knew that I couldn't just let her leave my life forever. I had to see her again.

"You still got some left?" she'd asked.

I nodded.

"Call me."

I called her. We saw each other the next night.

And let me tell you, the sex was aitch-oh-tee HOT.

I felt like one of those hermits who go up on a mountain and find god, except my god wasn't peace and love and being one with the universe; it was hot, sweaty fucking that was so intense I had to pull the sheets out of my ass when we finished.

I wasn't looking for emotional attachment. Neither was Leena. She wasn't the type. I knew she was using me, and that when she got bored she'd more on.

But before I understood what was happening, I was whipped. I would have done anything for her. So when she told me she needed some help, I fell all over myself volunteering.

Leena, I found out, didn't have a regular job. She got her money from men. Not like a prostitute; Leena never directly took money for sex. But there were certain men she dated, 'whales' she called them, who took her nice places and bought her nice things in exchange for being with her a few nights a month.

Tonight, one of these fat-cats was calling their relationship quits. He was wracked with guilt over his wife, or some crap like that. Since this particular whale was also paying for Leena's apartment, she was understandably miffed.

"No one leaves me. You have to help me, John."

"Help you do what?"

The plan was, after she boffed the whale goodbye, I was supposed to burst into the room pretending to be Leena's husband. I'd swing the crowbar around, threatening the guy, acting crazy. Leena assured me he'd be reaching for his checkbook to smooth things over.

"We'll get twenty grand at least," Leena said.

11:44.

One more minute.

A groan–a male groan–came from behind the door. Then a thumping sound.

I squeezed my eyes shut, wiped the sweat off the back of my neck. I'd never had a jealous minute in my whole life, but right then, right there, I wanted to bash this guy's head into the mattress. I wouldn't have to fake being angry, no sir. When I got done with him, he'd be offering a lot more than twenty large.

A giggle. High and feminine.

I ground my teeth.

11:45.

I burst in, crowbar raised.

The puke cleared my teeth before I even got the door closed behind me.

The whale was tied to bed. There was a big bloody hole where his stomach should have been, loops of shiny intestines pulled out and draped across all four bedposts like Christmas lights. All kinds of slimy glop soaked the sheets and pooled on the floor. The smell of blood and shit was so strong, I hurled again.

Leena–sexy, crazy Leena–was naked and squatting on his face, riding hard, her hands clenched on the headboard, making her cum sounds.

I dropped the crowbar.

Leena's back arched, and she shuddered and turned. Her perfect tits were coated with blood and dark bits of stuff. Her eyes were wide, manic, and the grin that creased her face scared the absolute fuck out of me.

She crawled, like a predatory cat, over the corpse and to the foot of the bed.

"Hi, John."

"Leena...jesus..."

She squatted, thighs spread, one hand rubbing gore between her legs.

"Come over here, John."

I took a step back, feeling the door knob hit me in the ass.

"Don't be scared. I'm harmless."

"Harmless?" I pointed at the mess behind her. "That's not harmless."

"He didn't complain. He died happy. See?"

She reached back and grabbed the guy by the joint, and damned if it wasn't stiffer than one of the bedposts. Leena began to stroke it, up and down.

"It's okay, John. He had it coming. I made it good for him."

As horrible, as revolting, as the whole scene was, I felt myself begin to respond.

"Come over here, Johnny. Come to Leena."

She licked something black and gooey off of her upper lip. Her hips humped the air. I had an urge to run away, to leave the apartment and run to the nearest bar and drink the last five minutes out of my memory.

But instead I took off my pants.

I fucked Leena, right there, on top of the dead guy.

And let me tell you, the sex was aitch-oh-tee HOT.

The Agreement

I wrote this in college, and never tried to publish it because I considered it too violent. But after selling several stories to Ellery Queen, I still couldn't crack its sister publication, Alfred Hitchcock. After a handful of rejections, I sent them this, and they bought it. I liked the last line so much I've reused it a few times in other stories.

Hutson closed his eyes and swallowed hard, trying to stop sweating. On the table, in the pot, thirty thousand dollars worth of chips formed a haphazard pyramid. Half of those chips were his. The other half belonged to the quirky little mobster in the pink suit that sat across from him.

"I'll see it."

The mobster pushed more chips into the pile. He went by the street nick Little Louie. Hutson didn't know his last name, and had no real desire to learn it. The only thing he cared about was winning this hand. He cared about it a great deal, because Bernard Hutson did not have the money to cover the bet. Seven hours ago he was up eighteen grand, but since then he'd been steadily losing and extending his credit and losing and extending his credit. If he won this pot, he'd break even.

If he didn't, he owed thirty thousand dollars that he didn't have to a man who had zero tolerance for welchers.

Little Louie always brought two large bodyguards with him when he gambled. These bodyguards worked according to a unique payment plan. They would hurt a welcher in relation to what he owed. An unpaid debt of one hundred dollars would break a finger. A thousand would break a leg.

Thirty thousand defied the imagination.

Hutson wiped his forehead on his sleeve and stared at his hand, praying it would be good enough.

Little Louie dealt them each one more card. When the game began, all six chairs had been full. Now, at almost five in the morning, the only two combatants left were Hutson and the mobster. Both stank of sweat and cigarettes. They sat at a greasy wooden card table in somebody's kitchen, cramped and red-eyed and exhausted.

One of Louie's thugs sat on a chair in the corner, snoring with a deep bumble-bee buzz. The other was looking out of the grimy eighth story window, the fire escape blocking his view of the city. Each men had more scars on their knuckles than Hutson had on his entire body.

Scary guys.

Hutson picked up the card and said a silent prayer before looking at it.

A five.

That gave him a full house, fives over threes. A good hand. A very good hand.

"Your bet," Little Louie barked. The man in the pink suit boasted tiny, cherubic features and black rat eyes. He didn't stand over five four, and a pathetic little blonde mustache sat on his upper lip like a bug. Hutson had joined the game on suggestion of his friend Ray. Ray had left hours ago, when Hutson was still ahead. Hutson should have left with him. He hadn't. And now, he found himself throwing his last two hundred dollars worth of chips into the pile, hoping Little Louie wouldn't raise him.

Little Louie raised him.

"I'm out of chips," Hutson said.

"But you're good for it, right? You are good for it?"

The question was moot. The mobster had made crystal clear, when he extended the first loan, that if Hutson couldn't pay it back, he would hurt him.

"I'm very particular when it comes to debts. When the game ends, I want all debts paid within an hour. In cash. If not, my boys will have to damage you according to what you owe. That's the agreement, and you're obliged to follow it, to the letter."

"I'm good for it."

Hutson borrowed another five hundred and asked for the cards to be shown.

Little Louie had four sevens. That beat a full house.

Hutson threw up on the table.

"I take it I won," grinned Little Louie, his cheeks brightening like a maniacal elf.

Hutson wiped his mouth and stared off to the left of the room, avoiding Little Louie's gaze.

"I'll get the money," Hutson mumbled, knowing full well that he couldn't.

"Go ahead and make your call." Little Louie stood up, stretched. "Rocko, bring this man a phone."

Rocko lifted his snoring head in a moment of confusion. "What boss?"

"Bring this guy a phone, so he can get the money he owes me."

Rocko heaved himself out of his chair and went to the kitchen counter, grabbing Little Louie's cellular and bringing it to Hutson.

Hutson looked over at Little Louie, then at Rocko, then at Little Louie again.

"What do you mean?" he finally asked.

"What do you mean?" mimicked Little Louie in a high, whiny voice. Both Rocko and the other thug broke up at this, giggling like school girls.

"You don't think I'm going to let you walk out of here, do you?"

"You said..."

"I said you have an hour to get the money. I didn't say you could leave to get it. I'm still following the agreement to the letter. So call somebody up and get them to bring it here."

Hutson felt sick again.

"You don't look so good." Little Louie furrowed his brow in mock-concern. "Want an antacid?"

The thugs giggled again.

"I...I don't have anyone I can call," Hutson stammered.

"Call your buddy, Ray. Or maybe your mommy can bring the money."

"Mommy." Rocko snickered. "You ought to be a comedian, boss. You'd kill 'em."

Little Louie puffed out his fat little chest and belched.

"Better get to it, Mr. Hutson. You only have fifty-five minutes left."

Hutson took the phone in a trembling hand, and called Ray. It rang fifteen times, twenty, twenty-five.

Little Louie walked over, patted Hutson's shoulder. "I don't think they're home. Maybe you should try someone else."

Hutson fought nausea, wiped the sweat off of his neck, and dialed another number. His ex-girlfriend, Dolores. They broke up last month. Badly.

A man answered.

"Can I speak to Dolores?"

"Who the hell is this?"

"It's Hutson."

"What the hell do you want?"

"Please let me speak to Dolores, it's real important."

Little Louie watched, apparently drinking in the scene. Hutson had a feeling the mobster didn't care about the money, that he'd rather watch his men inflict some major pain.

"Dolores, this is Hutson."

"What do you want?"

"I need some money. I owe a gambling debt and..."

She hung up on him before he got any farther.

Hutson squeezed his eyes shut. Thirty thousand dollars worth of pain. What would they start with? His knees? His teeth? Jesus, his eyes?

Hutson tried his parents. They picked up on the sixth ring.

"Mom?" This brought uncontrollable laughter from the trio. "I need some money, fast. A gambling debt. They're going to hurt me."

"How much money?"

"Thirty grand. And it need it in forty-five minutes."

There was a lengthy pause.

"When are you going to grow up, Bernard?"

"Mom..."

"You can't keep expecting me and your father to pick up after you all the time. You're a grown man Bernard."

Hutson mopped his forehead with his sleeve.

"Mom, I'll pay you back, I swear to God. I'll never gamble again."

An eternity of silence passed.

"Maybe you'll learn a lesson from this, son. A lesson your father and I obviously never taught you."

"Mom, for God's sake! They're going to hurt me!"

"I'm sorry. You got yourself into this, you'll have to get yourself out."

"Mom! Please!"

The phone went dead.

"Yeah, parents can be tough." Little Louie rolled his head around on his chubby neck, making a sound like a crackling cellophane bag. "That's why I killed mine."

Hutson cradled his face in his hands and tried to fight back a sob. He lost. He was going to be hurt. He was going to be very badly hurt, over a long period of time. And no one was going to help him.

"Please," he said, in a voice he didn't recognize. "Just give me a day or two. I'll get the money."

Little Louie shook his head. "That ain't the deal. You agreed to the terms, and those terms were to the letter. You still have half an hour. See who else you can call."

Hutson brushed away his tears and stared at the phone, praying for a miracle. Then he had an idea.

He called the police.

He dialed 911, then four more numbers so it looked like it was a normal call. A female officer answered.

"Chicago Police Department."

"This is Hutson. This is a matter of life and death. Bring 30,000 dollars over to 1357 Ontario, apartment 506."

"Sir, crank calls on the emergency number is a crime, punishable by a fine of five hundred dollars and up to thirty days in prison."

"Listen to me. Please. They want to kill me."

"Who does, sir?"

"These guys. It's a gambling debt. They're going to hurt me. Get over here."

"Sir, having already explained the penalty for crank calls..."

The phone was ripped from Hutson's hands by Rocko and handed to Little Louie.

"I'm sorry. It won't happen again." Little Louie hung up and waggled a finger at Hutson. "I'm very disappointed in you, Mr. Hutson. After all, you had agreed to my terms."

Hutson began to cry. He cried like a first grader with a skinned knee. He cried for a long time, before finally getting himself under control.

"It's time." Little Louie glanced at his watch and smiled. "Start with his fingers."

"Please don't hurt me..."

Rocko and the other thug moved in. Hutson dodged them and got on his knees in front of Little Louie.

"I'll do anything," he pleaded. "Anything at all. Name it. Just name it. But please don't hurt me."

"Hold it boys." Little Louie raised his palm. "I have an idea."

A small ray of hope penetrated Hutson.

"Anything. I'll do anything."

Little Louie took out a long, thin cigarillo and nipped off the end, swallowing it.

"There was a guy, about six years ago, who was in the same situation you're in now."

He put the end of the cigar in his mouth and rolled it around on his fat, gray tongue.

"This guy also said he would do anything, just so I didn't hurt him. Remember that fellas?"

Both bodyguards nodded.

"He finally said, what he would do, is put his hand on a stove burner for ten seconds. He said he would hold his own hand on the burner, for ten whole seconds."

Little Louie produced a gold Dunhill and lit the cigar, rolling it between his chubby fingers while drawing hard.

"He only lasted seven, and we had to hurt him anyway." Little Louie sucked on the stogie, and blew out a perfect smoke ring. "But I am curious to see if it could be done. The whole ten seconds."

Little Louie looked at Hutson, who was still kneeling before him.

"If you can hold your right hand on a stove burner for ten seconds, Mr. Hutson, I'll relieve you of your debt and you can leave without anyone hurting you."

Hutson blinked several times. How hot did a stove burner get? How seriously would he be hurt?

Not nearly as much as having thirty thousand dollars worth of damage inflicted upon him.

But a stove burner? Could he force himself to keep his hand on it for that long?

Did he have any other choice?

"I'll do it."

Little Louie smiled held out a hand to help Hutson to his feet.

"Of course, if you don't do it, the boys will still have to work you over. You understand."

Hutson nodded, allowing himself to be led into the kitchen.

The stove was off-white, a greasy Kenmore, with four electric burners. The heating elements were each six inches in diameter, coiled into spirals like a whirlpool swirl. They were black, but Hutson knew when he turned one on it would glow orange.

Little Louie and his bodyguards stepped behind him to get a better look.

"It's electric," noted Rocko.

Little Louie frowned. "The other guy used a gas stove. His sleeve caught on fire. Remember that?"

The thugs giggled. Hutson picked the lower left hand burner and turned it on the lowest setting.

Little Louie wasn't impressed.

"Hey, switch it up higher than that."

"You didn't say how high it had to be when we made the agreement." Hutson spoke fast, relying on the mobster's warped sense of fairness. "Just that I had to keep it on for ten seconds."

"It was inferred it would be on the hottest."

"I can put it on low and still follow the deal to the letter."

Little Louie considered this, then nodded.

"You're right. You're still following it to the letter. Leave it on low then."

It didn't matter, because already the burner was firey orange. Rocko leaned over and spat on it, and the saliva didn't even have a chance to drip through the coils before sizzling away and evaporating.

"It think it's hot," Rocko said.

Hutson stared at the glowing burner. He held his trembling hand two inches above it. The heat was excruciating. Hutson's palm began to sweat and the hair above his knuckles curled and he fought the little voice in his brain that screamed get your hand away!

"Well, go ahead." Little Louie held up a gold pocket watch. "I'll start when you do. Ten whole seconds."

"Sweet Jesus in heaven help me," thought Hutson.

He bit his lip and slapped his hand down on to the burner.

There was an immediate frying sound, like bacon in a pan. The pain was instant and searing. Hutson screamed and screamed, the coils burning away the skin on his palm, burning into the flesh, blistering and bubbling, melting the muscle and fat, Hutson screaming louder now, smoke starting to rise, Little Louie sounding off the seconds, a smell like pork chops filling Hutson's nostrils, pain beyond intense, screaming so high there wasn't any sound, can't keep it there anymore, jesus no more no more and...

Hutson yanked his hand from the burner, trembling, feeling faint, clutching his right hand at the wrist and stumbling to the sink, turning on the cold water, putting his charred hand under it, losing consciousness, everything going black.

He woke up lying on the floor, the pain in his hand a living thing, his mouth bleeding from biting his lower lip. His face contorted and he yelled from the anguish.

Little Louie stood over him, holding the pocket watch. "That was only seven seconds."

Hutson's scream could have woken the dead. It was full of heart-wrenching agony and fear and disgust and pity. It was the scream of the man being interrogated by the Gestapo. The scream of the woman having a Caesarean without anesthetic. The scream of a father in a burning, wrecked car turning to see his baby on fire.

The scream of a man without hope.

"Don't get upset." Little Louie offered him a big grin. "I'll let you try it again."

The thugs hauled Hutson to his feet, and he whimpered and passed out. He woke up on the floor again, choking. Water had been thrown in his face.

Little Louie shook his head, sadly. "Come on Mr. Hutson. I haven't got all day. I'm a busy man. If you want to back out, the boys can do their job. I want to warn you though, a thirty grand job means we'll put your face on one of these burners, and that would just be the beginning. Make your decision."

Hutson got to his feet, knees barely able to support him, breath shallow, hand hurting worse than any pain he had ever felt. He didn't want to look at it, found himself doing it anyway, and stared at the black, inflamed flesh in a circular pattern on his palm. Hardly any blood. Just raw, exposed, gooey cooked muscle where the skin had fried away.

Hutson bent over and threw up.

"Come on, Mr. Hutson. You can do it. You came so close, I'd hate to have to cripple you permanently."

Hutson tried to stagger to the door to get away, but was held back before he took two steps.

"The stove is over here, Mr. Hutson." Little Louie's black rat eyes sparkled like polished onyx.

Rocko steered Hutson back to the stove. Hutson stared down at the orange glowing burner, blackened in several places where parts of his palm had stuck and cooked to cinder. The pain was pounding. He was dazed and on the verge of passing out again. He lifted his left hand over the burner.

"Nope. Sorry Mr. Hutson. I specifically said it had to be your right hand. You have to use your right hand, please."

Could he put his right hand on that burner again? Hutson didn't think he could, in his muddied, agony-spiked brain. He was sweating and cold at the same time, and the air swam around him. His body shook and trembled. If he were familiar with the symptoms, Hutson might have known he was going into shock. But he wasn't a doctor, and he couldn't think straight anyway, and the pain, oh jesus, the awful pain, and he remembered being five years old and afraid of dogs, and his grandfather had a dog and made him pet it, and he was scared, so scared that it would bite, and his grandfather grabbed his hand and put it toward the dog's head...

Hutson put his hand back on the burner.

"One...............two..............."

Hutson screamed again, searing pain bringing him out of shock. His hand reflexively grabbed the burner, pushing down harder, muscles squeezing, the old burns set aflame again, blistering, popping...

"...............three..............."

Take it off! Take it off! Screaming, eyes squeezed tight, shaking his head like a hound with a fox in his teeth, sounds of cracking skin and sizzling meat...

"..............four...............five..............."

Black smoke, rising, a burning smell, that's me cooking, muscle melting and searing away, nerves exposed, screaming even louder, pull it away!, using the other hand to hold it down...

"..............six...............seven..............."

Agony so exquisite, so absolute, unending, entire arm shaking, falling to knees, keeping hand on burner, opening eyes and seeing it sear at eye level, turning grey like a well-done steak, meat charring...

"Smells pretty good," says one of the thugs.

"Like a hamburger."

"A hand-burger."

Laughter.

"................eight...............nine..............."

No flesh left, orange burner searing bone, scorching, blood pumping onto heating coils, beading and evaporating like fat on a griddle, veins and arteries searing...

"................ten!"

Take it off! Take it off!

It's stuck.

"Look boss, he's stuck!"

Air whistled out of Hutson's lungs like a horse whimpering. His hand continued to fry away. He pulled feebly, pain at a peak, all nerves exposed– pull dammit! –blacking out, everything fading...

Hutson awoke on the floor, shaking, with more water in his face.

"Nice job Mr. Hutson." Little Louie stared down at him. "You followed the agreement. To the letter. You're off the hook."

Hutson squinted up at the mobster. The little man seemed very far away.

"Since you've been such a sport, I've even called an ambulance for you. They're on their way. Unfortunately, the boys and I won't be here when it arrives."

Hutson tried to say something. His mouth wouldn't form words.

"I hope we can gamble again soon, Mr. Hutson. Maybe we could play a hand or two. Get it? A hand?"

The thugs tittered. Little Louie bent down, close enough for Hutson to smell his cigar breath.

"Oh, there's one more thing, Mr. Hutson. Looking back on our agreement, I said you had to hold your right hand on the burner for ten seconds. I said you had to follow that request to the letter. But, you know what? I just realized something pretty funny. I never said you had to turn the burner on."

Little Louie left, followed by his body guards, and Bernard Hutson screamed and screamed and just couldn't stop.

Well Balanced Meal

This is something I wrote back in college. It's the first time I ever did a story using only dialog. I read this at the infamous Gross Out Contest at the World Horror Con, but was pulled off the stage for not being gross enough The next year I came back with a truly disgusting story and won the contest, becoming the Gross Out Champion of 2004. The story that won the contest will never see print. If you're curious, the ending involved relations with a colostomy bag. This piece is much less extreme.

"Hi, welcome to Ranaldi's. You folks ready to order?"

"Not quite yet."

"How about we start you off with some drinks?"

"Sounds good. I'll have a rum and toothpaste."

"Flavor?"

"Pepsident."

"I'm sorry. We only have Aim, Close-Up, Gleem, and Tarter Control Crest."

"Give me the Crest, then."

"And you sir?"

"I'll take a Kahlua and baby oil."

"Miss?"

"Vodka and mayonnaise."

"How about you, Miss?"

"Just hot buttered coffee for me."

"I think I'm ready to order."

"What can I get you sir?"

"A pimpleburger."

"How would you like that cooked?"

"Until it turns brown and starts to bubble."

"You have a choice of soup or salad with that."

"What's the soup?"

"Cream of Menstruation. It's our special—we only get it once a month."

"That sounds good."

"How about you sir, ready to order?"

"Yeah. I'll take boils and eggs."

"Good choice. The chef has several big ones just waiting to be lanced."

"Is the ham fresh?"

"No ma'am."

"Okay, I'll take the ham. Can you cover it with vomit?"

"Of course. What kind?"

"How about from someone who has just eaten chicken?"

"I'll have the cook eat some chicken right now so he can puke it up for you."

"I'd like it to be partially digested, if possible."

"There will be a forty minute wait for that."

"No problem."

"And you miss? Have you decided?"

"Yeah. I think I'll just take a bowl of hot grease with a hair in it."

"Pubic or armpit?"

"Can I get one of each?"

"I think I can arrange that."

"Could we also get an appetizer?"

"Of course sir."

"Fresh rat entrails."

"How many orders?"

"How big are the rats?"

"They're a pretty good size."

"Okay, two. Do we get to dig them out ourselves?"

"Yep. We serve out rat entrails live and squirming."

"Make it three then."

"Can we get a cup of placenta for dipping?"

"Yes you can."

"Is it okay to order dessert now?"

"Of course miss."

"I'd like the sugar fried snot."

"Good choice. One of the busboys has a terrible cold."

"I think I'll have a slice of lung cake."

"Would you like spit sauce on that?"

"On the side."

"Sir, would you like to order your dessert now?"

"A blood sundae."

"What kind?"

"What kind do you have?

"Types A, B, and O."

"No AB?"

"I'm sorry. We're out."

"Could you mix A and B together?"

"It will clot."

"That's okay."

"And you, Miss? Dessert?"

"I think I'll skip dessert and eat my own stool when I get home."

"That's a good idea, honey. Cancel the lung cake, I think I'll just eat my wife's shit too."

"We do serve feces here. Regular and chunky style. We're also running a special on diarrhea. Two cups for the price of one."

"No thanks. Why buy something you can get for free at home?"

"Thrifty thinking, sir. Can I get you folks anything else?"

"Yeah. This fork has got water spots on it. Can I get a new one?"

"Absolutely sir. I'll be right back."

S.A.

I wrote this for the anthology Wolfsbane & Mistletoe, edited by Charlaine Harris and Toni L.P. Kelner. It was one of those stories that practically wrote itself. Werewolves have always been one of my favorite monsters, and I was thrilled to have a chance to cut loose and let my imagination run wild. Some quick notes: The Salvation Army is a wonderful organization with over 3.5 million volunteers, and I'm pretty sure none of them are cough syrup swilling psychotics. The names used in this story are all names of characters from famous werewolf movies. Unless someone tries to sue me, in which case I made all of them up. (L.L. Cool J also did a rocking version of "Who's Afraid of the Big Bad Wolf.") While the modern Bible is missing many of its original passages, the Book of Bob isn't one of them. You're probably getting it confused with the lost Book of Fred. Other than that, everything in this story is 100% true.

Robert Weston Smith walked across the snow-covered parking lot carrying a small plastic container of his poop.

Weston considered himself a healthy guy. At thirty-three years old he still had a six-pack, the result of working out three times a week. He followed a strict macrobiotic diet. He practiced yoga and tai chi. The last time he ate processed sugar was during the Reagan administration.

That's why, when odd things began appearing in his bowel movements, he became more than a little alarmed. So alarmed that he sought out his general practitioner, making an appointment after a particularly embarrassing phone call to his office secretary.

Weston entered the office building with his head down and a blush on his ears, feeling like a kid sneaking out after curfew. He used the welcome mat to stamp the snow off his feet and walked through the lobby to the doctor's office, taking a deep breath before going in. There were five people in the waiting room, two adults and a young boy, plus a nurse in pink paisley hospital scrubs who sat behind the counter.

Weston kept his head down and beelined for the nurse. The poop container was blue plastic, semi-opaque, but it might as well have been a police siren, blinking and howling. Everyone in the room must have known what it was. And if they didn't at first, they sure knew after the nurse said in a loud voice, "Is that your stool sample?"

He nodded, trying to hand it to the woman. She made no effort to take it, and he couldn't really blame her. He carried it, and a clipboard, over to a seat in the waiting room. Setting his poop on a table atop an ancient copy of *Good Housekeeping*, he got to work filling out his insurance information. When it came time to describe the nature of his ailment, he wrote down "intestinal problems." Which was untrue---his intestines felt fine. It's what came out of his intestines that caused alarm.

"What's in the box?"

Weston looked up, staring into the big eyes of a child, perhaps five or six years old.

"It's, um, something for the doctor."

He glanced around the room, looking for someone to claim the boy. Three people had their noses stuck in magazines, one was watching a car commercial on the TV hanging from the ceiling, and the last appeared asleep. Any of them could have been his parent.

"Is it a cupcake?" the boy asked.

"Uh... yeah, a cupcake."

"I like cupcakes."

"You wouldn't like this one."

The boy reached for the container.

"Is it chocolate?"

Weston snatched it up and set it in his lap.

"No. It isn't chocolate."

"Show it to me."

"No."

The boy squinted at the sample. Weston considered putting it behind his back, out of the child's sight, but there was no place to set it other than the chair. It didn't seem wise to put it where he might lean back on it.

"It looks like chocolate. I think I can see peanuts."

"Those aren't peanuts."

In fact, gross and disturbing as it sounded, Weston didn't know what those lumps were. Which is why he was at the doctor's office.

He glanced again at the three people in the waiting room, wondering why no one bothered to corral their son. Weston was single, no children. None of his friends had children. Being a mechanical engineer, he didn't encounter children at his job. Perhaps today's parents had no problems letting their kids walk up to strangers and beg for cupcakes.

"Mr. Smith?" the pink paisley nurse said. "Please come with me."

Weston stood, taking his poop through the door, following the nurse down a short hallway and into an examining room.

"Please put on the gown. I'll be back in a moment."

She closed the door behind him. Weston stared at the folded paper garment, setting on the edge of a beige examination table also lined with paper. He set the container down on next to a jar of cotton swabs. Then he removed his coat, shoes, jeans, boxer shorts, and polo shirt, placed them in a neat pile on the floor, and slipped his arms through the gown's sleeve holes. It felt like wearing a large, stiff napkin.

Weston shivered. It was cold in the room; examination rooms always seemed to be several degrees too cool for comfort. He stood there in his socks, rubbing his bare arms, waiting for the nurse to come back.

She eventually did, taking his temperature and blood pressure, then left him again with the promise that Dr. Waggoner would be there shortly.

A minute passed. Two. Three. Weston stared at the ceiling tiles, thinking about the hours he'd spent on the Internet looking for some sort of clue to what strange disease he had. There was plenty of disturbing content about bowel movements, including a website where people actually sent in pictures of theirs so others could rate them, but he'd found nothing even remotely close to the problem he was having.

The door opened, derailing his train of thought.

"Mr. Smith? I'm Dr. Waggoner. Please, sit down."

Weston sat on the table, the paper chilly under his buttocks. Dr. Waggoner was an older man, portly. Bald, but with enough gray hair growing out of his ears to manage a comb over. He had on trendy round eyeglasses with a faux tortoise shell frame, and a voice that was both deep and nasally.

"Your blood pressure is normal, but your temperature is 100.5 degrees." He snapped on some latex gloves. "How are you feeling right now?"

"Fine."

"Any aches, pains, problems, discomforts?"

"No. I'm a little chilly, but that's all."

Dr. Waggoner removed some sort of scope and checked Weston's eyes and ears as they talked.

"How long have you been having these intestinal problems?"

"Um, on and off for about three months. But they aren't really intestinal problems. I'm finding, uh, strange things in my bowel movements."

"Can you describe them for me?"

"Like little stones. Or things that look like strips of fabric."

Dr. Waggoner raised an eyebrow.

"Well, I have to ask the obvious question first."

Weston waited.

"Have you been eating little stones or strips of fabric?"

The doctor grinned like a Halloween pumpkin. Weston managed a weak smile.

"Not that I'm aware of, Doctor."

"Good to know. Tell me about your diet. Has it changed recently? Eating anything new or exotic?"

"Not really. I eat mostly health foods, have been for the last ten years."

"Been out of the country in the last six months?"

"No."

"Do you eat a lot of rare meat, or raw vegetables?"

"Sometimes. But I don't think I have a tapeworm."

Dr. Waggoner chuckled.

"Ah, the Internet. It gives everyone a doctorate in medicine."

Weston did the open his mouth and say "aaaaah" thing, then said, "I know I'm not a doctor, but I checked a lot of sites, and the things in my stool, they don't look like tapeworm segments."

"Stones and fabric, you said. Can you be more specific?"

"The stones are sort of white. Some very small, like flecks. Other times bigger."

"How big?"

"About the size of my thumb."

"And the fabric?"

"There have been different colors. Sometimes red. Sometimes black. Sometimes blue."

"How closely have you examined these items?"

Weston frowned. "Not too closely. I mean, I never took them out of the toilet and picked them up or anything. Except for that." Weston pointed to the stool on the table.

"We'll have the lab take a look at that. In the meantime, I'm going to have to take a look myself. Can you bend over the table and lift up your gown, please?"

Weston hoped it wouldn't have to come to this, but he assumed the position while Dr. Waggoner applied some chilly lubricating jelly to his hand and the point of entry.

"Just relax. You'll feel some pressure."

It was a hell of a lot worse than pressure, and impossible to relax. Weston clenched his eyes shut and tried to concentrate on something, anything, other than the fat fingers going up the down staircase.

"You said this began three months ago. Has it been non-stop? Intermittent?"

"Only two or three days out of the month," Weston grunted. "Then it goes back to normal."

"When during the month?"

"Usually the last week."

"Have you... wait a second. Stay still for a moment. I think I feel something."

Which is the absolute last thing you want to hear when a doctor has his hand inside you. Weston held his breath, scrunched up his face. He didn't know which was worse, the pain or the humiliation. Blessedly, mercifully, the hand withdrew.

"What is it, Doctor?"

"Hold on. I think there's more. I'm going in again."

Weston groaned, hating his life and everyone in it. The doctor went back in four additional times, so often that Weston was becoming used to it, a fact that disturbed him somewhat.

"I think that's the last of it."

"The last of what?"

Weston turned around, saw the physician staring at several objects on his palm.

Dr. Waggoner said. "A coat button, part of a zipper, and sixty three cents in change. Apparently you're not eating as healthy as you think."

Weston blinked, as if the act would make the objects disappear. They remained.

"This is going to sound like a lie," Weston said. "But I didn't eat those."

"I had a colleague who once examined a man who wanted to get into one of those world record books by eating a bicycle, one piece at a time. He removed a reflector from the man's rectum."

"I'm serious, Doctor. I'm not eating buttons or change. I certainly didn't eat a zipper."

"It looks like a fly from a pair of jeans." Dr. Waggoner chuckled again. "I know an old lady who swallowed a fly."

"I didn't eat a fly."

"Okay. Then there's only one alternative. Are you sexually active?"

Weston sighed. "I'm straight. Currently between girlfriends. And the only person who has been up there in my entire life has been you."

Dr. Waggoner placed the objects in a bedpan and said, "You can sit down now."

Weston got off all fours, but preferred to stand. He didn't think he'd ever sit again.

"You think I'm lying to you."

"These things didn't just materialize inside you from another dimension, Mr. Smith. And you probably don't have a branch of the US Treasury inside you, minting coins."

At least someone seemed to be enjoying this. Weston wondered when he'd ask him to break a dollar.

"I'm telling the truth."

"Do you have a roommate? One who likes practical jokes?"

"I live alone."

"Do you drink? Do any drugs?"

"I have an occasional beer."

"Do you ever drink too much? Have black outs? Periods where you don't remember what happened?"

Weston opened his mouth to say no, but stopped himself. There were a few moments during the last few weeks that seemed sort of fuzzy, memory-wise. He wouldn't call them black-outs. But he'd go to bed, but wake up in a different part of the house. Naked.

"I think I might sleep walk," he admitted.

"Now we're getting somewhere." Dr. Waggoner pulled off his gloves, put them in the hazardous materials bin. "I'm going to refer you to a specialist."

Weston scratched his head. "So you think I'm eating buttons and spare change in my sleep?"

"They're getting inside you, one way or another. Consider yourself lucky. I once had a patient who, while sleepwalking, logged onto an internet casino and blew seventy-eight thousand dollars."

"So he came to see you for help with sleepwalking?"

"He came to see me to set his broken nose, after his wife found out. Don't worry, Mr. Smith. I'm going to prescribe a sleep aid for you tonight, to help curb late-night snacking, and the specialist will get to the root of your problem. Sleepwalking is usually the result of stress, or depression."

Weston frowned. "This doctor you're referring me to. Is he a shrink

"His name is Dr. Glendon. He's a psychiatrist. My nurse will set up an appointment for you. In the meantime, try to lock up all the small, swallowable objects in your home."

* * *

Weston walked home feeling like an idiot. An idiot who sat on a cactus. His apartment, only a few blocks away from the doctor's office, seemed like fifty miles because every step stung.

The sun was starting to set, and Naperville had its holiday clothes on. Strands of white lights hung alongside fresh evergreen wreaths and bows, decorating every lamp post and storefront window. The gently falling snow added to the effect, making the street look like a Christmas card.

None of it cheered Weston. Since his job moved him to Illinois, away from his family and friends in Asheville, North Carolina, he'd been down. But not actually depressed. All Weston knew about depression came from watching TV commercials for anti-depressants. He'd never seen a commercial where the depressed person ate nickels, but maybe Dr. Waggoner was on to something.

Fishing his keys from his jeans, he was about to stick them in the lock of the security door when it opened suddenly. Standing there, all four feet of her, was his mean next door neighbor. Weston didn't know her name. She probably didn't know his either. She simply called him "Loud Man." Every twenty minutes she would bang on the wall between their apartments, screaming about him making noise. If he turned on the TV, she'd bang—even when it was at its lowest setting. If the phone rang, she'd bang. When the microwave beeped, she'd bang. She even banged while he was brushing his teeth.

He'd called the landlord about her, three times. Each occasion, Weston got the brush off.

"She's eccentric," he was told. "No family. You should ignore her."

Easy for the landlord to say. How do you ignore someone who won't let you into your own door?

Weston tried to step around her, but the old woman folded her arms and didn't budge. She had light brown skin, and some sort of fabric tied to the top of her head. Weston couldn't help staring at her ears, which had distinctive, gypsy-like gold hoops dangling from them. The ears themselves were huge, probably larger than Weston's hands. Maybe if his ears were that big, he'd complain all the time about noise too.

Her dog, some sort of tiny toy breed with long fur and a mean disposition, saw Weston and began to yap at him, straining against his leash. It had a large gold tag on his collar that read "ROMI."

"Excuse me," Weston said, trying to get by.

The old woman stayed put. So did Romi.

"I said, *excuse me.*"

She pointed a crooked old finger at him.

"Loud Man! You keep noise down!"

"They have these things called earplugs," Weston said. "I think they come in extra large."

She began to scream at him in a high-pitched native tongue that sounded a lot like "BLAAA-LAAAA-LAAAAA-LEEEE-LAAAA-BLAAA!" Romi matched her, yipping right along. Weston took it for about ten seconds, and then pushed past, heading for his apartment. The chorus followed him inside.

Though it was early, Weston yawned, then yawned again. He hung his keys on a hook next to the door, switched the TV on to one setting above MUTE, and sat on the sofa. There was dog hair on the carpet, which made no sense, because Weston had no dog.

But the crazy old lady had a dog.

Could she be getting in my apartment somehow?

Panicked, Weston did a quick tour, looking for anything missing or out of place. He came up empty, but to his shame he realized he was picking up everything smaller than a match book and sticking it in his pockets. He took these items and placed them in a junk drawer in the kitchen.

For some reason, this act drained him of his last drop of energy, and the sun had barely even gone down. He sat back down on the couch, switched to the SciFi Channel, and closed his eyes for just a few seconds.

* * *

A ringing sound woke Weston up. He was naked on the kitchen floor, the sun streaming in through the windows. Weston automatically smacked his lips, checking to see if he could taste anything odd. Then he got to his knees and reached for the phone on the counter.

"Mr. Smith? This is Dr. Waggoner's office calling. Please hold for the doctor."

Weston scratched his chest, listening to Neil Diamond singing to a chair who apparently didn't hear him.

"Weston? This is Dr. Waggoner. How did you sleep last night?"

"Not well," he said, noting his nude body.

"Remember to keep your appointment with the psychiatrist today. And also, it wouldn't hurt to see a dentist as well. We got the lab report from your stool sample. It contained three molars."

"Teeth?"

"Yes. Your teeth. There was also a shoelace, and a silver cross on a necklace. The lab is sending the cross over to my office later, in case you'd like to pick it up. It will be cleaned first, of course"

"Doctor, I…"

Dr. Waggoner hung up before Weston could finish, "…don't own a silver cross."

He got to his feet and padded over to the bathroom, opening wide for the mirror. Weston wasn't missing any molars. Each of his teeth was in its proper place.

What the hell is going on?

His abdomen grumbled. Weston sat on the toilet and rubbed his temples, trying to make sense of any of this. How could he have swallowed teeth, or a silver cross? Why did he keep waking up naked? What was going on?

He didn't want to look, but before he flushed he forced himself. And gasped.

At the bottom of the toilet bowl were two distinct, unmistakable objects: A gold hoop earring, and a silver tag that said ROMI.

* * *

When he stopped running around in a blind panic (which took the good part of twenty minutes) Weston forced himself to the computer and Googled "eating+disorder+neighbor." This led him to sites about anorexia, which certainly wasn't his problem. Next he tried "cannibal" and got hits for bad Italian horror movies and death metal rock bands. "Sleep+eating+people" produced articles about sleeping pills, and "I ate human beings" led to a YouTube video of some drunk Klan member who kept saying "I hate human beings" and apparently posted the video so wasted he misspelled the title of his own rant.

Various other word combination produced pages about Hannibal Lector, Alfred Packer, Sawney Bean, and ultimately Hansel and Gretel.

While on the site about fairy tales, Weston clicked from the old witch who wanted to eat children to the big bad wolf who wanted to eat children. This took him to a site about the history of lycanthropy, which featured several old paintings of wolf people running off with screaming babies in their mouths. Soon Weston was looking up "clinical lycanthropy" which was a real psychiatric term that pretty much meant "batshit crazy."

Could I really be crazy? he thought. *Do I subconsciously think I'm a werewolf?*

A quick click on a lunar calendar confirmed Weston's fears: The only time he'd had blackouts and found weird things in his poop was during the full moon.

Weston sat back, slack-jawed. He wondered if he should call someone. His parents? A doctor? The cops?

He searched his soul for remorse for eating his mean neighbor and her nasty dog, but couldn't find any.

But he must have killed other, nicer people. Right?

Weston slipped on some shorts and attacked the Internet again, looking through back issues of the local newspaper for accounts of murders or disappearances. He found five.

The first was from yesterday. A hand and partial skeleton found near the River Walk, a popular woodsy trail in Naperville. The prints on the hand belonged to Leon Corledo. His death was attributed to the Naperville Ripper.

How could I have missed hearing about that? Weston wondered. Too much work, probably. And the fact that the news depressed him, so he avoided it. Not to mention the fact that every time he turned on his TV, his recently digested neighbor banged.

Weston read on, found that Mr. Corledo was a registered sex offender. No big loss there. Weston followed the links to articles about the Ripper's other known victims. They included:

Waldemar Daminsky, 66, a local businessman with known ties to Polish organized crime.

Tony Rivers, 17, who was decapitated after robbing a liquor store and beating the owner unconscious.

Ginger Fitzgerald, who had recently lost custody of her daughter for locking her in a closet for a week without food or water.

And Marty Coslaw, a lawyer.

Weston felt zero guilt, and breathed a bit easier. But how many criminals and lawyers did Naperville have? Eventually, he'd run out of scumbags to eat. Then what?

He tried the search term "help for real lycanthropy" and, incredibly, got a hit. A single hit, for a website called *Shapeshifters Anonymous.*

Weston went to the site, and found it to be a home for werewolf jokes. After suffering through a spate of awful puns (Where do werewolves go on vacation? A Howliday Inn!) he had about given up when he noticed a tiny hotlink at the bottom of the page that read, "Real therianthropes click here."

He knew from his lycanthropy reading that therianthropes were humans who morphed into animals. He clicked.

The page took him to another site, which had a black background and only five large cryptic words on it.

THERIANTHROPES MUST VIEW THE SOURCE

Weston stared, wondering what it meant. Which source? The source of their affliction? The source of their food?

On a whim, he Googled "view the source" and came up with a bunch of websites about HTML programming. Then he got it.

View the webpage source.

He went back to the werewolf page, opened his Internet Explorer toolbar, and under the PAGE menu clicked VIEW SOURCE. The HTML and Javascript appeared in a new window. Weston read through the computer language gobbledygook until he came to this:

&ei=xY0_R6--CZXcigGGoPmBCA"+g}return true};window.gbar={};(function(){;var g=window.gbar,a,f,h;functionm(b,e,d){b.display=b.display=="block"?"none" :"block";b.left=e+"px";b.top=d+"px"}g.tg=function(b){**real therianthropes call 1-800-209-7219**}

Weston grabbed his phone and dialed with trembling hands.

"Therianthrope hotline, Zela speaking, may I help you?"

"I… uh… is this for real?"

"Are you a therianthrope, sir?"

"I think so. Is this really a werewolf hotline?"

"Is that what you turn into, sir? A wolf?"

"I have no idea. I black out beforehand, can't remember anything."

"Why do you think you're a therianthrope, sir?"

"I'm finding, um, things, in my, uh, toilet."

"Things like bone fragments, jewelry, eyeglasses, bits of clothing, coins, watches, and keys?"

"How did you know?"

"I'm a therianthrope myself, sir. Can I ask where you currently reside?"

"Naperville. Illinois."

"So I'm assuming you just realized you're the Naperville Ripper we've been hearing about?"

"They were all bad people," Weston said quickly. "I'm not sure about the lawyer, but I can make assumptions."

"We've been following the news. He was a defense attorney, defended child molesters. When given a choice, therianthropes usually prefer the wicked over the good. The creatures inside us find evil tastier."

"That's, uh, good to know. So… what are you, exactly? Are you a werewolf too?"

"I'm a weresquirrel, sir."

"When the full moon rises, you turn into a squirrel?"

"Yes."

"A squirrel with buck teeth with a big fluffy tail?

"That's the one."

Weston wasn't sure if he was supposed to laugh or not.

"Do you shrink? Or stay full size?"

"Full size."

"And you eat people?"

"No, sir. Not all therianthropes are carnivores."

"So, if you don't mind me asking, what do you do when you change?"

"I horde nuts."

Weston chose his next words carefully.

"Are they... evil nuts?"

"Sir, I'm going to put your sarcasm down as you being on the edge of a nervous breakdown, so I'll ignore it. Are you interested in getting help for your therianthropy?"

"Yes, please. Thank you, Zela."

"Let me check the meeting schedule. Okay, today, at noon, there's an SA meeting at St. Lucian's church in Schaumburg, approximately ten miles northwest of you. The secret word to gain entry is Talbot."

"What's SA?"

"Shapeshifters Anonymous."

"So I just go there, and they'll let me join them?"

"If you give the secret word. Yes."

"Do I have to bring anything?"

"Donuts are always nice."

"Donuts. I could bring donuts. Will you be there tonight, Zela? I can bring some with peanuts on them."

"That's very thoughtful of you sir, but I live in New Jersey. And I also think you're kind of a schmuck. Is there anything else I can help you with today?"

"No. Thanks, Zela."

"Thanks for calling the hotline."

Weston hung up, ending what was easily the most surreal conversation he ever had in his life. An hour ago, he'd been a normal guy with some odd bowel movements. Now, he was 99% sure he was some sort of therianthrope.

But what kind?

He went back to the sofa, picked up some of the hair. Long, grayish, fluffy.

Was he a weresheep?

No. He ate people. Had to be a carnivore of some sort.

So what gray animals ate other animals?

Wolves, obviously. Coyotes. Dogs. Cats. Were elephants carnivores?

The Internet told him they were herbivores, which was a relief. But then Weston thought of another gray carnivore.

Rats.

Weston didn't want to be a wererat. He hated rats. Hording nuts was one thing. Swimming in the sewers, eating garbage and feces and dead animals, that was awful. He held his armpit up to his face and sniffed, seeing if he could detect any sort of sewage smell. It seemed okay. Then he checked the time and saw he had two hours to get to the SA meeting. So he hopped in the shower, dressed, and got on his way.

* * *

It had snowed during the night, making Naperville seem even more Winter-Wonderlandish. The cold felt good on Weston's bare face. He attributed the slight fever to his condition: Google told him wolves had an average body temperature of 100.5.

His first stop was Dr. Waggoner's, to pick up the silver cross. Weston didn't want to keep it for himself, but it was evidence of a murder, so it was best to get rid of it.

The nurse handed it to him in an envelope.

"Are you going to put it on?" she asked, eyes twinkling.

"Not right now."

But when he stepped outside, he did open the envelope to take a look. It was, indeed, silver. But all of the movies, all the books, said silver killed werewolves. Weston took a deep breath and dumped it into his palm. It didn't burn his skin. Or was that only with vampires?

He was bringing it up to his face, ready to touch it to his tongue, when he remembered where it had been. Besides, it had already passed through his system without killing him. Obviously the legends were wrong.

He tucked the cross into his coat pocket and walked into town, toward the bakery. On his way, he passed a man dressed as Santa Claus, ringing a bell for some charity. Thinking of the cross, Weston approached and dropped it in the steel collection pot.

"Beware," Santa muttered, voice low and sinister.

Weston wasn't sure he heard correctly. "Excuse me?"

"There's a killer on the loose in Naperville." Weston could smell the NyQuil on Santa's breath. "Not an ordinary killer, either. Only comes out when the moon is full."

"Uh, thanks for the warning."

Weston began to walk away, but Santa's hand reached out and snatched his wrist, pinching like a lobster claw.

"Naughty boys get what they deserve," Santa intoned.

"Okay…"

Santa's eyes suddenly lit up, burning with some internal fire.

"They will be torn limb-from-limb! Their heads severed from their unholy bodies! Burned to ash on sacred ground! BURNED! BURRRRRRRRRNED!!!!!"

Weston pulled free, then walked briskly to the other side of the street, badly shaken. What kind of charity allowed cough syrup crazed psychotics out in public? Wasn't there some kind of screening process for volunteers?

He glanced once over his shoulder, and Psycho Santa was talking on a cell phone, still pointing at him like Donald Sutherland at the end of the first Invasion of the Bodysnatchers remake. It gave Weston the chills.

The uneasy feeling stayed with him all the way up to Russoff's Bakery, where he bought a dozen assorted donuts and a black coffee. When he stepped back onto the street, Weston considered taking another route home so he wouldn't have to see Looney Claus again, then chided himself for being afraid. After all, he was a werecreature. What did he have to fear? If that Santa was really a bad person, chances were good that Weston's inner therianthrope would eat him tonight during the full moon. Weston allowed himself a small smile at the thought of seeing a white beard in his toilet tomorrow morning.

So he steeled himself, and walked the regular path home. But when he passed the spot where Psycho Santa had been, he saw the volunteer was no longer there. Crazy Kringle had packed up his charity pot and left.

Weston walked to his apartment parking lot, hopped into his car, spent a minute programming his GPS, and headed for the suburb of Schaumburg. During the drive, he tried to get his mind around the events of the past twenty-four hours. But he wasn't able to focus. He kept seeing Santa's face. Kept hearing his threats. Once, in the rearview mirror, he swore he saw someone several car lengths behind him in a pointy red hat.

"You're being paranoid," he said to himself, refusing to drink any more coffee.

Just the same, he drove a little faster.

Ten minutes later he was at St. Lucian's, an unassuming Catholic church with a 1970's vibe to the architecture. It was orange with a black shingle roof, shaped like an upside down V. Two large stained glass windows flanked the double entry doors, and a statue of someone, possibly Jesus, perched atop the steeple. There were only six cars in the parking lot, which Weston appreciated because he wasn't good at remembering names, and no one would be short a donut. He parked behind an SUV and took a deep breath to calm his nerves. It was 10:46.

"Here goes nothing."

Bakery goods in hand, he approached the double doors and let himself into St. Lucian's.

The church was dark, quiet. It smelled of scented candles, many of which were burning on a stand next to a charity box. Weston looked down the aisle, to the altar, seeing no one. Then he caught a handwritten sign taped to the back of a pew that read, "SA MEETING IN BASEMENT."

He did a 360, opened a storage closet, then a confessional booth, before finding the door to the stairs next to a baptism font. The concrete staircase wasn't lit, but at the bottom he heard voices. Weston descended, the temperature getting warmer the lower he went. At the bottom he walked past a large furnace, down a short hall, and over to a meeting room.

A bored looking man whose gray hair and loose skin put him somewhere in the sixties, peered at Weston through thick glasses. He wore jeans and a faded turtleneck sweater. From his stance, and his severe haircut, Weston guessed he was ex-military. He stood guard over the doorway, preventing Weston from seeing inside.

"Sorry, sir. This is a private meeting."

The conversation in the room stopped.

"This is SA, right?"

"Yeah. But it's invitation only."

Weston was momentarily confused, until he remembered the hotline conversation.

"Talbot," he said.

"Tall what?"

"Talbot. Isn't that the password?"

"No."

"It's last week's password," someone from in the room said.

"Sorry, buddy." Old Guy folded his arms. "That was last week's password."

"That's the one I was told to use."

"By whom?"

"The SA hotline woman. Tina or Lena or someone."

"Sorry. Can't let you in."

"I brought you donuts." He meekly held up the box.

Old Guy took them.

"Thanks."

"So I can come in?"

"No."

Weston didn't know what to do. He could call the hotline back, but he didn't have the number handy. He'd have to find Internet access, find the website, and by then the meeting could be over.

"Listen." Weston lowered his voice. "You have to let me in. I'm a thespianthrope."

Several snickers from inside the room.

"Does that mean when the moon rises you start doing Shakespeare?" someone asked.

More laughs. Weston realized what he said.

"A therianthrope," he corrected. "I'm the Naperville Ripper."

"I don't care if you're Mother Theresa. You don't get in without the correct password."

Weston snapped his fingers. "Zela. Her name was Zela. She liked to grab people's nuts."

Old Guy remained impassive.

"I mean, she said she was a weresquirrel. She horded nuts."

"I'll call Zela." It was woman's voice. Weston waited, wondering what he would do if they turned him away. For all of his Googling, he'd found precious little information about his condition. He needed to talk to these people, to understand what was going on. And to learn how to deal with it.

"He's okay," the woman said. "Zela gave him the wrong password. Said he's kind of a schmuck, though."

Old Guy stared hard at Weston. "We don't allow for schmuckiness at SA meetings. Got it?"

Weston nodded.

"Oh, lighten up, Scott." The woman again. "Let the poor guy in."

Scott stepped to the side. Weston took his donuts back and entered the room. A standard church basement. Low ceiling. Damp smell. Florescent lights. Old fashioned coffee percolator bubbling on a stand in the corner, next to a trunk. A long, cafeteria style table dominated the center, surrounded by orange plastic chairs. In the chairs were five people, three men and two women. One of the women, a striking blonde, stood up and extended her hand. She had apple cheeks, a tiny upturned nose, and Angelina Jolie lips.

"Welcome to Shapshifters Anonymous. I'm Irena Reed, chapter president."

The one who called Zela. Weston reached his hand out to shake hers, but she bypassed it, grabbing the donuts. She brought them to the table, and everyone gathered round, picking and choosing. Irena selected a jelly filled and bit into, soft and slow. Weston found it incredibly erotic.

"So what's your name?" she purred, mouth dusted with powdered sugar.

"I thought this was anonymous."

Irena motioned for him to come closer, and they walked over to the coffee stand while everyone else ate.

"The founders thought Shapeshifters Anonymous had gravitas."

"Gravitas?"

"You know. Depth. Sorry, I'm a school teacher, that's one of our current vocab words. When this group was created, they thought Shapeshifters Anonymous sounded better than the other potential names. We were this close to calling ourselves Shapeshifters R Us."

"Oh. Okay then." He looked at the group and waved. "My name is Weston."

Weston waited for them all to reply in unison, "Hi, Weston." They didn't.

"You're welcome," Weston tried.

Still no greeting.

"They aren't very social when there's food in front of them," Irena said.

"I guess not. So... you're a therianthrope?"

"A werecheetah. Which is kind of ironic, being a teacher."

He stared blankly, not getting it.

"We expel cheetahs." Irena put a hand to her mouth and giggled.

Weston realized he was already in love with her. "So who is everyone here?"

"The ex-marine, Scott Howard, he's a weretortoise."

Weston appraised the man anew. Long wrinkled neck. Bowed back. "It suits him."

"The small guy with the big head, that's David Kessler. He's a werecoral."

Weston blinked. "He turns into coral?

"Yeah."

"Like a coral reef?"

"Shh. He's sensitive about it."

"How about that older woman?" Weston indicated a portly figure with a huge mess of curly black hair.

"Phyllis Allenby. She's a furry."

"What's that?"

"Furries dress up in animal costumes. Like baseball team mascots."

Weston was confused. "Why?"

"I'm not sure. Might be some sort of weird sex thing."

"So she's not a therianthrope?"

"No. She likes to wear a hippo outfit and dance around. Personally, I don't get it."

"Why is she allowed into meetings?"

"We all kind of feel sorry for her."

A tall man with his mouth around something covered in sprinkles called over to them.

"You two talking about us?"

Irena shot him with her thumb and index finger. "Got it in one, Andy."

Andy strutted over, his grin smeared with chocolate. He shook Weston's hand, pumping enthusiastically.

"Andy McDerrmott, wereboar."

"You... become a pig?" Weston guessed.

"Actually, when the full moon rises, I change into someone vastly self-interested, and I talk incessantly about worthless minutiae going on in my life."

Weston wasn't sure how to answer. Andy slapped him on the shoulder, hard enough to rock him.

"A bore! Get it? Were-bore!" Andy laughed, flecking Weston with sprinkles. "Actually, kidding, I turn into a pig."

"You mean a bigger pig, right Andy?"

Andy shot Irena a look that was pure letch.

"God, you're so hot, Irena. When are we going to get together, have ourselves a litter of little kiggens?"

"On the first of never, Andy. And they wouldn't be kiggens. They'd be pities."

"Snap," Phyllis said. "Shoot that pig down, girl."

"So who's the last guy?" Weston asked. "The big one?"

The trio glanced at the heavily muscled man sitting at the end of the table, staring off into space.

"That's Ryan."

"Just Ryan?"

Andy wiped his mouth on the sleeve of his sports jacket. "That's all he's ever told us. Never talks. Never says a word. Comes to every meeting, but just sits there, looking like the Terminator."

"What does he change into?"

"No one knows. Has to be something, though, or Zela wouldn't have sent him here." Andy faced Weston. "So you're the Naperville Ripper, huh? What kind of therianthrope are you? Wererat?"

Andy frowned. "I'm not sure. I think I'm a werewolf."

This provoked laughter from the group.

"What's funny?"

"Everyone thinks they're a werewolf at first," Irena explained, patting him on the arm. "It's because werewolves are the most popular therianthropes."

"They get all the good press," Andy said. "All the books. All the movies. Never gonna see a flick called An American Wereboar in London."

"Or The Oinking," Phyllis added.

Furry or not, Andy was starting to like Phyllis.

Irena's hand moved up Weston's arm, making him feel a little light-headed.

"Because we can't remember what we do when we've changed, we all first assume we're werewolves."

"So how can I find out what I change into?"

"I set up a video camera and recorded myself." Andy reached into his jacket, took out a CD. "We can pop it in the DVD if you want."

"Don't say yes," Phyllis warned. "The last time he put in a tape of himself and some woman doing the nasty. And it was real nasty."

"An honest mistake." Andy leaned closer to Weston and whispered, "She was a college cheerleader, studying massage therapy. I was bow-legged for a week afterward."

"She was an elderly woman," Phyllis said. "With a walker."

"Mind your own business, you furvert. You're not even a real therianthrope."

Phyllis stuck out her jaw. "I am in my heart."

"When there's a full moon, you don't turn into hippo. You turn into an idiot who puts on a hippo outfit and skips around like a retarded children's show host."

Phyllis stood up, fists clenched.

"I'm 'bout to stick an apple in your talk-hole and roast you on a spit,

Ham Boy."

"Enough." Irena raised her hands. "We're adults. Let's act like it."

"Does anyone want the last donut?" It was David, the werecoral, talking. "Weston? You haven't had one yet."

Weston patted his stomach. "No thanks. I just ate my neighbor and her dog."

"I ate a Fuller Brush Salesman once," Andy said.

"Did not," Phyllis countered. "You ate your own toilet brush. And a pack of them Ty-D-Bowl tablets. That's why your poo was blue."

"So I can have the last donut?" David had already taken a bite out of it.

Weston looked at Irena, felt his heart flutter.

"Other than video, is there another way to find out what I am?"

Irena's eyes sparkled. "Yes. In fact, there is."

* * *

The group, except for Ryan, gathered in front of the chest sitting in the corner of the room.

"Testing equipment." Irena twisted an old fashion key in the lock and opened the lid.

Weston expected some sort of medical supplies, or maybe a chemistry set. Instead, the trunk was filled with dried plants, broken antiques, and assorted worthless-looking junk.

"Hold out your hand."

Weston did as told. Irena held his wrist, and then ran a twig lightly across his palm.

"Feel anything?"

Other than getting a little aroused, Weston felt nothing. He shook his head.

"Cat nip," Irene said. "It's a shame. You would have made a cute kitty."

She brought the branch to her lips, sniffed it, and a tiny moan escaped her throat. Andy took it away from her and tossed it back in the trunk.

"If we let her, she'll play with that all day, and the meeting starts in five minutes. Here, touch this."

Andy handed him a longer, darker twig. Weston touched it, and immediately felt like his entire arm had caught on fire. There was a puff of smoke, and a crackling sound. He recoiled.

"Jesus! What the hell was that, a burning bush?"

Andy cocked his head to the side. "It was wolfsbane. I'll be damned. You are a lycanthrope."

Everyone's expressions changed from surprise to awe, and Weston swore that Irena's pupils got wider. He shrugged.

"Okay, so I'm a werewolf."

"We've never had a werewolf in the group," David said. "How did you become a werewolf?"

"I have no idea."

Weston recalled the masturbation scare tales from his youth, many of which involved hairy palms. He almost asked if that may have caused it, but looked at Irena and decided to keep it to himself.

"Is your mother or father a werewolf?" Scott, the weretortise asked. "I inherited a recessive gene from my mother, Shelly. Been a therianthrope since birth."

"No. This only started three months ago."

"Were you bitten by a therianthrope?" David asked. "That's how they got me."

Weston didn't think that coral could actually bite, but he didn't mention it. Instead he shook his head.

"How about a curse?" Irena asked. "Were you cursed by a gypsy recently?"

"No, I..." Then Weston remembered his evil next door neighbor. He'd been wondering about her ethnic background, and now it seemed obvious. Of course she was a gypsy. How could he have missed the signs? His shoulders slumped.

"Oh, boy. I think maybe I was cursed, for brushing my teeth too loudly."

"You're lucky." David smiled. "That's the easiest type of therianthropy to cure."

"Who wants to be cured?" Scott's eyes narrowed. "I like being a weretortise."

"That's because when you change all you do is eat salad and swim around in your bathtub," Andy said. "I root through the garbage and eat aluminum cans. You ever try to crap out a six pack of Budweiser tall boys?"

David put his hands on his hips. "I'm saying that Weston's a carnivore, like Irena. They eat people. It has to weigh heavy on the conscience."

"Do you feel guilty about it?" Weston asked Irena.

"Nope." Irena smiled. "And I have the added benefit of not having to put up with any bad kids in my class for more than a month."

Weston wondered if it was too soon to propose marriage. He squelched the thought and turned to David.

"So, assuming I want to go back to normal, how do I do it?"

"Just go back to the gypsy that cursed you and pay her to take the curse off."

Oops.

"That might be a problem, seeing as how I ate her."

Andy slapped him on the shoulder. "Tough break, man. But you'll get used to it. Until then, it's probably a good idea to get yourself a nice, sturdy leash."

"It's time to begin the meeting. Let's get started." Irena leaned into Weston and softly said, "We can talk more later."

Weston sincerely hoped so.

* * *

"Let's begin by joining hands and saying the Shapeshifters Anonymous Credo."

Everyone around the table joined hands, including the silent Ryan. Weston noted that Irena's hand was soft and warm, and she played her index finger along the top of his as she talked. So did Phyllis.

Irena began.

"I, state your name, agree to abide by the rules of ethics as set forth by Shapeshifter's Anonymous."

Everyone, including Weston, repeated it.

"I promise to do my best to use my abilities for the good of man and therianthrope kind."

They repeated it.

"I promise to do my best to help any therianthrope who comes to me in need."

They repeated it. Weston thought it a lot like being in church. Which, technically, they were.

"I promise to do my best to not to devour any nice people."

Weston repeated this verse with extra emphasis.

"I promise to avoid Kris Kringle, the dreaded Santa Claus, and his many evil helpers."

"Hold on," Weston interrupted. "What the hell does that mean?"

"Santa Claus is a therianthrope hunter," David said. "He kills shapeshifters."

"You're kidding. Right?"

An uncomfortable silence ensured. Everyone stopped holding hands. Scott cleared his throat, then pushed away from the table and stood up.

"No one is sure how our kind got started. Some say black magic. Some say interspecies breeding, though I don't buy into that malarkey. Some say therianthropes date back the very beginning, the Garden of Eden, where man and werebeast lived in harmony. But the Bible doesn't tell the whole story. Certain religious leaders over the years have edited it as they see fit. Entire books were taken out. Like the Book of Bob."

Weston looked around to see if anyone was smiling. All faces were serious.

"The Book of Bob?"

"The Book of Bob is a lost chapter of the Old Testament, dating back to the Hellenistic period. It tells the story of God's prophet, Bob, son of Jakeh, who is the first werewolf mentioned in the Bible."

"The first? There aren't any."

"They were edited out. Pay attention, son. You'll learn something. See, Bob was a werewolf, blessed by the Lord with the gift of lycanthropy to do His work by eating evildoers. But after eating his one thousandth sinner, Bob became prideful of his accomplishments, and that angered God."

"Why would that anger God?"

"This was the Old Testament. God got pissed off a lot. Didn't you ever read Job?"

"I'm just saying…"

Irena shushed him. Scott continued.

"So to put Bob in his place, God granted one of Bob's enemies---Christopher, son of Cringle---a red suit of impenetrable armor, and ordered him to smite all therianthropes. God also blessed domesticated beasts with the power to fly through the sky, to pull Christopher's warship of destruction throughout the world."

Weston again looked around the room. Andy was examining his fingernails. Ryan was staring off into space. But David looked like a child listening to his favorite bedtime story.

"Bob and Christopher fought, and Bob proved victorious. Upon triumphing, he begged God to forgive his pridefulness, and God agreed. But Christopher, God's chosen avenger, felt betrayed. So he turned to the other side, begging for assistance."

"The devil?"

"Lucifer himself, the Son of the Morning Star. Lucifer gave Christopher a fearsome weapon, shaped like the talons of an eagle, forged in the fires of hell. He called the weapon Satan's Claws. And Christopher recruited an army of helpers to rid the world of Bob and his kind, claiming he was bringing about salvation."

"Let me see if I got this right," Weston said. "Kris Kringle and his magic red suit are using Satan's Claws---which I'm guessing became Santa Claus over time---to kill therianthropes with the help of... the Salvation Army?"

Everyone nodded. Weston laughed in disbelief.

"So how did this whole toy thing get started?"

"Kringle has killed millions of therianthropes, leaving many children orphans. He began to feel some remorse, so after he slaughtered their parents he began to leave toys behind, to take away some of the sting."

"And this is for real?"

Scott reached up and pulled down his collar, exposing a terrible scar along is neck.

"Kringle gave this to me when I was seven years old, right after murdering my parents."

"I thought he gave orphans toys."

"He also gave me a train set."

Weston shook his head. "Look, I can accept this whole shapeshifting thing. And touching the wolfsbane, that was creepy. But you want me to believe that every volunteer on the street corners with a bell and a Santa suit is out to murder us? I just saw one of those guys this morning, and while he was kind of odd---"

Scott reached across the table, grabbing Weston by the shirt. His face was pure panic.

"You saw one! Where?"

"Back in Naperville."

"What did he say to you?"

"Something about naughty boys and being beheaded and burned on sacred ground. He was obviously out of his mind."

Irena clutched Weston's hand. "The only way we can die is old age or beheading."

"Think carefully, Weston." Scott actually looked frightened. So did everyone else. "Were you followed here?"

"I don't think so. I mean, maybe I saw him talking on a cell phone. And maybe there was someone in a Santa suit a few cars behind me on the expressway…"

A shrill whistle cut Weston off. It sounded like a teapot.

But it wasn't a teapot. It was an alarm.

"They've found us." David's voice was quavering. "They're here."

* * *

"Battle stations!" Irena cried, causing everyone to scurry off in different directions.

Scott hurried to the coffee table, pushed the machine aside, and pressed a red button on the wall. An iron gate slammed closed across the entry door, and three TV monitors rose up on pedestals from hidden panels in the floor.

"Jesus." Phyllis squinted at one of the screens. "There have to be forty of them."

Weston looked, watching as the cameras switch from one view to another around the church. Santa's helpers, dozens of Santa's helpers. Wielding bats and axes and swords. They had the place surrounded.

"We need to call the police." David's voice had gone up an octave.

Irena already had the phone in her hand. "Line's been cut."

"Cell phones?"

"We're in a basement. No signals."

Scott knelt before the trunk, removing the top section and revealing a cache of handguns underneath. He tossed one to Weston, along with an extra clip.

"Are guns safe to throw?"

"Safety is on. Ever used a 9mm before?"

"No."

"Thumb off the safety on the side. Then pull back the top part. That's the slide, loads the bullet into the chamber. Now all you have to do is pull the trigger. Those red suits they're wearing are Kevlar, so aim for the face."

Weston had more questions, but Scott was too busy distributing the guns.

"Place your shots carefully, people. We don't have a lot of ammo. Ryan! Can you fire a weapon?"

Ryan remained sitting, staring into space.

"Dammit, man! We need you!"

Ryan didn't move.

"Can't we escape?" Weston asked Irena.

Irena worked her slide, jacking in a round.

"That's the only door."

"But those are steel bars. They can't get through it."

"They'll get through." Phyllis pointed. "See?"

Weston checked out the monitor, saw a group of Santa's storming down the stairs with a battering ram. The first CLANG! made everyone in the room jump.

"The table! Move!"

Weston helped Andy and Scott push the cafeteria table in front of the door. Then the group, except for Ryan, huddled together in the back of the room, guns pointed forward.

"I hope we live through this," Weston told Irena, "because I'd really like to ask you out."

"I'd like that too."

"Living through this, or going out with me?"

"Both."

Another CLANG! accompanied by a CREAK! which shook the table.

"Wait until you see the whites of their beards, people."

CLANG!

CLANG!

The table lurched forward.

CLANG!

They were in.

The room erupted in gunfire. It was louder than anything Weston had heard in his life, and he'd seen Iron Maiden in concert when he was seventeen. The kick of the gun surprised him, throwing off his aim, but Weston kept his head, kept sighting the targets, kept pulling the trigger.

The first Santa only made it a step inside.

The next three only made it two steps.

Then it got bad. A dozen of Santa's helpers burst into the room, swinging their weapons, their HO HO HO! warcries cutting through the cacophony of gunfire.

Weston fired until his pistol was empty. He tried to tug the empty clip out of the bottom of the gun, but it didn't budge. He wasted valuable seconds looking for the button or switch to release it, and then a helper tackled him.

His eyes were crazed, and his breath smelled like cough syrup, and Weston knew that this was the Santa who threatened him on the street corner in Naperville.

"Naughty boy! Naughty boy!" he screamed, both hands clasped on a curved dagger poised above Weston's eye.

Weston blocked with his elbows, trying to keep the knife away, but the crazy old elf possessed some sort of supernatural strength, and the knife inched closer and closer no matter how hard he resisted. Weston saw his terrified expression reflected in the polished steel blade as the tip tickled his eyelashes.

"Hey! Santa! Got some cookies for you!"

Weston watched, amazed, as someone jammed a gun into the Santa's snarling mouth and pulled the trigger. Psycho Santa's hat lifted up off his head, did a pirouette in the air, and fell down onto his limp body.

Weston followed the hand that held the gun, saw Irena staring down at him. She helped him to his feet.

"Thanks."

She nodded, taking his pistol and showing him the button to release the empty clip.

"Where did you learn how to shoot?" he asked.

"I teach high school."

Weston slammed the spare clip home and pulled the slide, firing six times at a Santa's helper swinging, of all things, a Grim Reaper scythe. The neck shot did him in.

"Hold your fire! They're retreating!"

As quickly as it began, the attack stopped. The gun smoke cleared. Weston winced when he saw the piles of dead Santa's helpers strewn around the room. At least two dozen of them. A Norman Rockwell painting it was not.

"Everyone okay?" Scott asked.

Everyone said yes except for Ryan, who remained sitting in the same chair, and David, who had a nasty gash on his shoulder that Phyllis was bandaging with duct tape and paper towels.

"Well, we sure kicked some Santa ass." Andy walked next to one of the fallen helpers and nudged him with his foot. "Try climbing down a chimney now, shit head."

"It's not over."

Everyone turned to look at Ryan.

"Did you saw something, Ryan?" Irena asked.

Ryan pointed to the monitor.

They all stared at a wide angle shot of the parking lot and watched eight reindeer racing down from the sky and using the blacktop like a landing strip. Behind them, a massive sleigh. It skidded to a stop and a hulking figure, dressed in red, climbed out and stared up at the camera.

"It's Santa Claus," Ryan whispered. "He's come to town."

* * *

Weston watched, horrified, as Santa headed for the church entrance, his remaining helpers scurrying around him.

"My God," Phyllis gasped. "He's huge."

Weston couldn't really judge perspective, but it seemed like Santa stood at least a foot taller than any of the Salvation Army volunteers.

"Who has ammo left?" Scott yelled.

"I'm out."

"Me too."

"So am I."

Weston checked his clip. "I've got two bullets."

It got very quiet. Scott rubbed his neck.

"Okay. We'll have to make do. Everyone grab a weapon. Kris Kringle is a lot more powerful than his helpers. Maybe, if we all strike at once, we'll have a chance."

From the sound of Scott's voice, he didn't believe his own words.

Andy didn't buy it either. "David is wounded. Ryan is sitting there like a pud. You think three men and two woman can fend off Kringle and his Satan's Claws? He's going to cut us into pieces!"

"We don't have a choice."

"But I don't want to get sliced up!" Andy said. "I'm too pretty to die like that!"

"Calm down, son. You're not helping the situation."

Andy knelt next to one of the helpers and began undressing him.

"You guys fight. I'm going to put on a red suit and pretend to be dead."

Weston locked eyes with Irena, saw fear, wondered if she saw the same in him.

"There's a way."

It was Ryan again, still staring off into space.

"You actually going to get up off your ass and help?" Phyllis asked.

Ryan slowly reached into his pants pocket, pulling out five tiny vials of liquid.

"I've been saving these."

Andy grabbed one, unscrewed the top. "Is it cyanide? Tell me it's cyanide, because I'm so drinking it."

"It's a metamorphosis potion. It will allow you to change into your therianthrope forms, while still retaining your human intellect."

Scott took a vial, squinting at it.

"Where did you get these?"

"I've had them for a long time."

"How do you know they work?"

"I know."

"Guess it can't hurt to try." Irena grabbed the remaining vials. She handed one to Weston, and one to David. She also held one out for Phyllis.

"But I'm not a therianthrope," Phyllis said. "I'm just a furry."

"You're one of us," Irena told her.

Phyllis nodded, and took the vial.

"Are you taking one?" Scott asked Ryan.

Ryan shook his head.

Scott shrugged. "Okay. Here goes nothing."

He downed the liquid. Everyone watched.

At first, nothing happened. Then Scott twitched. The twitching became faster, and faster, until he looked like a blurry photograph. Scott made a small sound, like a sigh, dropped his gun, and fell to all fours.

He'd changed into a turtle. A giant turtle, with vaguely human features. His face, now green and scaled, looked similar to his human face. And his body retained a roughly humanoid shape; so much so that he was able to push off the ground and stand on two stubby legs.

"I'll be damned." Scott reached up and tapped the top of his shell. "And I can still think. Hell, I can even talk."

Irena had already drunk her vial, and her clothes ripped, exposing the spots underneath. While in final werecheetah form she retained her long blonde hair, and---Weston could appreciate this---her breasts. He could suddenly understand the appeal furries saw in anthropomorphic costumes.

"You look great," Weston told her.

Her whiskers twitched, and she licked her arm and rubbed it over her face.

An oink, from behind, and Andy the wereboar was standing next to the overturned table, chewing on the cardboard donut box.

"What?" he said. "There's still some frosting inside."

"This sucks."

Weston turned to David, who had become a greenish, roundish, ball of coral. Weston could make out his face underneath a row of tiny, undulating tentacles.

"I think you're adorable," Irena told him. "Like Humpty Dumpty."

"I don't have arms or legs! How am I supposed to fight Santa?"

"Try rolling on him," Andy said, his snout stuck in the garbage can.

"I guess it's my turn." Phyllis drank the potion.

Everyone waited.

Nothing happened.

"Well, shit," Phyllis said. "And I don't even have my hippo suit here. At least give me the damn gun."

Weston handed it to her, then looked at his vial.

"You'll be fine," Irena said.

She walked a circle around him, then nuzzled against his chest. Weston stroked her chin, and she purred.

"Better hurry," Scott was eyeing the monitor. "Here comes Santa Claus."

Weston closed his eyes and lifted the vial to his lips.

* * *

It was kind of like being born. Darkness. Warmth. Then turmoil, sensory overload, a thousand things happening at once. It didn't hurt, but it didn't tickle either. Weston coughed, but it came out harsh. A bark. He looked down at his arms and noted they were covered with long, gray fur. His pants stayed on, but his clawed feet burst through the tops of his shoes.

"Hello, sexy."

Weston stared at Irena and had an overpowering, irrational urge to bark at her. He managed to keep it in check.

"Remember," Scott said. "He's wearing armor. It's claw-proof. Go for his head and neck, or use blunt force."

They formed a semi-circle around the door, except for the immobile David and the still-seated Ryan. Then they waited. Weston heard a licking sound, traced it to Andy, who had his nose buried between his own legs.

"Andy," he growled. "Quit it."

"Are you kidding? I don't think I'm ever going to stop."

Then the crazed Santa's helpers burst into the room, screaming and swinging weapons. Weston recoiled at first, remembered what he was, and then lashed out with a claw. It caught the helper in the side of the head, snapping his neck like a candy cane.

Andy quit grooming—if you could call it that—long enough to gore a helper between his red shirt and pants, right in the belly. What came out looked a lot like a bowlful of jelly.

Phyllis fired twice, then picked up the scythe and started swinging it like a mad woman and swearing like a truck driver with a toothache.

Scott had two helpers backed up against the wall, using his enormous shell to squeeze the life out of them.

Even David had managed to get into the act, snaring a helper with his tiny, translucent tentacles. Judging from the screams, those tentacles had stingers on them.

Weston searched for Irena, and saw her hanging onto a helper's back, biting at his neck.

Two more Santa's helpers rushed in, and Weston lunged at them, surprised by his speed. He kept his arms spread out and caught each one under the chin. His canine muscles flexed, tightened, and their heads came off like Barbie dolls.

And then, there he was.

Kris Kringle was even bigger up close than he was on the TV monitors. So tall he had to duck down to fit through the doorway. When he entered the room and reared up, he must have been eight feet tall. And wide, with a chest like a whiskey barrel, arms like tree trunks. His long white beard was flecked with blood, and his tiny dark eyes twinkled with malevolent glee.

But the worst thing were his hands. They ended in horrible metal claws, each blade the length of a samurai sword. One of his helpers, the one Irena had bitten, staggered over to Kringle, clutching his bleeding neck. Kringle lashed out, severing the man into three large pieces, even with the Kevlar suit on.

It was so horrible, so outrageously demonic, that Weston had to laugh when he saw it. In spite of himself.

Scott waddled over to Kringle and pointed his stubby fingers at him.

"Your reign of evil ends today, Kringle."

Kringle laughed, a deep, resonating croak that sounded like thunder. Then his huge black boot shot out, kicking Scott in the chest, knocking him across the room and into the back wall. Scott crashed through it like a turtle-shaped meteor.

Andy said, "Holy shit," then tore ass through the hole in the wall after Scott.

Kringle took a step forward, and Weston had an urge to pee; an urge so strong he actually lifted a leg. There was no way they could defeat Santa Claus. He was a monster. He'd tear through them like tissue paper.

Kringle appraised Weston, eyeing him head to toe, and said, "Robert Weston Smith. Werewolf. You're on my list."

Then he looked at Irena, who'd come to Weston's side, clutching his paw.

"Irena Reed. Werecheetah. You're on my list too. Want to sit on Santa's lap, little girl?"

Irena hissed at him. Kringle's eyes fell upon David next.

"And what the hell are you? A were-onion?"

David released the dead helper. "I'm David Kessler. Werecoral."

"David Kessler. Yes. You're also on my list. Now who is this crazy bitch?"

Phyllis put her hands on her hips and stuck out her jaw. "Phyllis Lawanda Marisha Taleena Allenby. Am I on your stupid ass list too?"

"No."

"No? You sure 'bout that, fat man?"

Kringle smiled. "I checked it twice."

Phyllis's eyes went mean. "You saying I'm not one of them? I'm one of them. I'm one of them in my heart, you giant sack of—"

"Enough!"

Ryan stood up and walked over to Kringle.

"And who are you, little human?"

"I'm tired of running, Christopher. I've been running for too long."

Kringle's brow furrowed.

"That voice. I know that voice."

"I had some work done. Changed my human face. But I'm sure you'll recognize this one."

Ryan's body shook, and then he transformed into a werewolf. A giant werewolf, several feet taller than Weston.

Kringle took a step back, his face awash with fear.

"Bob."

* * *

Weston watched, awestruck, as this millennia-old battle played out before him.

Kringle snarled, raising up his awful Satan Claws.

Bob bared his teeth and howled, a gut-churning cry that reverberated to the core of Weston's very soul.

But before either of them attacked, before either of them even moved, Kris Kringle's head rolled off his shoulders and onto the floor by Bob's feet.

Phyllis Lawanda Marisha Taleena Allenby, scythe in hand, brought the blade down and speared the tip into Kringle's decapitated head, holding it up so it faced her.

"Am I on your list now, mutha fucker?"

Bob peered down at Phyllis, his lupine jaw hanging open.

"You just killed Kris Kringle."

"Damn easy too. Why the hell didn't you do that five thousand years ago?"

Scott, a round green hand pressed to his wrinkled old head, stumbled back into the room.

"What happened?"

"Phyllis killed Kris Kringle," Irena said.

"You go, girl." Scott gave Phyllis a high-five.

"You all fought bravely." Bob stood tall, addressing the group. "Except for the pig. For your courage, you'll now have full control over your therianthrope powers. You can change at will, and shall retain control of your inner creatures."

"So how do we turn back?" Irena asked.

"Concentrate."

Scott went first, morphing back into his human form.

Weston and Irena changed while holding hands.

David's face scrunched up, but nothing happened.

"It's not working," he said. "I'm still coral."

"How about me?" Phyllis asked. "I'm the one that killed that jolly old bastard."

"I can turn you into a werewolf, if you so desire."

"These guys offered me that before. But I don't want to be no wolf, or no cheetah, or no turtle, or no dumb ass coral. No offense, David."

"None taken. I'm concentrating, but nothing's happening."

Phyllis folded her arms. "My inner animal is a hippopotamus. That's what I want to be."

Bob's shoulders slumped. "I'm sorry, Phyllis. That's the extent of my power. But... maybe... just maybe..."

"Maybe what?"

"I don't know if this will work, because he's dead."

"Just spill the beans, Lon Chaney."

"Try sitting on Santa's lap."

Phyllis raised a drawn-on eyebrow. "You serious?"

"He might still have some magic left. Try it."

Phyllis walked over to the fallen Kringle and sat on one of his massive thighs.

"Now what?"

"Make a Christmas wish, Phyllis. Make your most heartfelt Christmas wish ever."

She closed her eyes, and her lips whispered something Weston couldn't hear.

And then Weston felt something. Kind of like a breeze. A breeze made of Christmas magic. It swirled around the room, touching each of them, and them coming to rest on Phyllis.

But nothing happened. She didn't morph into a hippo. She didn't morph into anything. A minute passed, and she was still the same old Phyllis.

"I'm sorry, Phyllis." Bob helped her up. "I wish there was something else I could do."

A sad silence blanketed the room.

Then badboy rapper LL Cool J strutted into the basement, sans shirt. He took Phyllis's hand, gave her a deeply passionate kiss, and cupped her butt.

"Gonna take you back to the crib and make love to you all night, girl. But first we gonna stop by the bank, get your hundred million dollars."

LL picked her up and carried her out.

"See you guys next week," Phyllis called after them.

"Someone push me over to Santa's lap," David said. "This coral wants a house in Hawaii."

"What about all of these corpses?" Scott made a sweeping gesture with his hands. "The police are gonna have a field day."

"I'll take care of it." Bob rubbed his stomach. "I didn't have any of the donuts."

"Little help here." David wiggled in place.

Weston felt a tug on his hand. He stared into Irena's eyes.

"Want to, maybe, grab some coffee?" he asked.

"No."

Weston died a little inside. Irena's nose twitched, showing him a brief glimpse of her inner cheetah.

"Instead of coffee, I want you to come to my place. I've got a leash and a king sized bed."

God bless us, everyone, Weston thought as they walked hand-in-hand out the door.

Dear Diary

Here's another old story that I eventually rewrote to flesh it out a bit. It's an epistolary peace, entirely done as journal entries written by a teen girl. I revisited the epistolary form for a section in an upcoming Jack Kilborn book.

Sept 15

Dear Diary,

First day of school! I hope this doesn't turn into a repeat of last year, when Sue Ellen Derbin and Margaret "Superbitch" Dupont decided to try and kick me off of Pom-Pons. When I think about all those things they said about me it makes me soooo mad! Who cares if my parents never had a lot of money or anything, and so what if I don't have any stupid designer clothes, I'm still a better person than them. They were so jealous of my blonde hair and blue eyes and my heritage. I hated those phonies soooo much!!! It's so nice they don't bother me anymore.

My schedule is English, Algebra, Biology, Lunch, Gym, History, Art, and Music. It's nice to finally be an eighth grader and get the classes I want. But I still don't want to be here, and if I ever have kids I'll let them decide if they want to go school or not. I don't care if it's a law, the law stinks and so does school!!!

But it's not all bad. Robert Collins is in my math class and he's sooooo cute! He's got the best butt I've ever seen on a thirteen-year-old, and when he smiles with those dimples I sincerely want to die! We got to choose our own seats and I sat next to him. Tomorrow I'll wear more perfume and see if he notices.

Sept 16

Dear Diary,

Pom-Pon tryouts were today, and I'm Captain of the first squad! With Sue Ellen and Margret Superbitch gone, it was waaaaay too easy. Debbie Baker made squad two leader, and I could tell she was pissed that I beat her out. Tough titties, Deb!!!

But even better than that, Robert commented that he liked my perfume today! I wore a little extra, and while we were doing our problems he wrote me a note that said "Is that you who smells so good?" I almost died, right there in class.

I know I'm going to save that note forever.

Then I did something that was totally unlike me. I asked him if he was still going out with Pam Escher. He said no, Pam was now dating Stu Dorman. It seems Stu dumped Melissa for Pam and Pam dumped poor Robert. I feel bad for him, but not for me. Wouldn't it be great if he asked me out?

Sept 17

Dear Diary,

HE ASKED ME OUT!!!!!!!!!!!!!!

I couldn't believe it. We were done checking our homework and he leaned over so his lips were almost touching my ear and asked if I wanted to go out after school! So I skipped Pom-Pon practice and we walked over to Barro's Pizza and shared a small pepperoni. I didn't actually eat any, because of my special diet, but he didn't notice. We talked a lot about school and about how everyone is too concerned about appearance rather than being real and he told me about his family that came from New York and I told him that my family actually came from Scandinavian. He was super intelligent and serious. I never would have guessed he was so smart because he's so cute. I wonder if he'll be THE ONE. He's so cute it would be great if he was.

Sept 18

Dear Diary,

I got in BIG trouble for skipping Pom-Pon practice. Debbie Baker kept sucking up to Mrs. Meaker, saying how I shouldn't be squad captain if I didn't show up. The little bitch. Mrs. Meaker didn't say much, other than I had to make sure I didn't miss it again.

Robert and I passed notes back and forth during math. Nothing lovey-dovey, just talk because math is sooooo boring. I wish he had the same lunch period as I did. He said he would ask me out again after school but he has football practice. I told him I had Pom-Pons, and maybe we could meet after. He said great. But my practice ran late (practicing Debbie's stupid new drills) so when I got to Barro's he wasn't there. I hope he isn't mad.

Sept 19

Dear Diary,

Robert looked hurt in Math today, but I wrote him a note in English to explain everything and when he read it he forgave me. He asked me out again after school, and I agreed, even though I would miss another practice. Practicing five times a week is too much, if you ask me. We met at Barro's and got another pepperoni (which I didn't eat), and we talked for two hours. I told him all about runestones and Viking mythology and the Heimskringla and he really seemed interested. Then halfway during our talk he reached out and held my hand. I thought I would die!!!!! His hands are so strong and big.

Maybe he is THE ONE.

Sept 20

Dear Diary,

WEEKEND!!!!! I'm gonna spent it all in my basement, getting stronger and watching my diet. If you want to be the best, that's what you have to do.

Sept 22

Dear Diary,

That bitch Debbie got me kicked off as squad one leader!!!!!!!!! I just missed two stupid days! I cried in the bathroom for a half hour. I want to kill her! She talked to Mrs. Meaker and Mrs. Meaker said I wasn't meeting up to my responsibilities. I hate them both.

Robert waited for me after practice so I had a shoulder to cry on. He even kissed me, but it was only on the cheek. He's such a doll. He invited me over to his house for dinner, but I lied to him and said my parents already had plans. I couldn't tell him about the basement. But maybe I will soon.

Sept 23

Dear Diary,

Debbie didn't come to school today. I wonder why? (Ha!) I asked Mrs. Meaker if I could have my squad leader position back, and she said maybe. She'll say yes when Debbie misses another practice.

Robert kissed me on the mouth today, for the first time! It was weird and exciting! He even used his tongue!!!!! He's soooo sophisticated. It was right after practice. He waited for me, and wanted to walk me home. I lied and said my parents didn't allow visitors. He believed me, and then he leaned over and kissed me. I thought my knees turned to Jell-O. I now know that he is THE ONE.

Sept 24

Dear Diary,

I've been thinking about it a lot and I've decided to show Robert the basement. I invited him over after practice and lied and said my parents weren't home. I said I'd make dinner. He was impressed that I could cook. I didn't tell him that I couldn't.

By the time we got to my place it was already getting dark, and Robert said he should call home and check in. But I told him to look at my basement first, because I had a big surprise.

When I turned on the basement light, the hissing started. Robert asked if it was the furnace, and I giggled. Then I pulled the cover off the cages.

Debbie Baker was tied up in the first one, naked, lying in a smelly puddle of her own piss. She twisted and banged her head on the cage door and looked so funny I had to laugh. Robert just stared.

Then I pulled the tarp off the other cage. Margret "Superbitch" Dupont hissed. Sue Ellen Derbin was crying, like always. Sue Ellen had no arms or legs, and was lying naked on the hay I put down for her, which she messed again. Gross! I had to stop feeding her so much dog food.

Superbitch Margret had one stump of an arm left, severed at the elbow. Both had those awful brown scars where I had to burn them to seal the wound after I cut off a limb. I couldn't let them bleed to death. That wouldn't be right.

Robert got really freaked out, and I explained to him they were hissing because I cut out their vocal cords. That way they couldn't attract attention. He turned around and tried to go up the stairs but I had locked the basement door. I told him I thought he was staying for dinner. That's how you get strong. By eating your enemies. One piece at a time. That's what my Viking ancestors did. But the people have to be alive when you eat them, or else you don't ingest their souls. Their souls are what really made you strong. They made me strong. That's why I was Pom-Pon captain. And that's why I was going out with the cutest boy in school.

As I explained this to Robert, he started to yell for help. I tried to tell him not to be scared, because he was THE ONE. THE ONE to share this secret with me. Together we could live forever. It was okay. You didn't have to eat them all at once. You just do it a little bit at a time. I told him I had already eaten my parents. It took two years before I finished the last of Dad.

But Robert just kept on screaming, and I finally had to hit him over the head to shut him up. I guess he wasn't THE ONE after all.

I stripped off his clothes and tied him up and used the long scissors to snip his vocal chords. Then I looked over his trim body and decided what I wanted to eat first. I plugged in the electric saw and built a fire in the pit to heat the cauterizing iron.

I didn't want Robert to bleed to death. That wouldn't be right. I couldn't ingest his strength then. And he looks strong enough to be able to feed me for a looooooooooong time.

Mr. Spaceman

A humorous horror story that harkens back to the alien invasion movies of the 1950s. I wondered what would happen if an alien landed in modern day California.

"I have traveled many billions of light years to mate with an earth woman."

Debbi eyed the john and licked her cherry red lips. *Freak,* she thought. But all the freaks were out tonight. Halloween in LA was crazier than Mardi Gras.

He was dressed up like some kind of gooey alien, and she had to admit his make-up was pretty good. His mask had scales on it, like a fish, and his mouth had little dangly things that moved when he spoke. The spacesuit, made of some kind of metallic silvery fabric, was Hollywood-quality—not surprising, considering they were on the Sunset Strip. It was probably an old movie prop.

The only fake thing about the costume was the eyes; big yellow orbs that were attached to his head on stalks. They looked like tennis balls.

The freak leaned closer to Debbi. "Will you mate with me?"

Any other night, she would have told him to take a hike. Weirdos were best avoided. But rent was due tomorrow, and business had been slow. Besides, her horoscope said today was a day for taking chances, and Debbi always put her faith in the stars. She launched into her pitch.

"Straight is twenty-five, half and half is fifty. And for seventy-five I'll take you around the world, sugar."

"I have already been in orbit around your world eight hundred and forty-two times."

"Couldn't find a parking space, huh?" Debbi smacked her gum. "How much money you got, Mr. Spaceman?"

Mr. Spaceman stuck one of his lobster claws into his tunic and pulled out a roll of cash that would choke a horse.

"Don't flash money like that around here!" Debbi looked up and down the street, scanning for predators. "This isn't a nice neighborhood."

"I thought this was the city of angels."

"The angels carry knives and guns."

She took the john by the claw and led him down the block to the flop house. The desk clerk, a fat, greasy guy named Larry, raised an eyebrow.

"Does Mars need women?"

"Screw you, Larry. Gimme 214 for the rest of the night."

Larry handed her the key and winked.

The room was dark, dingy, the bed still rumpled from the previous rental. Debbi took off her halter top and hot pants, nudifying herself.

"See anything you like, ET?"

The john nodded several times. "I am aroused at the sight of your mammalian infant feeding vessels."

"You should be. They cost six grand."

She sidled up to him, her hand seeking the front of his shiny outfit.

The things I do for a buck...

"So, can Mr. Spock come out and play?"

"Who is this Mr. Spock? My name is Gnerlok. I am from the planet

Norbulon in the second quadrant of the Xaldorgia Galaxy."

"A tourist, huh? I had a feeling. Isn't Norbulon somewhere east?"

To a Los Angeleno, everyplace was east.

Gnerlok narrowed his bulbous eyes. "Yes. It is east. Near the state called Florida."

"I can spot an out-of-towner a mile away. How about slipping out of those tin foil pants?"

With the deft move of a pro, Debbi southicated Gnerlok's zipper. His outfit fell with a clanging sound.

"Oh my." Debbi bit her lower lip to keep from laughing, Fire Engine Red #03 rubbing off on her teeth. "I've never seen one that small before."

Gnerlok frowned.

"I assure you, that this is an average size for a male from Norbulon. I'm actually a bit larger than most."

"Go ahead and think that, sugar. You want to take a shower, get all that make-up off?"

"I am fine."

You're about as far from fine as you can get, Debbi thought.

"Okay, Mr. Spaceman. What would you like to do first?"

"Please give my full access to your urteran cavity."

Debbi laid back on the bed. "Like this?"

"That is perfect."

Gnerlok climbed on, then immediately climbed off.

Debbi frowned at him. "What's the matter, sugar?"

"Nothing is the matter. The coupling was most enjoyable."

"You're done?"

"Yes I am. Was our mating pleasurable for you?"

Debbi sighed. She sat up, giving him a pat on the claw. "You're a machine, honey. I'll never have better."

Gnerlok pulled up his pants and dug out his wad O'bills.

"Here is three hundred earth dollars. Thank you for procreating with me."

Debbi reached for the cash. "Anytime, sug—"

Her words were cut off by a rumbling sound. It came from her abdomen, loud enough for them both to hear.

"Excuse me. I had a couple chili dogs for dinner, and it sounds like those dogs are barking."

"That is not the sound of your digestive system."

The sound repeated, louder this time. Debbi looked down, unable to comprehend what she saw.

Her belly was expanding.

"What the hell is going on?"

"We have successfully mated. My brood incubates inside of you."

Her stomach was now the size of a basket ball, and the growth showed no signs of stopping.

Even worse, Debbi felt something deep within.

Something moving.

"You freak!" Debbie screamed. "Take off that stupid mask and tell me what you've done to me!"

She bolted to her feet and reached for Gnerlok's face, her fist closing around one of his eye stalks.

"Please do not tug at my face, earth-woman."

Debbi recoiled. It wasn't a mask.

"My God! What part of Florida are you from?"

"I am not from Florida. I have used deception to gain admission to your birthing portal. Now my progeny shall be born, and we shall enslave the world and—"

"I'm not ready to be a mother!" Debbi cried. "I haven't finished Junior College yet!"

"Nor shall you ever, earth-woman. My species shall destroy—"

Debbi slapped Gnerlok across the face.

"Our agreement was for sex, not motherhood! You owe me a lot more money!"

Gnerlok held his cheek, his bulbous eyes widening.

"But money will not be necessary when we take over—"

There was a popping sound, and a flood of green cascaded down Debbi's legs.

She stared, horrified, as her uterus contracted and a tiny yellow crustacean, the size of a golf ball, shot out of her and plopped onto the floor.

"Waaa," it cried.

Debbi's eyes got moist. She swallowed back the lump forming in her throat. "My baby."

She bent down to pick it up, and the motion caused more creatures to shoot rapid-fire from her womanhood.

"Don't just stand there like an idiot!" she hissed at Gnerlok. "Pick my children up!"

Gnerlok didn't move until Debbi slapped him again. Then he moved as fast as he could.

It was hard to keep up. Debbie's body spit them out like watermelon seeds.

For five minutes, the room was a combat zone. Multi-colored alien crayfish flew through the air—*BING! BING! BING!*—Gnerlok scurrying after them, mindful where he stepped.

Debbi finally expelled the last child and let out a huge sigh of relief. She felt like an empty corn popper.

"How many is that?" she asked.

Gnerlok placed the final three on the bed and tugged at his dangly mouth thingies.

"One hundred and seventeen."

"Did you get the one that flew behind the TV?"

"Yes I did."

"Check to make sure."

"I am sure."

Debbi clenched her teeth. "Are you sassing back?"

Gnerlok checked behind the TV again.

"None of my progeny reside behind the TV," he said.

"*Your* progeny? Don't you mean *our* progeny? I'm the one that did all the work."

Debbi approached the bed and picked up one of the kids. *Her* kids. It looked like a crawfish, complete with lobster claws and a tail. But its tiny face was almost human.

"They're kind of cute. What do they eat?"

"They are supposed to feast on your rotting corpse until they are large enough to dominate—"

Debbi grabbed Gnerlok by the eye stalk once again, squeezing out a stream of tears.

"Let's get one thing straight, Mr. Spaceman. All this talk of taking over the world, it ends right now. Got it?"

"But I've traveled for billions—"

Debbie yanked. Gnerlok screamed.

"Enough! You're a father now. You have responsibilities. I hope you have a damn good job, because diapers alone are going to cost a fortune."

"My job is to dominate—" Gnerlok cast his free eye, fearfully, at Debbi. "I mean—I currently have no means of employment."

"But you're rich, right? Where did you get that big roll of money?"

Gnerlok mumbled something.

"Speak up, Mr. Spaceman, or I'll tie these eye things into a big bow on your ugly head."

"A scratch-and-win lottery ticket."

Debbi scowled. "So that's how it is. You come up to me all slick, flashing your cash like you're a real player. Then you knock me up, and you don't even have a job. Do you at least have a place to live?"

"I arrived on this planet only two earth hours ago, and have not had a chance to establish a permanent residence."

Debbi sighed. *Ugly, hung like a Chihuahua,* and *a homeless deadbeat.*

"How about a car? No! Wait! A space ship! You've got a space ship, right?"

Gnerlok glanced, one-eyed, at the floor.

"When I landed, a group of three disaffected youths assaulted me and absconded with my interstellar vessel."

Welcome to LA.

Debbi needed to think, and she mentioned as much.

"While you are thinking, could you please release my—"

"I got it! My brother-in-law works for a furniture place. I bet he can get you a job in upholstery. But first, we have to go to City Hall and get married."

"Married? But I am not ready for marriage. I still require a few more years to play the field."

"Should have thought of that before you started mating with earth women. This is your responsibility, Yoda. And you're not weaseling out of it."

Debbi released Gnerlok's eye and turned her attention to the kids on the bed. A feeling of pure joy welled up in her chest, a place she hadn't had much feeling since getting the implants.

"Hello, my darlings. I'm Mama."

"Mama!" several of them cried.

"Yes. Mama. And this is your homeless deadbeat father. He's going to do good by you, or else your Uncle Joey will break his knees. Say hello to your children, Hubbie."

"Hello, children." Gnerlok frowned and gave them a half-hearted wave.

"Tracy! Jerry! Don't eat your brother! Daddy will get you some food." Debbi jabbed a finger at Gnerlok's chest. "There's a pizza place down the street. Get an extra large with anchovies. I bet they'll like anchovies."

"Anchovies," Gnerlok repeated.

"And I'm starving too. Get me a meatball sandwich. And move your alien butt, or I'm picking up the phone and calling the CIA. I'm sure they'd love to hear about your plans to dominate the world."

"Yes, earth-woman."

Gnerlok slunk out the door.

Debbi sat on the bed and tickled little Alphonse under the chin. He giggled.

So did Debbi.

She'd always put her faith in the stars. And for good reason, it turned out.

"You know what, kids?" Debbi's eyes became moist. "I think we can make this work. We can be a big, happy family."

And if it gets too weird, Debbi decided, *I can always make a big pot of gumbo and eat the little buggers.*

"Come to Mama, my delicious little babies. When your father gets home we're going house hunting. We're going to get a nice, big place in Beverly Hills."

With an extra large stove, Debbi decided.

Just in case.

Appalachian Lullaby

My friend John Weagley asked me if I had any radioactive monkey stories for his collection Requiem For A Radioactive Monkey. Naturally, I did.

At first, they were all kind of excited when JoJo got into the Uranium.

"He's gonna mutate, I bet," said Gramps. "Maybe grow another monkey head. Or teats."

"Could easily quadruple in size," said Pops. "Go on a rampage, killin' folks and rapin' women."

Uncle Clem disagreed. "I'm bettin' invisibility. A seeable monkey causes enough trouble, running around, bitin' and chitterin', throwin' feces. An invisible money would be a hunnerd times worse."

"Would the feces be invisible?" Aunt Lula asked.

"Likely so. Wouldn't know it was there 'till you sat in it."

Gramps packed his lower lip with a wad of Skoal and spat brown juice into Aunt Lula's coffee mug.

"Shoulda kept that uranium locked up. Leavin' it on the counter like that, monkey was gonna mess with it sooner or later."

Uncle Clem disagreed. "JoJo ain't never fooled with it before."

"Them glowin' isotopes, they're like a magnet to the lower primates.

Shoulda kept it locked up."

Pops scratched his head. "Where'd we get the uranium anyway?"

They all sat around and had a think about that. No one said nothin' for a while, the only sound being the slurp-slurp of Aunt Lula and her coffee.

"Well," Gramps finally said, "whatever strange mutation happens to JoJo, I'm guessin' we all agree it'll be speck-tack-ler."

Somethin' did happen to JoJo, and it happened fast. An hour after messin' with the Uranium, JoJo's hair all fell out, and then he died.

"Didn't see that comin'," Uncle Clem said.

Pops scratched his head. "Where'd we get a monkey anyway?"

No one could answer that. Only one who could have was JoJo, and he didn't say much on account of his deceasedness. Plus, JoJo was a monkey, and monkeys don't talk.

The next day, Gramps lost all of his hair, even the hair growin' from his ears, and got sick something fierce.

"Gramps?" Pops asked him, side-steppin' the chunk-streams gushing from Gramps's dip-hole. "You been messin' with that Uranium?"

Gramps answered between expulsions. "Wanted...another...head."

Later that night, after Gramps hemorrhaged, they buried him in the garden, next to JoJo. The family grieved and grieved, and Aunt Lula made some Uranium cookies to cheer everyone up, but Uncle Clem hoarded them all for himself.

"Thad a dab thine thookie," Uncle Clem said, not speakin' clearly because most of his teeth had worked themselves free of his bleedin' gums.

When Uncle Clem coughed up his pancreas, they buried him in the garden, next to Gramps and JoJo.

Not long after, Aunt Lula's hands turned black and plum fell off, on account she didn't wear no lead gloves when she made the uranium cookies. "Because lead is poisonous," she had said, smartly.

When Aunt Lula died, Pops buried her in another part of the garden, not too close to Uncle Clem and Gramps and JoJo, because that part was all took up.

When he was done, Pops scratched his head. "Where'd we get a garden anyway?"

Convinced the Curse of the Radioactive Uranium would claim him next, which would have been a very bad thing because there was nobody left to bury him in the garden, Pops played it smart.

He buried himself in the garden with the uranium.

When the milkman came by later that week, with the milk and eight ounces of farmer's cheese, he noticed the five new mounds in the garden. Being a curious milkman, he dug them all up.

"Well, will you lookit that," said the mailman. "Where'd they get that uranium?"

He found some tin foil in the kitchen, and wrapped up the Uranium and took it home, for his pet monkey to play with.

Treatment

Written years ago, this eventually sold to Blood Lite 2 edited by Kevin J. Williamson. It's a fun piece where things aren't what they appear to be.

"It all goes back to the time I was bitten by that werewolf."

Dr. Booster's pencil paused for a moment on his notepad, having only written a 'w.'

"A werewolf?"

Tyler nodded. Booster appraised the teenager; pimples, lanky, hair a bit too long for the current style. The product of a well-to-do suburban couple.

"This is the reason your grades have gone down?"

"Yeah. Instead of studying at night, I roam the neighborhood, eating squirrels."

"I see...and how do squirrels taste, Tyler?"

"They go down dry."

Booster wrote 'active imagination' on his pad.

"What makes you say you were bitten by a werewolf?"

"Because I was."

"When did this happen?"

Tyler scratched at the pubescent hairs on his chin. "Two weeks ago. I was out at night, burying this body..."

"Burying a body?"

The boy nodded.

"Tyler, for therapy to work, we have to be honest with each other."

"I'm being honest, Dr. Booster."

Booster made his mouth into a tight line and wrote 'uncooperative' on his pad.

"Fine, Tyler. Whose body were you burying?"

"It was Crazy Harold. He was a wino that hung out in the alley behind the liquor store on Kedzie."

"And why were you burying him?"

Tyler furrowed his brow. "I had to get rid of it. I didn't think digging a grave would be necessary. I thought they disintegrated after getting a stake in the heart."

Booster frowned. "Crazy Harold was a vampire?"

Tyler shifted on the couch to look at him. "You knew? Shouldn't they turn into dust when you kill them?"

Booster glanced the diplomas on his wall. Eight years of education, for this.

"So you're saying you hammered a stake into Crazy Harold—"

"It was actually a broken broom handle."

"—and then buried him."

"In the field behind the house. And just when I finished, that's when the werewolf got me." Tyler lifted up his right leg and hiked up his pants. Above the sock was a raised pink scar, squiggly like an earthworm.

"That's the bite mark?"

Tyler nodded.

"It looks old, Tyler."

"It healed fast."

"Your mother told me you got that scar when you were nine-years-old. You fell off your bike."

Tyler blinked, then rolled his pants leg back down.

"Mom's full of shit."

Booster wrote 'animosity towards mother' in his pad.

"Why do you say that, Tyler? Your mother is the one who recommended therapy, isn't she? It seems as if she wants to help."

"She's not my real mother. Her and Dad were replaced by aliens."

"Aliens?"

"They killed my parents, replaced them with duplicates. They look and sound the same, but they're actually from another planet. I caught them, once, in their bedroom."

Booster raised an eyebrow. "Making love?"

"Contacting the mother ship. They're planning a full scale invasion of earth. But I thought you wanted to know about the werewolf."

Booster pursed his lips. WWSFD? He appealed to the picture of Sigmund hanging above the fireplace. The picture offered no answers.

"Tyler, with your consent, I'd like to try some hypnotherapy. Have you ever been hypnotized?"

"No."

Booster dimmed the lights and sat alongside the couch. He held his pencil in front of Tyler's face at eye level.

"Take a deep breath, then let it out. Focus on the pencil..."

It took a few minutes to bring Tyler to a state of susceptible relaxation.

"Can you hear me, Tyler?"

"Yes."

The boy's jaw was slack, and a thin line of drool escaped the corner of his mouth. Booster was surprised at the child's halitosis—perhaps he had been eating squirrels after all.

"I'd like you to remember back a few weeks, when you told me about burying Crazy Harold."

"Okay."

"Tell me what you see."

"It's cold. There are a lot of rocks in the dirt, and the shovel won't go in very far."

Booster used his pen light to check Tyler's pupils. Slow response. The child was under.

"What were you digging?"

"Grave. For the vampire."

Booster frowned. He'd studied cases of patients lying under hypnosis, but had never had one on his couch.

"What about the werewolf?"

"Came out of the field. It was big, had red eyes, walked on two legs."

"And it bit you?"

"Yeah. I thought it was going to kill me, but Runs Like Stallion saved me."

"Runs Like Stallion?"

"He's a ghost of a Sioux brave. The field is an old Indian burial ground."

Booster decided he'd had enough. He wrote 'treatment' in his notebook and went over to his desk, unlocking the top drawer. The plastic case practically leapt up at him. He took it over to Tyler.

"Tyler, your parents are tired of these stories."

"My parents are dead."

"No, Tyler. They aren't dead. They care about you. That's why they brought you to me."

Booster opened the case. The gnerlock blinked its three eyes and crawled into Booster's hand. It would enter Tyler's mouth and burrow up into his brain, taking over his body.

"Soon, it will all be better. You'll have no more worries. You're going to be a host, Tyler, for the new dominant species on this planet. Are you scared?"

"No."

"Open your mouth, Tyler."

Tyler stretched his mouth wide.

Wider than humanly possible, crammed with sharp teeth.

The gnerlock nesting in Dr. Booster's brain crawled out through his neck after the wolf decapitated the host body.

Its eleven legs beelined for the door, antennae waving hysterically, telepathically cursing that quack Freud.

Halfway there, a green ghostly foot came down on its oblong head, smashing it into the carpeting.

The Indian gave the wolf a thumbs up, but Tyler was already leaping out the window, eyes locked on a juicy squirrel in the grass below.

A Sound of Blunder

It's no secret I'm a huge F. Paul Wilson fan. When we were both invited into the Blood Lite anthology, I asked him if he would like to collaborate on a funny horror short. He graciously agreed, and we produced this slapstick bit of schtick. It was a lot of fun to write.

"We're dead! We're freakin' dead!"

Mick Brady, known by the criminal underground of Arkham, Pennsylvania as "Mick the Mick," held a shaking fist in front of Willie Corrigan's face. Willie recoiled like a dog accustomed to being kicked.

"I'm sorry, Mick!"

Mick the Mick raised his arm and realized that smacking Willie wasn't going to help their situation. He smacked him anyway, a punch to the gut that made the larger man double over and grunt like a pig.

"Jesus, Mick! You hit me in my hernia! You know I got a bulge there!"

Mick the Mick grabbed a shock of Willie's greasy brown hair and jerked back his head so they were staring eye-to-eye.

"What do you think Nate the Nose is going to do to us when he finds out we lost his shit? We're both going to be eating *San Francisco Hot Dogs,* Willie."

Willie's eyes got wide. Apparently the idea of having his dick cut off, boiled, and fed to him on a bun with a side of fries was several times worse than a whack to the hernia.

"We'll…we'll tell him the truth. Maybe he'll understand."

"You want to tell the biggest mobster in the state that your Nana used a key of uncut Columbian to make a pound cake?"

"It was an accident," Willie whined. "She thought it was flour. Hey, is that a spider on the wall? Spiders give me the creeps, Mick. Why do they need eight legs? Other bugs only got six."

Mick the Mick realized that hitting Willie again wouldn't help anything. He hit him anyway, a slap across his face that echoed off the concrete floor and walls of Willie's basement.

"Jesus, Mick! You hit me in my bad tooth! You know I got a cavity there!"

Mick the Mick was considering where he would belt his friend next, even though it wasn't doing either of them any good, when he heard the basement door open.

"You boys playing nice down there?"

"Yes, Nana," Willie called up the stairs. He nudged Mick the Mick and whispered, "Tell Nana yes."

Mick the Mick rolled his eyes, but managed to say, "Yes, Nana."

"Would you like some pound cake? It didn't turn out very well for some reason, but Bruno seems to like it."

Bruno was Willie's dog, an elderly beagle. He tore down the basement stairs, ran eighteen quick laps around Mick the Mick and Willie, and then barreled, full-speed, face-first into the wall, knocking himself out. Mick the Mick watched as the dog's tiny chest rose and fell with the speed of a weed wacker.

"No thanks, Nana," Mick the Mick said.

"It's on the counter, if you want any. Good night, boys."

"Night, Nana," they answered in unison.

Mick the Mick wondered how the hell they could get out of this mess. Maybe there was some way to separate the coke from the cake, using chemicals and stuff. But they wouldn't be able to do it themselves. That meant telling Nate the Nose, which meant San Francisco Hot Dogs. In his twenty-four years since birth, Mick the Mick had grown very attached to his penis. He'd miss it something awful.

"We could sell the cake," Willie said.

"You think someone is going to pay sixty thousand bucks for a pound cake?"

"It's just an idea."

"It's a stupid idea, Willie. No junkie is going to snort baked goods. Ain't gonna happen."

"So what should we do? I—hey, did you hear if the Phillies won? Phillies got more legs than a spider. And you know what? *They catch flies too!* That's a joke, Mick."

"Shaddup. I need to think."

Mick the Mick couldn't think of anything, so he punched Willie again, even though it didn't solve anything.

"Jesus, Mick! You hit my kidney! You know I got a stone there!"

Mick the Mick walked away, rubbing his temples, willing an idea to come.

"That one really hurt, Mick."

Mick the Mick shushed him.

"I mean it. I'm gonna be pissing red for a week."

"Quiet, Willie. Lemme think."

"It looks like cherry Kool-Aid. And it burns, Mick. Burns like fire."

Mick the Mick snapped his fingers. *Fire.*

"That's it, Willie. Fire. Your house is insured, right?"

"I guess so. Hey, do you think there's any pizza left? I like pepperoni. That's a fun word to say. *Pepperoni.* It rhymes with *lonely.* You think pepperoni gets lonely, Mick?"

To help Willie focus, Mick the Mick kicked him in his bum leg, even though it really didn't help him focus much.

"Jesus, Mick! You know I got gout!"

"Pay attention, Willie. We burn down the house, collect the insurance, and pay off Nate the Nose."

Willie rubbed his shin, wincing.

"But where's Nana supposed to live, Mick?"

"I hear the Miskatonic Nursing Home is a lot nicer, now that they arrested the guy who was making all the old people wear dog collars."

"I can't put Nana in a nursing home, Mick!"

"Would you rather be munching on your vein sausage? Nate the Nose makes you eat the whole thing, or else you also get served a side of meatballs."

Willie folded his arms. "I won't do it. And I won't let you do it."

Mick the Mick took aim and punched Willie in his bad knee, where he had the metal pins, even though it did nothing to fix their problem.

"Jesus, Mick! You hit me in the…"

"Woof!"

Bruno the beagle sprang to his feet, ran sixteen laps around the men, then tore up the stairs.

"Bruno!" they heard Nana chide. "Get off the counter! You've had enough pound cake!"

Mick the Mick put his face in his hands, very close to tears. The last time he cried was ten years ago, when Nate the Nose ordered him to break his mother's thumbs because she was late with a loan payment. When he tried, Mom had stabbed Mick the Mick with a meat thermometer. That hurt, but not as much as a wiener-ectomy would.

"Maybe we can leave town," Willie said, putting a hand on Mick the Mick's shoulder.

That left Willie's kidney exposed. Mick the Mick took advantage, even though it didn't help their situation.

Willie fell to his knees. Bruno the beagle tore down the stairs, straddled Willie's calf, and began to hump so fast his little doggie hips were a blur.

Mick the Mick began searching the basement for something flammable. As it often happened in life, arson was really the only way out. He found a can of paint thinner on a dusty metal shelf and worked the top with his thumbnail.

"Mick, no!"

Mick couldn't get it open. He tried his teeth.

"You can't burn my house down, Mick! All my stuff is here! Like my comics! We used to collect comics when we were kids, Mick! Don't you remember?"

Willie reached for a box, dug out a torn copy of Amazing Spiderman #146, and traced his finger up and down Scorpion's tail in a way that made Mick the Mick uncomfortable. So he reached out and slapped Willie's bad tooth. Willie dropped the comic and curled up fetal, and Bruno the beagle abandoned the calf for the loftier possibilities of Willie's head.

Mick managed to pop the top on the can, and he began to sprinkle mineral spirits on some bags labeled *Precious Photos & Memories.*

Willie moaned something unintelligible through closed lips—he was probably afraid to open his mouth until he disengaged Bruno the beagle.

"Mmphp-muummph-mooeoemmum!"

"We don't have a choice, Willie. The only way out of this is fire. Beautiful, cleansing fire. If there's money left over, we'll bribe the orderlies so Nana doesn't get abused. At least not as much as the others."

"Mick!" Willie cried. It came out "Mibb!" because Bruno the beagle had taken advantage. Willie gagged, shoving the dog away. Bruno the beagle ran around Willie seven times then flew up the stairs.

"Bruno!" they heard Nana chide. "Naughty dog! Not when we have company over!"

Willie hacked and spit, then sat up.

"A heist, Mick. We could do a heist."

"No way," Mick the Mick said. "Remember what happened to Jimmy the Spleen? Tried to knock over a WaMu in Pittsburgh. Cops shot his ass off. His whole ass. You want one of them creepy poop bags hanging on your belt?"

Willie wiped a sleeve across his tongue. "Not a bank, Mick. The Arkham Museum."

"The museum?"

"They got all kinds of expensive old stuff. And it ain't guarded at night. I bet we could break in there, get away with all sorts of pricey antiques. I think they got like a T-rex skull. That could be worth a million bucks. If I had a million bucks, I'd buy some scuba gear, so I could go deep diving on shipwrecks and try to find some treasure so I could be rich."

Mick the Mick rolled his eyes.

"You think Tommy the Fence is going to buy a T-rex skull? How we even gonna get it out of there, Willie? You gonna put it in your pocket?"

"They got other stuff too, Mick. Maybe gold and gems and stamps."

"I got a stamp for you."

"Jesus, Mick! My toe! You know I got that infected ingrown!"

Mick the Mick was ready to offer seconds, but he stopped mid-stomp.

"You ever been to the Museum, Willie?"

"Course not. You?"

"Nah."

But maybe it wasn't a totally suck-awful idea.

"What about the alarms?"

"We can get past those, Mick. No problem. Hey, you think I need a haircut? If I look up, I can see my bangs."

Willie did just that. Mick the Mick stared at the cardboard boxes, soaked with paint thinner. He wanted to light them up, watch them burn. But insurance took forever. There were investigations, forms to fill out, waiting periods.

But if they went to the museum and pinched something small and expensive, chances are they could turn it around in a day or two. The faster they could pay off Nate the Nose, the safer Little Mick and the Twins were.

"Okay, Willie. We'll give it a try. But if it don't work, we torch Nana's house. Agreed?"

"Agreed."

Mick the Mick extended his hand. Willie reached for it, leaving his hernia bulge unprotected. Now that they had a plan, it served absolutely no purpose to hit Willie again.

He hit him anyway.

* * *

"I don't like it in here, Mick." Willie said as they entered the great central hall of the Arkham Pennsylvania Museum of Natural History and Baseball Cards.

Mick the Mick gave him a look, which was pretty useless since Willie couldn't see his face and he couldn't see Willie's. The only things they could see were whatever lay at the end of their flashlight beams.

Getting in had been a walk. Literally. The front doors were unlocked. And no alarm. Really weird. Unless the museum had stopped locking up because nobody ever came here. Mick the Mick had lived in Arkham all his life and never met anyone who'd ever come here except on a class trip. Made a kind of sense then to not bother with locks. Nobody came during the day when the lights were on, so why would anyone want to come when the lights were out?

Which made Mick the Mick a little nervous about finding anything valuable.

"It's just a bunch of rooms filled with loads of old crap."

Willie's voice shook. "Old stuff scares me. Especially *this* old stuff."

"Why?"

"'Cause it's old and—hey, can we stop at Burger Pile on the way home?"

"Focus, Willie. You gotta focus."

"I like picking off the sesame seeds and making them fight wars."

Mick the Mick took a swing at him and missed in the dark.

Suddenly the lights went on. They were caught. Mick the Mick feared prison almost as much as he feared Nate the Nose. He was small for his size, and unfortunately blessed with perfectly-shaped buttocks. The cons would trade him around like cigarettes.

Mick the Mick ducked into a crouch, ready to run for the nearest exit. He saw Willie standing by a big arched doorway with his hand on a light switch.

"There," Willie said, grinning. "That's better."

Mick wanted to punch his hernia again but he was too far away.

"Put those out!"

Willie stepped away from the wall toward one of the displays. "Hey, look at this."

Mick the Mick realized the damage had been done. Sooner or later someone would come to investigate. Okay, maybe not, but they couldn't risk it. They'd have to move fast.

He looked up and saw a banner proclaiming the name of the exhibit: *Elder Gods and Lost Races of South Central Pennsylvania.*

"What's this?" Willie said, leaning over a display case.

Suddenly a deep voice boomed: *"WELCOME!"*

Willie cried, "Whoa!" and Mick the Mick jumped—high enough so as if he'd been holding a basketball he could have made his first dunk.

Soon as he recovered, he did a thorough three-sixty but saw no one else but Willie.

"What you see before you," the voice continued, *"is a rare artifact that once belonged to an ancient lost race that dwelled in the Arkham area during prehistoric times. This, like every other ancient artifact in this room, was excavated from a site near the Arkham landfill."*

After recovering from another near dunk, plus a tiny bit of pee-pee, Mick noticed a speaker attached to the underside of the case.

Ah-ha. A recording triggered by a motion detector. But the sound was a little garbled, reminding him of the voice of the aliens in an old black-and-white movie he and Willie had watched on TV last week. The voice always began, "People of Earth . . ." but he couldn't remember the name of the film.

"We know little about this ancient lost race but, after careful examination by the eminent archeologists and anthropologists here at the Arkham Pennsylvania Museum of Natural History and Baseball Cards, they arrived at an irrefutable conclusion."

"Hey, Willie said, grinning. "Sounds like the alien voice from *Earth versus the Flying Saucers.*"

"The ancient artifact before you once belonged to an ancient shaman."

"What's a shaman, Mick?"

Mick the Mick remembered seeing something about that on TV once. "I think he's a kind of a witch doctor. But forget about—"

"A shaman, for those of you who don't know, is something of a tribal wise man, what the less sophisticated among you might call a 'witch doctor.' "

"Witch doctor? Cooool."

Mick the Mick stepped over to see what the voice was talking about. Under the glass he saw a three-foot metal staff with a small globe at each end.

"The eminent archeologists and anthropologists here at the Arkham Pennsylvania Museum of Natural History and Baseball Cards have further determined that the object is none other an ancient shaman's scepter of

power."

Willie looked a Mick the Mick with wide eyes. "Did you hear that? A scepter of power! Is that like He-Man's Power Sword? He-Man was really strong, but he had hair like a girl. Is the scepter of power like a power sword, Mick?"

"No, it's more like a magic wand, but forget—"

"The less sophisticated among you might refer to a scepter of power as a 'magic wand,' and in a sense it functioned as such."

"A magic wand! Like in the Harry Potter movies? I love those movies, and I've always wanted a magic wand! Plus I get crazy hot thoughts about Hermoine. She's a real fox. Kinda like Drew Barrymore. In E.T. Hey, why does the wand have a deep groove in it?"

Mick the Mick looked again and noticed the deep groove running its length.

"Note, please, the deep groove running the length of the scepter of power. The eminent archeologists and anthropologists here at the Arkham Pennsylvania Museum of Natural History and Baseball Cards believe that to be what is knows as a fuller. . .

A fuller? Mick thought. Looks like a blood channel.

"...which the less sophisticated among you might call a 'blood channel.' The eminent archeologists and anthropologists here at the Arkham Pennsylvania Museum of Natural History and Baseball Cards believe this ancient scepter of power might have been used by its shaman owner to perform sacred religious ceremonies—specifically, the crushing of skulls and ritual disemboweling."

Mick the Mick got a chill. He hoped Nate the Nose never got his hands on something like this.

"What's disemboweling, Mick?"

"When someone cuts out your intestines."

"How do you dooky, then? Like squeezing a toothpaste tube?"

"You don't dooky, Willie. You die."

"Cool! Can I have the magic wand, Mick? Can I?"

Mick the Mick didn't answer. He'd noticed something engraved near the end of the far tip. He leaned closer, squinting until it came into focus.

Sears.

What the—?

He stepped back for a another look at the scepter of power and—

"A curtain rod . . . it's a freakin' curtain rod!"

Willie looked at him like he was crazy. "Curtain rod? Didn't you hear the man? It's, like, a magic wand, and—hey, what's that over there?"

Mick the Mick slapped at Willie's kidney as he passed but missed because he couldn't take his eyes off the Sears scepter of power. Maybe they could steal it, return it to Sears, and get a brand new one. That wouldn't help much with Nate the Nose, but Mick the Mick did need a new curtain rod. His old one had broken, and his drapes were attached to the wall with forks. That made Thursdays—spaghetti night—particularly messy.

"WELCOME!" boomed the same voice as Willie stopped before another display. *"What you see before you is a rare artifact that once belonged to an ancient lost race that dwelled in the Arkham area during prehistoric times. This, like every other ancient artifact in this room, was excavated from a site near the Arkham landfill."*

"Hey, Mick y'gotta see this."

After some biblical thinking, Mick the Mick spared the rod and moved along.

"We know little about this ancient lost race but, after careful examination by the eminent archeologists and anthropologists here at the Arkham Pennsylvania Museum of Natural History and Baseball Cards, they arrived at an irrefutable conclusion: The artifact before you was used by an ancient shaman of this lost race to perform surrogate sacrifices. (For those of you unfamiliar with the term 'shaman,' please return to the previous

display.)"

"I know what a shaman is, 'cause you just told me," Willie said. "But what's a surrogate—?"

"A surrogate sacrifice was an image that was sacrificed instead of a real person. Before you is a statuette of a woman carved by the ancient lost race from a yet-to-be-identified flesh-colored substance. Note the head is missing. This is because the statuette was beheaded instead of the human it represented."

Mick the Mick stepped up to the display and immediately recognized the naked pink figure. He'd used to swipe his sister Suzy's and make it straddle his rocket and go for a ride. Only Suzy's had a blonde head.

"That's a freakin' Barbie doll!" He grabbed Willie's shoulder and yanked him away.

"Jesus, Mick! You know I got a dislocating shoulder!"

Willie stumbled, knocking Mick the Mick into another display case, which toppled over with a crash.

"WELCOME! What you see before you is a rare tome of lost wisdom that once belonged—"

Screaming, Mick the Mick kicked the speaker until the voice stopped.

"Look, Mick," Willie said, squatting and poking through the broken glass, "it's not a tome, it's a book. It's supposed to contain lost wisdom. Maybe it can tell us how to keep Nate the Nose off our backs." He rose and squinted at the cover. *"The Really, Really, Really Old Ones."*

"It's a paperback, you moron. How much wisdom you gonna find in there?"

"Yeah, you're right. It says, 'Do Not Try This at Home. Use Only Under Expert Supervision or You'll Be Really, Really, Really Sorry.' Better not mess with *that.*"

"Oh, yeah?" Mick the Mick had had it—really had it. Up. To. Here. He opened to a random page and read. "'Random Dislocation Spell.'"

Willie winced. "Not my shoulder!"

" 'Use only under expert supervision.' Yeah, right. Look, it's got a bunch of gobbledygook to read."

"You mean like 'Mekka-lekka hi—?"

"Shaddap and I'll show you what bullshit this is."

Mick the Mick started reading, pronouncing the gobbledygook as best he could, going slow and easy so he didn't screw up the words like he normally did when he read.

When he finished he looked at Willie and grinned. "See? No random dislocation."

Willie rolled his shoulder. "Yeah. Feels pretty good. I wonder—"

* * *

The smell hit Mick the Mick first, hot and overpowering, reminding him of that time he stuck his head in the toilet because his older brother told him that's where brownies came from. It was followed by the very real sensation of being squeezed. But not squeezed by a person. Squeezed all over by some sort of full-body force like being pushed through a too-small opening. The air suddenly became squishy and solid and pressed into every crack and pore on Mick the Mick's body, and then it undulated, moving him, pushing him, through the solid marble floor of the Arkham Pennsylvania Museum of Natural History and Baseball Cards.

The very fabric of reality, or something like that, seemed to vibrate with a deep resonance, and the timbre rose to become an overpowering, guttural groan. The floor began to dissolve, or maybe he began to dissolve, and then came a horrible yet compelling farting sound and Mick the Mick was suddenly plopped into the middle of a jungle.

Willie landed next to him.

"I feel like shit," Willie said.

Mick the Mick squinted in the sunlight and looked around. They were surrounded by strange, tropical trees and weird looking flowers with big fat pink petals that made him feel sort of horny. A dragonfly the size of a bratwurst hovered over their heads, gave them a passing glance, then buzzed over to one of the pink flowers, which snapped open and bit the bug in half.

"Where are we, Mick?"

Mick the Mick scratched his head. "I'm not sure. But I think when I read that book I opened a portal in the space-time continuum and we were squeezed through one of the eleven imploded dimensions into the late Cretaceous Period."

"Wow. That sucks."

"No, Willie. It doesn't suck at all."

"Yeah it does. The season finale of *MacGyver: The Next Generation* is on tonight. It's a really cool episode where he builds a time machine out of some pocket lint and a broken meat thermometer. Wouldn't it be cool to have a time machine, Mick?"

Mick the Mick slapped Willie on the side of his head.

"Jesus, Mick! You know I got swimmer's ear!"

"Don't you get it, Willie? This book *is* a time machine. We can go back in time!"

Willie got wide-eyed. "I get it! We can get back to the present a few minutes early so I won't miss MacGyver!"

Mick the Mick considered hitting him again, but his hand was getting sore.

"Think bigger than MacGyver, Willie. We're going to be rich. Rich and famous and powerful. Once I figure out how this book works we'll be able to go to any point in history."

"You mean like we go back to summer camp in nineteen seventy-five? Then we could steal the candy from those counselors so they couldn't lure us into the woods and touch us in the bad place."

"Even better, Willie. We can bet on sports and always win. Like that movie."

"Which one?"

"The one where he went to the past and bet on sports so he could always win."

"*The Godfather?*"

"No, Willie. *The Godfather* was the one with the fat guy who slept with horse heads."

"Oh yeah. Hey Mick, don't you think those big pink flowers look like...

"Shut your stupid hole, Willie. I gotta think."

Mick the Mick racked his brain, but he was never into sports, and he couldn't think of a single team that won anything. Plus, he didn't have any money on him. It would take a long time to parlay the eighty-one cents in his pocket into sixty grand. But there *had* to be other ways to make money with a time machine. Probably.

He glanced at Willie, who was walking toward one of those pink flowers, leaning in to sniff it. Or perhaps do something else with it, because Willie's tongue was out.

"Willie! Get away from that thing and try to focus! We need to figure out how to make some money."

"It smells like fish, Mick."

"Dammit, Willie! Did you take your medicine this morning like you're supposed   to?"

"I can't remember. Nana says I need a stronger subscription. But every time I go to the doctor to get one I get distracted and forget to ask."

Mick the Mick scratched himself. Another dragonfly—this one shaped like a banana wearing a turtleneck—flew up to one of those pink flowers and was bitten in half too. Damn, those bugs were stupid. They just didn't learn.

Mick the Mick scratched himself again, wondering if the crabs were back. If they were, it made him really angry. When you paid fifty bucks for a massage at Madame Yoko's, the happy ending should be crab-free.

Willie said, "Maybe we can go back to the time when Nate the Nose was a little boy, and then we could be real nice to him so when he grew up he would remember us and wouldn't make us eat our junk."

Or we could push his stroller into traffic, Mick the Mick thought.

But Nate the Nose had bosses, and they probably had bosses too, and traveling through time to push a bunch of babies in front of moving cars seemed like a lot of work.

"Money, Willie. We need to make money."

"We could buy old stuff in the past then sell it on eBay. Hey, wouldn't it be cool to have four hands? I mean, you could touch twice as much stuff."

Mick the Mick thought about those old comics in Willie's basement, and then he grinned wider than a zebra's ass.

"Like Action Comics #1, which had the first appearance of Superman!" Mick the Mick said. "I could buy it with the change in my pocket, and we can sell it for a fortune!"

Come to think of it, he could buy eight copies. Didn't they go for a million a piece these days?

"I wish I could fly, Mick. Could we go back into time and learn to fly like Superman? Then we could have flown away from those camp counselors before they stuck their…"

"Shh!" Mick the Mick tilted his head to the side, listening to the jungle. "You hear something, Willie?"

"Yeah, Mick. I hear you talkin' to me. Now I hear me talkin'. Now I'm singing *a sooooong, a haaaaaaaaappy soooooong.*"

Mick the Mick gave Willie a smack in the teeth, then locked his eyes on the treeline. In the distance the canopy rustled and parted, like something really big was walking toward them. Something so big the ground shook with every step.

"You hear that, Mick? Sounds like something really big is coming."

A deafening roar from the thing in the trees, so horrible Mick the Mick could feel his curlies straighten.

"Think it's friendly?" Willie asked.

Mick the Mick stared down at his hands, which still held the *Really, Really, Really Old Ones* book. He flipped it open to a random page, forcing himself to concentrate on the words. But, as often happened in stressful situation, or even situations not all that stressful, the words seemed to twist and mash up and go backward and upside-down. Goddamn lesdyxia—shit—*dyslexia.*

"Maybe we should run, Mick."

"Yeah, maybe…wait! No! We can't run!"

"Why can't we run, Mick?"

"Remember that episode of *The Simpsons* where Homer went back in time and stepped on a butterfly and then Bart cut off his head with some hedge clippers?"

"That's two different episodes, Mick. They're both Treehouse of Horror episodes, but from different years."

"Look, Willie, the point is, evolution is a really fickle bitch. If we screw up something in the past it can really mess up the future."

"That sucks. You mean we would get back to our real time but instead of being made of skin and bones we're made entirely out of fruit? Like some kind of juicy fruit people?"

Another growl, even closer. It sounded like a lion's roar—if the lion had balls the size of Chryslers.

"I mean really bad stuff, Willie. I gotta read another passage and get us out of here."

The trees parted, and a shadow began to force itself into view.

"Hey, Mick, if you were made of fruit, would you take a bite of your own arm if you were really super hungry? I think I would. I wonder what I'd taste like?"

Mick the Mick tried to concentrate on reading the page, but his gaze kept flicking up to the trees. The prehistoric landscape lapsed into deadly silence. Then, like some giant monster coming out of the jungle, a giant monster came out of the jungle.

The head appeared first, the size of a sofa—a really big sofa—with teeth the size of daggers crammed into a mouth large enough to tear a refrigerator in half.

"I think I'd take a few bites out of my leg or something, but I'd be afraid because I don't know if I could stop. Especially if I tasted like strawberries, because I love strawberries, Mick. Why are they called strawberries when they don't taste like straw? Hey, is that a T-Rex?"

Now Mick the Mick pee-peed more than just a little. The creature before them was a deep green color, blending seamlessly into the undergrowth. Rather than scales, it was adorned with small, prickly hairs that Mick the Mick realized were thin brown feathers. Its huge nostrils flared and it snorted, causing the book's pages to ripple.

"I really think we should run, Mick."

Mick the Mick agreed. The Tyrannosaur stepped into the clearing on massive legs and reared up to its full height, over forty feet tall. Mick the Mick knew he couldn't outrun it. But he didn't have to. He only had to outrun Willie. He felt bad, but he had no other choice. He had to trick his best friend if he wanted to survive.

"The T-Rex has really bad vision, Willie. If you stay very still, it won't be able to---Willie, come back!"

Willie had broken for the trees, moving so fast he was a blur. Mick the Mick tore after him, swatting dragonflies out of the way as he ran. Underfoot he trampled on a large brown roach, a three-toed lizard with big dewy eyes and a disproportionately large brain, and a small furry mammal with a face that looked a lot like Sal from *Manny's Meats* on 23rd street, which gave a disturbingly human-like cry when its little neck snapped.

Behind them, the T-Rex moved with the speed of a giant two-legged cat shaped like a dinosaur, snapping teeth so close to Mick the Mick that they nipped the eighteen trailing hairs of his comb-over. He chanced a look over his shoulder and saw the mouth of the animal open so wide that Mick the Mick could set up a table for four on the creature's tongue and play Texas Hold 'em, not that he would, because that would be fucking stupid.

Then, just as the death jaws of death were ready to close on Mick the Mick and cause terminal death, the T-Rex skidded to a halt and craned its neck skyward, peering up through the trees.

Mick the Mick continued to sprint, stepping on a family of small furry rodents who looked a lot like the Capporellis up in 5B—so much so that he swore one even said "Fronzo!" when he broke its little furry spine—and then he smacked smack into Willie, who was standing still and staring up.

"Willie! What the hell are you doing? We gotta move!"

"Why, Mick? We're not being chased anymore."

Mick looked back and noticed that, indeed, the thunder lizard had abandoned its pursuit, focusing instead on the sky.

"I think it's looking at the asteroid," Willie said.

Mick the Mick shot a look upward and stared at the very large flaming object that seemed to take up a quarter of the sky.

"I don't think it was there a minute ago," Willie said. "I don't pay good attention but I think I woulda noticed it, don't you think?"

"This ain't good. This ain't no good at all."

"Look how big it's getting, Mick! We should hide behind some trees or something."

"We gotta get out of here, Willie." Mick the Mick said, his voice high-pitched and uncomfortably girlish.

"Feel that wind, Mick? It's hot. I bet that thing is going a hundred miles an hour. Do you feel it?"

"I feel it! I feel it!"

"Do you smell fish, Mick? Hey, look! Those pink flowers that look like—"

Willie screamed. Mick the Mick glanced over and saw his lifelong friend was playing tug of war with one of those toothy prehistoric plants, using a long red rope.

No. Not a red rope. Those were Willie's intestines.

"Help me, Mick!"

Without thinking, Mick the Mick reached out a hand and grabbed Willie's duodenum. He squeezed, tight as he could, and Willie farted.

"It hurts, Mick! Being disemboweled hurts!"

A bone-shaking roar, from behind them. The T-Rex had lost interest in the asteroid and was sniffing at the newly spilled blood, his sofa-sized head only a few meters away and getting closer. Mick the Mick could smell its breath, reeking of rotten meat and bad oral hygiene and dooky.

No, the dooky was coming from Willie. Pouring out like brown shaving cream.

Mick the Mick released his friend's innards and wiped his hand on Willie's shirt. The pink flower made a *pbbbthh* sound and did the same, without the wiping the hand part.

"I gotta put this stuff back in." Willie began scooping up guts and twigs and rocks and shoving them into the gaping hole in his belly.

Mick the Mick figured Willie was in shock, or perhaps even stupider than he'd originally surmised. He considered warning Willie about the infection he'd get from filling himself with dirt, but there were other, more pressing, matters at hand.

The asteroid now took up most of the horizon, and the heat from it turned the sweat on Mick the Mick's body into steam. They needed to get out of here, and fast. If only there was someplace to hide.

Something scurried over Mick the Mick's foot and he flinched, stomping down. Crushed under his heel was something that looked like a beaver. The animal kind. Another proto-beaver beelined around its dead companion, heading through the underbrush into...

"It's a hole, Willie! I think it's a cave!"

Mick the Mick pushed aside a large fern branch and squatted down. The hole led to a diagonalish path, dark and rocky, deep down into the earth.

"It's a hole, Willie! I think it's a cave!"

"You said that, Mick!"

"That's an echo, Willie! Hole must go down deep."

Mick the Mick watched as two more lizards, a giant mosquito, and more beaver things poured into the cave, escaping the certain extinction the asteroid promised.

"That's an echo, Willie! Hole must go down deep."

"You're repeating yourself, Mick!"

"I'm not repeating myself!" Mick yelled.

"Yes you are!"

"No I'm not!"

"I'm not repeating myself!"

"Yes you are!"

"No I'm not!"

"You just did!"

"I'm not, Willie!"

"I'm hurt bad, Mick!"

"I'm not, Willie!"

"I said *I'm* hurt, Mick! Not you!"

Mick the Mick decided not to pursue this line of conversation anymore. Instead, he focused on moving the big outcropping of rock partially obscuring the cave's entrance. If he could budge it just a foot or two, he could fit into the cave and maybe save himself.

Mick the Mick put his shoulder to the boulder, grunting with effort. Slowly, antagonizingly slowly, it began to move.

"You got your cell phone, Mick? You should maybe call 911 for me. Tell them to bring some stitches."

Just a little more. A little bit more…

"I think my stomach just fell out. What's a stomach look like, Mick? This looks like a kidney bean."

Finally, the rock broke away from the base with a satisfying crack. But rather than rolling to the side, it teetered, and then dropped down over the hole, sealing it like a manhole cover.

Mick the Mick began to cry.

"Do kidneys look like kidney beans, Mick?" Willie made a smacking sound. "Doesn't taste like beans. Or kidneys. Hey, the T-Rex is back. He doesn't look distracted no more. You think he took is medication?"

The T-Rex opened its mouth and reared up over Mick the Mick's head, blotting out the sky. All Mick the Mick could see was teeth and tongue and that big dangly thing that hangs in the back of the throat like a punching bag.

"Read to him, Mick. When Nana reads to me, I go to sleep."

The book. They needed to escape this time period. Maybe go into the future, to before Nana baked the cake so they could stop her.

Mick the Mick lifted the *Really, Really, Really Old Ones* and squinted at it. His hands shook, and his vision swam, and all the vowels on the page looked exactly the same and the consonants looked like pretzel sticks and the hair still left on his comb-over was starting to singe and the T-Rex's jaws began to close and another one of those pink flowers leaned in took a big bite out of Little Mick and the Twins but he managed to sputter out:

"OTKIN ADARAB UTAALK!"

* * *

Another near-turd experience and then they were excreted into a room with a television and a couch and a picture window. But the television screen was embedded—or growing out of?—a toadstoollike thing that was in turn growing out of the floor. The couch looked funny, like who'd sit on that? And the picture window looked out on some kind of nightmare jungle.

And then again, maybe not so weird.

No, Mick the Mick thought. Weird. Very weird.

He looked at Willie.

And screamed.

Or at least tried to. What came out was more like a croak.

Because it wasn't Willie. Not unless Willie had grown four extra eyes—two of them on stalks—and sprouted a fringe of tentacles around where he used to have a neck and shoulders. He now looked like a conical turkey croquette that had been rolled in seasoned breadcrumbs before baking and garnished with live worms after.

The thing made noises that sounded like, "Mick, is that you?" but spoken by a turkey croquette with a mouth full of linguini.

Stranger still, it sounded a little like Willie. Mick the Mick raised a tentacle to scratch his—

Whoa! *Tentacle?*

Well, of course a tentacle. What did he expect?

He looked down and was surprised to see that he was encased in a breadcrumbed, worm-garnished turkey croquette. No, wait, he *was* a turkey croquette.

Why did everything seem wrong, and yet simultaneously at the same time seem not wrong too?

Just then another six-eyed, tentacle-fringed croquette glided into the room. The Willie-sounding croquette said, "Hi, Nana." His words were much clearer now.

Nana? Was this Willie's Nana?

Of course it was. Mick the Mick had known her for years.

"There's an unpleasant man at the door who wants to talk to you. Or else."

"Or else what?"

A new voice said, "Or else you two get to eat cloacal casseroles, and guess who donates the cloacas?"

Mick the Mick unconsciously crossed his tentacles over his cloaca. In his twenty-four years since budding, Mick the Mick had grown very attached to his cloaca. He'd miss it something awful.

A fourth croquette had entered, followed by the two biggest croquettes Mick the Mick had ever seen. Only these weren't turkey croquettes, these were chipped-beef croquettes. This was serious.

The new guy sounded like Nate the Nose, but didn't have a nose. And what was a nose anyway?

"Oh, no," Willie moaned. "I don't want to eat Mick's cloaca."

"I meant your own, jerk!" the newcomer barked.

"But I have a hernia—"

"Shaddap!"

Mick the Mick recognized him now: Nate the Noodge, pimp, loan shark, and drug dealer. Not the sort you leant your bike to.

Wait . . . what was a bike?

"What's up, Nate?"

"That brick of product I gave you for delivery. I had this sudden, I dunno, bad feeling about it. A *frisson* of malaise and apprehension, you might say. I just hadda come by and check on it, knome sayn?"

The brick? What brick?

Mick the Mick had a moment of panic—he had no idea what Nate the Noodge was talking about.

Oh, yeah. The *product*. Now he remembered.

"Sure Nate, it's right in here."

He led Nate to the kitchen where the brick of product lay on the big center table.

Nate the Noodge pointed a tentacle at it. One of his guards lifted it, sniffed it, then wriggled his tentacle fringe that it was okay. Mick the Mick had expected him to nod but a nod would require a neck, and the guard didn't have a neck. Then Mick the Mick realized he didn't know what a neck was. Or a nod, for that matter.

What was it with these weird thoughts, like memories, going through his head? They were like half-remembered dreams. Nightmares, more likely. Pink flowers, and giant lizards, and big rocks in the sky, and stepping on some mice that looked like a lot like the Capporellis up in 5B. Except the Capporellis lived in 4B, and looked like jellyfish. What were mice anyway? He looked at Willie to see if he was just as confused.

Willie was playing with his cloaca.

Nate the Noodge turned to them and said, "A'ight. Looks like my frisson of malaise and apprehension was fer naught. Yer cloacas is safe . . . fer now. But you don't deliver that product like you're apposed to and it's casserole city, knome sayn?"

"We'll deliver it, Nate," Willie said. "Don't you worry. We'll deliver it."

"Y'better," Nate said, then left with his posse

"Where we supposed to deliver it?" Willie said when they were alone again.

Mick the Mick kicked him in his cloaca.

"The same place we always deliver it."

"Ow!" Willie was saying, rubbing his cloaca. "That hurt. You know I got a—hey, look!" He was pointing to the TV. "*The Toad Whisperer* is on! My favorite show!"

He settled onto the floor and stared.

Mick the Mick hated to admit it, but he was kind of addicted to the show himself. He settled next to Willie.

Faintly, from the kitchen, he heard Nana say, "Oh dear, I was going to bake a cake but I'm out of flour. Could one of you boys—oh, wait. Here's some. Never mind."

A warning glimp chugged in Mick the Mick's brain and puckered his cloaca. Something bad was about to happen . . .

What had Nate the Noodge called it? "A *frisson* of malaise and apprehension." Sounded like a dessert, but Mick the Mick had gathered it meant a worried feeling like what he was having right now.

But about what? What could go sour? The product was safe, and they were watching *The Toad Whisperer*. As soon as that was over, they'd go deliver it, get paid, and head on over to Madam Yoko's for a happy ending endoplasmic reticulum massage. And maybe a cloac-job.

The *frisson* of malaise and apprehension faded. Must have been another nightmare flashback.

Soon the aroma of baking cake filled the house. Right after the show he'd snag himself a piece.

Yes, life was good.

BIO

J.A. Konrath is the author of seven novels in the Jack Daniels series, along with dozens of short stories. The eighth, STIRRED, will be available in 2011.

Under the name Jack Kilborn, he wrote the horror novels AFRAID, ENDURANCE, TRAPPED, SERIAL UNCUT (written with Blake Crouch) and DRACULAS (written with Blake Crouch, Jeff Strand, and F. Paul Wilson.)

Under the name Joe Kimball, he wrote two novels in the TIMECASTER sci-fi series which feature Jack Daniels's grandson as the hero, and Harry McGlade III.

Visit Joe at www.JAKonrath.com.

BIBLIOGRAPHY

The Jack Daniels Novels

Shot of Tequila
Whiskey Sour
Bloody Mary
Rusty Nail
Dirty Martini
Fuzzy Navel
Cherry Bomb
Shaken
Stirred

In the Jack Daniels Universe

Jack Daniels Stories (Collected Stories)
Truck Stop
Suckers by JA Konrath and Jeff Strand
Planter's Punch by JA Konrath and Tom Schreck
Serial Uncut by Blake Crouch and JA Konrath
Floaters by JA Konrath and Henry Perez
Killers Uncut by Blake Crouch and JA Konrath
Banana Hammock - A Harry McGlade Adventure

As Jack Kilborn

Afraid
Trapped
Endurance
Draculas by J.A. Konrath, Blake Crouch, Jeff Strand, and F. Paul Wilson
Horror Stories (Collected Stories)

Other Work

Origin
The List
Disturb
55 Proof (Short Story Omnibus)
Crime Stories (Collected Stories)
Dumb Jokes & Vulgar Poems

As Joe Kimball

Timecaster
Timecaster Supersymmetry

Made in the USA
Lexington, KY
15 July 2011